THE HALF-CROWN HOUSE

THE
HALF-CROWN
HOUSE

By

HELEN ASHTON

DODD, MEAD & COMPANY
NEW YORK

ᏗHE HORNBEAM FAMILY

RICHARD HORNBEAM, wool merchant of Wilchester, obtained the Abbey lands after the Dissolution of the Monasteries.

His grandson, Lucius Hornbeam, took the Royalist side in the Civil War.

His son Henry (Mad Harry) killed at the first battle of Newbury, 1643, left a posthumous son,

Charles, ancestor of a line of eighteenth-century squires, one of these, 'Sensibility' Hornbeam, rebuilt the house in 1780.

Colonel Sir George ('Waterloo') Hornbeam
  m. (1) 1820, Lavinia d. of James Hornbeam (2) Maria Sowerby
    of Anatto Grove, Barbados

Charles, James, Rupert
Beatrice, Alice, Amelia,
Charles, First Baron Hornbeam   Alfred
  b. 1822–1887 m. Helen Jones
    seven children   great-grandfather of
                     Cousin Charles

Charles, Second Baron, b. 1853, d. 1904
  m. Lady Mary, third d. of the tenth
      Duke of Wilchester
      ("Lady Hornbeam")

Edward, Third Baron, b. 1897, d. 1934 (shooting accident)
  m. Sylvia, d. of Canon Kingswood

                     Harriet b. 1899
{ Henrietta b. 1923
{ Harry, her twin brother, killed at Arnhem 1944. Fourth Baron
  m. 1944 Maureen, d. of J. Smith
Victor, b. VE Day, 1945. Fifth Baron Hornbeam

I

It WAS the thirtieth day of October, 1954, a Saturday and the last afternoon in that year on which Fountain Court was open to the public. *"Foundations of Cistercian Priory,"* boasted the local guide, *"incorporated in seventeenth-century mansion, with Regency and Victorian additions. Waterloo wing with portraits, glass, china, furniture; bedroom of Queen Henrietta Maria (starred); eighteenth-century landscape garden. Open April 7th to Oct. 30th; Wednesdays and Saturdays 2.30–6. Other days by appointment. Admission; House 2/6, Queen's Room 6d. Garden 1/–. Children half-price. Reduction for parties. Church adjoins, with interesting monuments of Hornbeam family. Wilchester 4 miles; 'bus and coach services 90 and 47. Alight at Lambscot Corner, ½ mile. Teas at Rising Sun."* The same particulars appeared in the Wilchester Clarion during the summer months and the Hornbeam family might hope for anything from twenty up to fifty visitors on a fine Saturday. If they could get that they could keep the roof on the house for a little longer.

The County History, tracing the story of England in bricks and mortar, was more explicit; speaking of a small Cistercian Abbey, built *ad fontes*, among the water-springs, founded in the eleventh century, fallen into decay at the time of the Reformation and granted to Richard Hornbeam, cloth-merchant of Wilchester. He retained the barn, fish-ponds and chapel, but pulled down the monastic buildings and built himself a gabled house of the apricot-coloured local stone on the foundations. The family flourished, took the Royalist side in the Civil War and were visited by Queen

Henrietta Maria; the eldest son raised a troop of horse for King Charles, and was killed at the first battle of Newbury.

The Hornbeams fell on evil times during the Commonwealth, but revived after the Restoration; they became a race of comfortable hunting and farming squires. A younger son, transported for his share in Monmouth's rebellion, prospered in Barbados and brought West Indian money into the family. A Sir Charles Hornbeam, nicknamed 'Sensibility' Hornbeam by his friends, remodelled the old house in the classical taste in 1780, employing an architect to lay him out a woodland garden, adorned with vistas and temples, to display a load of statues which he had purchased in Italy when making the Grand Tour. In 1818 Colonel Sir George Hornbeam ('Waterloo' Hornbeam) married his cousin Lavinia, a West Indian heiress and with her money added a late-Regency suite of State apartments on the east side of the house.

Colonel George married twice and left nine children; his eldest son, Lavinia's only child, appears in the Peerage as Charles, First Lord Hornbeam, the Conservative statesman, the friend of Peel and Wellington. His portrait hung in the ballroom in Garter robes, a stupid sheep-faced man with an obstinate jaw. It was he who added the Victorian south front, in the Gothic style, with a ballroom, a billiard room, a great hump-backed conservatory full of palm trees, plate-glass windows, stone mullions, massive chimney stacks and a parapet with a motto detached against the sky. *"Created first Baron Hornbeam"* says the peerage, *"in 1865. Arms; argent, a chevron gules, between three hornbeam leaves proper, erased. Crest; a hornbeam leaf; motto Viresco."* This first Baron lived to a prodigious age. He married the daughter of a Liverpool ship-owner and sired seven children. In his time everything went well with the family.

It was in his son's time that things began to go wrong. Charles, the second Lord Hornbeam, who did not succeed till he was forty, took no part in public affairs; after a few years in the Army he devoted himself entirely to field sports. He was one of the wild hard-riding Hornbeams, hunted with the Wilchester hounds for twenty years and married in 1896 one of the six red-headed long-legged daughters of the tenth Duke of Wilchester. He had picked her up, they said, out of a ditch with a broken arm, at the end of the famous run from Walker's Gorse to the Standing Stones at Melbury. It was not a happy marriage. Lady Hornbeam, as reckless as he, spent his money like water; she gave him three children before they finally quarrelled and parted, in 1905, not without scandal.

Within two years Lord Hornbeam, riding harder than ever, had broken his neck at a fence and Mary, Lady Hornbeam, returned from the Continent to take up her dowager state at Fountain Court.

She was there still, had been there, a widow, for nearly fifty years; in her time she had been a frightful tyrant and had ruled the place with a rod of iron. Nowadays she had dwindled into a legend. She lay comfortably upstairs in her big Victorian bedroom overlooking the south terrace and was waited upon hand and foot by a devoted Swiss maid. She had outlived two minorities and a couple of wars. Her son Edward, the third Baron, touched in the lungs by gas in the First World War, had died by a shooting accident in 1934, leaving twin children. Harry the boy had grown up in time to be killed at Arnhem in 1944 on his twenty-first birthday; Henrietta, his twin sister, unmarried at twenty-nine, now ran the place. The present Lord Hornbeam was Victor, a posthumous child, nine years old. Lady Hornbeam had had a long run for her money, she had not done so badly for herself when she married the owner of Fountain Court.

The house stood in a mild Midland landscape, farming and hunting country, rolling windswept uplands with thin hedges and small plantations, stone villages and farms, all spread under a wide sky. The big southern windows of the Victorian front looked over a terrace into a valley with a nameless brook in it; the water had come out of the Abbot's Fish-pond behind the house and would eventually meander into the headwaters of the Thames. Wilchester, the county town, was four miles away; a by-road from Lambscot village led down to the classical north front of Fountain Court, a circular approach walled in by yew hedges. On the east the Regency wing overlooked a neglected rose-garden; to the west lay the kitchens, the stable yard, the Abbot's Barn and Tower and the fish-ponds. From the air American pilots, climbing up from Lambscot airfield, saw the place as a neat toy house, a hollow square among lawns, with a straggle of secondary buildings, a wood and a crooked elbow of water reflecting the sky. Once they were over Fountain Court they could change course and turn westward, beginning a clockwise circuit of the aerodrome, tying a knot of black smoke in the air, where their two double trails of exhaust fumes had sharply altered direction and been folded one upon another. At the same moment the roar of the engines changed its note and began to fade away and somebody or other in house or village would probably raise a head to grumble, "There's another of 'em . . . price of peace . . . that was a low one. Some day we'll get one of the nasty things on the roof, I suppose."

2

On this thirtieth of October the sun came up just before seven at the end of the Waterloo Avenue, a double row of limes, a mile long; it had at first been planted to reach the old coach-road to London, but nowadays it was grass-grown and lost itself among the fields. Morning light struck the eastern windows and turned them to gold; one or two moorhens got busy on the fish-ponds and a flag was run up on a mast in the stable yard. This was the self-imposed ritual of Commander Hornbeam, R.N. retired on a disability pension; Cousin Charles, who had lost an arm and an eye in the war and now ran a market-garden for the family. He lived by himself in a couple of rooms over the old stable, which he kept as neat as a new pin, employed a landgirl and an Irish labourer, with local help for the fruit-picking and grew tomatoes and peas in the glass-houses, filling in with lettuces, bulbs, cut flowers and potted chrysanthemums for the Christmas trade. He drove into Wilchester on three mornings a week, did a delivery-round of the shops and the three hotels and on Thursday, market-day, sold his produce from the tail of his van at a pitch behind St. Blaizey's church. He was a neat cheerful lively little fellow; it was amazing how well he managed with his one arm, nipping along a row of cloches, sowing seed out of a bag at his waist, thrusting in young plants with finger and thumb, going along with a sideways scramble, twice as fast as either Tim or the landgirl. Cousin Charles was usually up and about before anybody else; by seven-thirty he had brewed himself a pot of tea, eaten a hunk of bread and cheese and driven away to Wilchester.

About the same time Roote, the old gardener, was lighting his fire in his cottage, opening his window and squinting up at the sky. Leaf the butler in his room on the third floor was shaving with his unsteady old hand, thinking, "Visitors to lunch and the house open all afternoon; my legs won't hardly carry me to the end of the day. I can't stand another summer like this one; people in and out all the time, growling and complaining, thinking they've bought the place for half-a-crown. I shall have to give up, I'm too old for it." He cut himself and dabbed at his chin, frowning in the glass. Mrs. Peppercorn the cook came grumbling down the back stairs in a dirty apron and a man's cap, to wrestle with the kitchen range. Poking in the ashes, trying to start a spark with twigs and paper, reaching for the paraffin can, she muttered to herself, as she did most mornings, "Didn't ought to be made to do this, at my time of life. They ought to put in a proper stove, Aga or Esse or something o' that, or else employ a proper kitchen-maid to light me fire for me; 'tisn't fair after thirty years' service in this great place, only to get that useless slut Gladys Moss from the village." She filled the electric kettle and switched it on; presently Roote would be at the back door with vegetables; after him Gladys Moss the kitchen-maid and Jean Furze the landgirl would come skimming into the yard on their bicycles, prop them insecurely against the wall and cry, "Morning, Mrs. Peppercorn; did you 'ear the latest?" Boffin the kitchen cat, a young and handsome tabby, appeared from nowhere and wound himself about her feet. "You get out of my way, boy," she said to him fondly, rattling the poker. "I got no time for you; I'm busy. Company to lunch. Miss Henrietta's American gentleman, coming down with a Bond Street dealer to buy a picture. Got to find something fit to put on the table for 'em. Oh! drat this range, it'll be the death of me."

3

Henrietta Hornbeam almost overslept. She had had a bad night, tossing and turning, getting up two or three times to look out at the blazing October stars, Orion striding across the heavens, Jupiter like a great blue diamond on top of the Twins. She had heard an owl hooting, a pheasant complaining, a fox barking in the woods. There had been the distant muffled roar from Lambscot aerodrome as the engines warmed up, hour after hour; later in the night there was a big bomber droning round and round high overhead, but none of that would have kept the tired girl awake if she had not been worrying herself sick about what was to become of Fountain Court. She was heavily asleep, with her auburn head buried in the pillow, when her Cousin Charles drove his lorry out of the yard at seven-thirty. The noise of his departure under her window broke into her sleep and made her toss to and fro. She slept another minute or two, then woke with a start from an uneasy dream, rubbing her hands over her screwed-up eyes. "Harry," she called out before she knew where she was; "Harry, do be careful."

She never called anyone by that name nowadays, seldom ever pronounced it: the name of her dead twin brother, the paratrooper who had been killed at Arnhem. She did not often dream about him nowadays, though in the first year after they got the news she had seen him often at night, sitting with his parachute on his shoulders, smiling at her from the edge of the hatch, putting his feet through the hole that went down into darkness, slipping out as neat as a fish, jerking like a hooked trout as the parachute opened like a flower above him, hovering and swaying like a hawk in empty air. Then the dream would change into a nightmare of smoke and bursting shells, with men like dolls turning over and over in the sky, bundles of clothes with dead men in them falling, a rain of bodies, into the dykes.

Henrietta had not dreamt that dream for some years now, but lately it had come back to plague her in a different form. She would dream pleasantly at first of their twin childhood, Harry and she running wild in the woods, feeding rabbits, saddling up ponies, pushing out an old boat on the fish-ponds, doing everything together as they used to do; but nowadays this dream ended in Harry climbing along the battlements of the old wall by the Abbot's Tower, while she stood below watching him. Then he would let go with one hand, turn and wave to show how safe he was and come crashing down. The dream turned back this morning into Henrietta's picture of Arnhem and she woke with a start. "God!" she told herself, "that was a nasty one. I must be out of sorts." She shook herself and the dream faded. She was awake in her old schoolgirl bedroom, with the morning light betraying the worn carpet, the dented golden-ash furniture, the school photographs, the gymkhana ribbons and medals treasured from childhood, his and hers. Harry had drowned in a dyke at Arnhem, with mud in his smiling mouth. Now Henrietta was rising thirty, tall, pale, red-headed, his living image; she had his work to do this day and every day, she had no time to lie in bed. The stable clock startled her, with its mellow half-hour chime. "Lord! they're all coming to-day," she remembered. "Victor and his mother, John and Mr. Birnbaum. I must hurry."

4

Mrs. Branch, whom everybody called Nanny at Fountain Court, was dressing briskly in the nursery tower, lacing her grey corsets tightly, pulling down her cotton frock under her starched belt, tying on her apron, screwing her white hair into a neat knot; transforming herself into her daytime figure of brisk authority. She set the room to rights while her kettle sang and her egg boiled, then sat down by the fire to eat her breakfast. The old room in the tower with the barred windows and the cupboards full of toys had been her kingdom for thirty years. She had come there as a young widow in 1923 when the twins were born; after they went from her to Miss Thorn in the schoolroom she had still remained there, mending linen, keeping an eye on the young housemaids, nursing anyone who fell sick, waiting for another generation of Hornbeam children to spring up. This morning she was all in a fluster, though she concealed it well, for now at last she would have something young to fuss over again. Little Lord Hornbeam, Victor Carolus, the fifth Baron, aged nine, was coming to live at Fountain Court.

Her own dear Harry, the fair smiling boy, had astonished his family by marrying all in a scramble, on his last leave, six weeks before he was killed. He had chosen a girl never seen or heard of before by his family, a pretty little dark-haired, dark-eyed thing, picked out from behind the counter of an ice-cream parlour in Manchester. "M. 1944. Maureen, daughter of J. Smith," said Burke's Peerage austerely. Nobody knew who J. Smith had been. Young Lady Hornbeam declared herself an orphan, brought up by an aunt in Wales; she certainly had a Welsh look. "She's no lady," the elder servants had told each other. "Look at her clothes, look at her hands, listen to the way she talks. She's pretty as a picture, I grant you; but where did he find her? Manicure girl . . . dance hostess . . . shopgirl . . . cinema usherette perhaps," they speculated, before they heard about the ice-cream parlour. "Good as gold, I daresay, but his Lordship should never have married her. He should have thought of the disgrace to the family. Her Ladyship won't never forgive or forget, that's certain."

Old Lady Hornbeam had put a good face on the matter at the time, but after the young woman had been down for a terrifying visit of inspection she banished her smoothly to the aunt in Wales until after the birth of Harry's child. "We really can't open up the old nurseries just at present," she told her friends. "We've no servants left, the house has been shut up for the duration; all the State rooms are piled up to the ceiling with packing cases; archives, you know and art-treasures from one of the museums. The stuff has had to be stored somewhere and I regarded it as a patriotic duty to offer the house; we have all those big rooms and I'm too old to run it as a hospital again. I had more than enough of that," said she firmly, "in the First World War. Of course we've had an extra fuel-allowance, which has been most useful to keep out the damp; and it's been a great deal better than evacuees or expectant mothers or D.P.s, but we really have nowhere to sit until the stuff goes back to London and who knows how long that may be, even after the war's over." This was during the last fierce winter of the fighting in the Ardennes. "Henrietta's out all day working at Wood's farm," Lady Hornbeam would explain, "and Dr. Bayes says I mustn't be going up and down stairs all the time, it's bad for my poor heart. So I just live in my bedroom and Maria waits on me. It would be dreadfully dull for poor little Maureen; much better to let her go to her aunt in Wales for the present. She'll be perfectly safe and comfortable there, well out of the way of air-raids if we have any more of them and most luckily the aunt has had a great deal of hospital experience." The woman had in fact been a district nurse.

The posthumous boy was born on VE Day and the rejoicings for his birth were the red, white and blue flowers, the flag-flying and bell-chiming, the dancing and bonfires for victory. He was christened Charles, as the eldest Hornbeam son was supposed to be in each generation; but his mother insisted on adding the second name of Victor, quite unknown in the family and she always called him by it; though when old Lady Hornbeam remonstrated she changed for a time to Charley-boy, which was worse. "So common," Lady Hornbeam complained, "but of course we shall change it to Charles when we get him here to live with us later on," and she would add with a sigh, "I wish the child were less like his mother;" for Victor as he grew, became a small-boned dark-eyed timid boy, quite unlike his father's family.

Harry had left instructions that the boy should remain in his mother's charge until he was old enough to go to school. She used to bring him for a duty visit twice a year, at Christmas and in the summer holidays. For the rest of the time she lived at Putney on her jointure, in what Lady Hornbeam described as "a horrid little villa, all roses and rockeries"; it was half-way up the hill, on the way to Roehampton, two-storeyed and semi-detached, with a neat little back garden where Victor could play with his toys until he grew old enough to be taken out for walks on Putney Heath. "Such a pity not to bring the boy up in the country," his great-grandmother said and Nanny had been dreadfully disappointed to miss Victor's early years; she considered that his mother was turning him into a dull and tidy little boy, quite unlike his father.

Quite lately, however, the story had taken another turn. Young Lady Hornbeam, after ten years of most respectable widowhood, had married again. She was now Mrs. Pine, the wife of a builder, in a very good way of business, had sold the Putney villa and was going to live in the outskirts of Stafford. Lady Hornbeam seized the opportunity to claim Victor. He was to have a holiday until Christmas, because he had just had measles. He could go to his father's old preparatory school in January, owing to a most fortunate vacancy; he had been put down for Winchester in six years' time. In future he was to spend his holidays at Fountain Court and only visit his mother occasionally. "We shall soon make a man of him," she told her granddaughter Henrietta, "once we get him away from that dreadful mother." The Pines were bringing him by car that morning from Stafford and Nanny had everything ready for him.

Generations of Hornbeam children had used the room in the nursery tower. The faded roses and figures of a Kate Greenaway wallpaper scarcely showed any longer between the framed Christmas supplements which covered the walls, *Bubbles, Cherry Ripe* and *Miss Muffet*. The dappled tail-less rocking horse, which his father and grandfather had ridden upon, waited for Victor by the window; the intricate fantasies of the faded scrap-screen, which his great-aunt had made in the seventies, kept off the draught from an ill-fitting door. His great-grandmother's dolls' house stood by the wall, foursquare and Palladian, with pediment and portico, made by the estate carpenter in imitation of Wilchester Castle, demolished these ten years. All its bright windows glittered; Nanny had rubbed them up faithfully, because even a boy ought to be amused by this copy of an ancestral house. The mantelpiece held children's treasures, brought back from seaside holidays, fifteen, twenty, thirty years ago; the glass lighthouse striped with coloured sand from Alum Bay, the paper-weight with the view of the Brighton Pavilion underneath, the glass ball waiting for Victor to shake up the snowstorm inside, the ship-in-a-bottle made by Nanny's sailor brother, the cracked Staffordshire jug with the heads of Admiral Nelson and Captain Hardy on its bulging sides. In the big toy-cupboard the child would find his father's toy fort and boxes of soldiers, the model theatre, the red-and-white bricks, the maps and puzzles with the pieces missing, the boats, spades and buckets, the small bats and cricket-stumps, the toy tricycle with one pedal gone. Nanny did hope that some of this junk would please him. He was a dreadfully quiet little boy and during his

earlier visits had always seemed frightened of everybody. "He's
sure to miss his mother at first," thought she sagely, "but in time
he'll get used to us;" and she took out of her cupboard the mug
with South African flags and generals upon it, which had belonged
to Edward, third Lord Hornbeam, her Ladyship's son, Victor's
grandfather. "The boy shall have his milk in it," she thought, "at
supper time. Maybe it'll amuse him."

5

Latest of all, Lady Hornbeam's blinds went up in the Victorian
south front. Maria Camin, her Swiss maid, tiptoed in, a little hard-
faced woman, almost as old as her mistress, in a black gown and
sateen apron, with a knitted shawl about her bony shoulders. She
drew the curtains, raised one faded scarlet linen blind after another, let in the fresh morning light upon a frivolous confusion of
padded blue satin Edwardian chairs and sofas, gilded mirrors, billowing draperies of blue satin with frilled muslin and crowds of
photographs in silver frames. The room had not changed in essen-
tials since Lady Hornbeam first came to it as a bride from Wilchester Castle, some sixty years earlier. It smelt this morning of
flowers and face-powder, of peppermint drops and caraway seeds,
of the medicines ranged along the marble chimney-piece; beneath
all that there was a faint stale smell of sickness and decay. The old
woman lay fast asleep in a nest of embroidered pillows, with her
toothless mouth open, her head on one side, her night-cap askew.
She breathed so quietly that Maria looked twice, as she often did
in the mornings, to make sure that her mistress was still alive.

Then she dropped on her knees to stir the fire into a blaze. She
had tended it last at five in the morning, slipping in like a mouse
to add lumps of coal with her gloved fingers. She had lifted the
old woman up then, turned and plumped up the pillows, poured
a drink of hot milk out of the Thermos, told her the time; like all

those who are approaching their last hours, the old woman always wanted to know what time it was and would ask for it three or four times in a night.

The crackle of the fire, the beam of morning sunlight, roused her now to say, "Is that you, Maria? How late is it?" "Almost nine, milady," said Maria. "Wait, I'll make you comfortable in a minute." She rose from her knees, lifted the fragile bag of bones up the bed in her strong peasant arms, pushed a pillow under each elbow, brought scented warm water to wash the famous face, which had once shown a classical beauty, but was now little more than wax-yellow skin clothing a skull. Lady Hornbeam whimpered fretfully, "Let me alone," pushed the ministering hands aside, talked a little foolishly about the past, as she often did on waking, pronouncing the names of friends long-dead. "Now just let me dry your face," coaxed Maria, "and then I'll go down and fetch you up your breakfast."

6

These were the human inhabitants of the house; Lady Hornbeam, Henrietta Hornbeam above stairs, below stairs Leaf the butler, Mrs. Peppercorn the cook, Maria the lady's maid, and Nanny; with Cousin Charles in the stables, besides Roote the gardener in his cottage and Jean the landgirl from the farm; but the old house had many other inhabitants, not human, living under floors, inside walls, among beams, up chimneys. At night the rats came out and frisked boldly through the attics, gnawed and scratched their way under doors, ran about with thumping noises in empty rooms. The house-mice scampered up and down their own long corridors under the floor-boards; they squeaked and fought among the joists, made themselves nests out of nibbled paper and rags. Every autumn, when the corn had been carried, there was an invasion of field-mice; one year they got into the velvet pillows of the State bed in the Queen's Room, shut up for the winter, and nibbled holes in the embroidered curtains; cats and traps could not keep pace with the field-mice. They would get into the larder and drown themselves in the cream-pans.

Many birds used the house as their own. Sparrows nested continually under tiles and in leaky rain-heads, producing floods and overflows in stormy weather. The young birds sat in rows along the edges of the gutters. Swallows and house-martins came every spring from Africa to the mud-nests under the eaves; this year there had been thirty nests with small sweet black-and-white faces looking out of them. There were always swifts hawking and screaming in the summer round the Abbot's Tower. The disused chimneys housed jackdaws and starlings, sometimes an owl or two; they became blocked with mountains of sticks in the older part of the house. Wrens and titmice occupied holes in the masonry; flycatchers and yellow wagtails hunted flies on the roof or the window-sills and sometimes attacked their own reflections in the glass.

There were toads in the damp groined and pillared cellars, once part of the monastery building, and there was often a frog or two in the stone corner-trough; it had formerly been used for pig-curing and the water came up and filled it every winter. Crickets chirped behind the kitchen range and an army of cockroaches lived behind the copper; at night they came out and ran about the kitchen flags.

Bats hung like fruit among the rafters in the attics, spiders wrapped the beams in felted cobwebs; in the furthest part of the roof, where nobody ever went, there was a hive of wild bees. They had been there for longer than anybody could remember, nobody could smoke them out; the bees went in and out by a narrow slit, like the opening of a letter-box, high up under the eaves. On warm days you heard them humming busily like a simmering kettle and the honey from the old black rotten combs had run down between two walls into a disused bedroom on the third floor, making a sticky stain on the ceiling. Charles had had better luck with a wasps'-nest, which he had smoked out of a spare-room chimney. Houseflies and bluebottles infested the kitchen, haunted the bedrooms, slept out the winter behind the shutters or died on closed window-sills. Tortoiseshell and peacock butterflies clung to the corners of ceilings, or beat themselves to death against closed panes on the first day of spring sun. Silver fish wriggled in and out of cracks in the plaster; death-watch beetles had established themselves in the beams above the Chestnut Staircase, gnawing and ticking quietly at night; woodworm tunnelled the furniture in the attics; dry rot and fungus had a firm hold behind the skirting boards in several rooms on the third floor and behind the minstrels' gallery in the old ballroom. All this quiet eager life fulfilled itself yearly, ignoring the human owners; some day no doubt it would inherit the ruined house.

II

OLD LADY LINDEN, in the Dower House at Gooseground, six miles away, was wondering that morning how best to entertain a visiting niece from London and her little girl. "Poor Mrs. Holly, she used to be such a pretty girl," the neighbours told each other. "Don't you remember how all the men ran after her, before the war? We used to say she'd done well for herself, marrying that handsome Captain Holly; he had money and he was supposed to be coming in for his uncle's place; but the war spoilt all that. They didn't see each other for ages; he went to Burma and was taken prisoner and she was doing war-work in one of the Ministries, when peace came they didn't get on too well together. He would make her go off to Kenya and of course she hated it; now she's been home again for over a year. She's quite lost her nerve and says she'll never go back to Africa and all those blacks; well, really you can't blame her. I suppose they'll have a divorce. She's got some job in London, works on one of these fashion-papers, I believe; she was always very smart. The girl lives with her. Oh! a dear little thing, Lucy, the image of her father, mad about horses, loves the country. It's a shame she should have to live in London. She's at school now, I hear; comes down to Lady Linden a good deal in the holidays, the old lady's been very kind to her. They're at the Dower House this week-end, for the child's half-term, I suppose."

And there they sat, after breakfast, in the sunny dining-room, looking out on Lady Linden's rose garden. Lucy Holly, thin and sunburnt, in a school uniform, was still eating toast and marmalade, encouraged by the old lady. "Do have some more coffee, dear, there's plenty in the pot; you want to make a good breakfast," she urged Lucy, who passed up her cup. "That child eats like a horse," said Elsa Holly, from the window seat. "I don't know how she does it. She never puts on any weight." "She's growing," said Lady Linden firmly. "She's going to be tall like her father." Lucy blushed and looked imploringly at her mother, who was smoking in the window seat and flipping over the pages of *The Times* as if a gale were blowing.

Lady Linden surveyed the young woman with anxiety. She was as thin as a rake and restless as a starling, she wore a tweed dress as soft as silk, her stockings were gossamer, her shoes just toes and heels; her hair was cut quite short and curled all over her head like a poodle's coat. She never stopped smoking and talked continually, in a high peevish voice; but she laughed rarely, and then with a mirthless rippling titter. She seemed dreadfully unhappy. "There never was anybody so changed from what she used to be," Lady Linden thought. "In the old days she was a darling; but the child is a good child, she's like her father." And she said aloud, "Take some more marmalade, Lucy; it's our own. I believe we shall have a lovely day, Elsa; the forecast was most favourable. Would you like to take a deck-chair out in the garden now and have a nice rest, while Lucy comes down to the village with me, or has a ride on the old pony; then after lunch I thought we might drive over and see Fountain Court. It's open from half-past two till six and it's the last day of the season."

"What's that in aid of?" yawned Elsa Holly, turning the pages of *Country Life* with a clawed forefinger. "The Nurses, or something?" "Well, really in aid of themselves," said Lady Linden. "They've been doing it for the last three years; half-a-crown for the house and a shilling extra for the gardens, because of all those Follies." "Everybody seems to be in that racket nowadays," said Elsa crossly. "Does it pay? I shouldn't have thought it was worth the fag. Fancy having hundreds of people tramping over our carpets and making rude remarks about your family treasures. I daresay it's all right if you have an enormous house with State

Apartments you never use; but what have they got to show at Fountain Court that's worth half-a-crown?" "Well, not a great deal," confessed Lady Linden, doing her best for her idea; "but it's a sweet old house and there are family portraits and nice bits of furniture and they show the Queen's Room. Lucy ought to see that, it'll help her with her history. Queen Henrietta Maria slept there, dear," she instructed Lucy, attending with her mouth full. "You must know about her." Lucy chewed an apple and looked blank. "Of course the house is rather shabby nowadays and the gardens aren't kept up as they ought to be, but they haven't the staff; they only grow the easy things. It's all rather sad when you think how lovely it used to be. Lucy would like the Follies, and the fish-ponds and the Abbot's Tower. I always try to take my visitors over and Henrietta would give us tea afterwards, I'm sure." Lucy's eyes brightened at this thought, her mother commented, "That's going to make a bit of a hole in the half-crown, isn't it? unless they make you pay for your tea."

"Oh! they don't do teas," said Lady Linden. "I've often told Henrietta they should, but she says it would be too difficult. She runs the whole place really nowadays, you know. I'm afraid she finds it fearfully hard to make ends meet. They've had three lots of death duties in fifty years and they've had to sell off all the farms. You'll find it a good deal changed."

"Is old Lady Hornbeam still alive?" yawned Elsa, turning a page. "I always heard she was the one who made the money fly in the gay nineties." "Yes, she's still alive, dear; but nobody ever sees her. She's pretty well bedridden, I believe, anyhow she lives upstairs in her room and that Swiss maid looks after her. Harry's little boy will come in for the place when he grows up——" "I didn't know Harry *had* a little boy," objected Elsa. "I never heard he was married even." "Oh! yes, dear, he married somebody or other when he was training at that parachute school near Manchester, just before he went off to be killed at Arnhem; rather a dreadful little person, I believe, nobody knows where he picked her up.

Somebody said she served behind the counter in an ice-cream parlour. There's a boy called Victor, he's just come to live at Fountain Court, I daresay Lucy will see him at tea. He's going to his father's old prep-school after Christmas and Henrietta will have to look after him in the holidays."

"She must have a lot on her plate, poor girl," said Elsa indifferently, flapping over the advertisement pages of *Country Life*. There they all were, the stately mansions, the historic manors, the old rectories, standing in beautiful easily-maintained grounds; the substantial, old-world, stone-built unmarketable properties hopefully advertised as suitable for hotels, for offices, for schools or convalescent homes. "No reasonable offer refused," recited Elsa scornfully. "Genuine Tudor, Georgian, Regency gems, given away with a pound of tea; the country's lousy with old houses that nobody wants. Here's a man with the right idea, he specialises in dismantling and demolishing uneconomic properties. Henrietta had better contact him, I should think. Fountain Court must be a white elephant. What's she like nowadays? I remember her as a leggy schoolgirl with red plaits, cleaning tack in the stables, she was always mad about horses then. That was donkey's years ago; Good Lord! the girl must be getting on for thirty. Why hasn't she married? Didn't she get away in the war?" Lady Linden shook her head. "She went into the Land Army. Woods had just bought the Home Farm and she worked for him; she's been running the place since the war. I don't know why she hasn't married, I'm sure, I suppose the right man didn't come along. She's very handsome, in that red-headed Hornbeam way, but rather managing. She and Harry were so devoted to each other; he was a glorious fellow, Shakespearean rather. You know how it is with twins. She was quite queer for a bit after he was killed, I was worried about her; however, she got over it. Now she seems to think it's her job to take his place and I must say she does it very well." She added thoughtfully, "Of course the Commander helps her." "What Commander?" yawned Elsa. "I never heard of him either;" but she sat up and put her paper down when her aunt said, "Charles, dear; the old Admiral's second boy, the one who was in the Navy. You must remember him."

"Oh! Lord, yes," cried Elsa, looking young and lively all of a sudden. "When I was about twenty I had quite a swing round with Charles. I was down for Christmas and he was here on leave. We used to meet out hunting and I always kept the supper dances for him; he was quite a charmer. I haven't seen Charles for ages, I thought he was married and settled long ago. He was such a heart-breaker. What's he doing back at Fountain Court?" "Why, he runs the gardens for Henrietta," said the old lady. "They sell their produce in Wilchester, I believe he makes quite a good thing out of it. He lives in a flat they made for him, out in the stables. He did marry, just before the war, a very nice girl, I believe; but I never saw her. She and the little boy were killed in the London blitz."

Elsa lit another cigarette and blew out a cloud of smoke. "Why don't he and Henrietta make a match of it, then," said she crossly. "It sounds suitable."

"Oh! they've known each other all their lives," Lady Linden dismissed the notion. "They're like brother and sister, I don't suppose it's ever occurred to either of them. Besides, poor Charles was most frightfully knocked about in the war. His ship was torpedoed and he was hours in the water before he was picked up and then they drifted about in an open boat. Simply dreadful it must have been; he never talks about it but Henrietta told me once. Poor Charles, he lost his left arm and eye. He nearly died and then while he was in hospital they had to tell him his wife and child had been killed. After that of course he had to leave the Navy. He'd nowhere to go, that's when the Hornbeams took him in. He's been here ever since, poor fellow!"

Elsa's face clouded. "I daresay he wishes he had died," said she morosely, but Lady Linden contradicted this. "Oh! no, dear, Charles isn't like that; he's always very cheerful, one of the most cheerful people I know. He wears a black patch on his eye, like Nelson and still manages to look quite handsome. If we go over this afternoon he'll very likely take us round." "I don't know that I'm so keen," said Elsa. "You'd almost persuaded me that half-a-crown would be worth it to see dear old Charles again, but I don't know that I want to if he's only got one arm and half a face. Still, it might amuse Lucy; all right, let's go."

2

On visiting days Grace Thorn, who had formerly been the governess at Fountain Court, did the flowers for the house in her old realm, the schoolroom; a period piece. Four generations of Hornbeam children had learnt their lessons there; it was cool, dark and high and looked into a laurel shrubbery. It was furnished with some battered chairs, a solid table carved with dead boys' initials and covered with an ancient ink-stained serge cloth, in one corner was an old upright piano on whose yellowed keys many reluctant fingers had thumped out scales and Czerny's five-finger exercises; the Hornbeams were not a musical family. A couple of big bookcases housed out-of-date primers, history, geography, arithmetic, Greek and Latin grammars; in the cupboards underneath were old exercise books with marbled covers, slates and chalks, pencil boxes, piles of music, stamp-collections and text-books about shells and flowers. There was a blackboard in the wall-cupboard which had not been used since Henrietta was a child, there were faded maps on rollers, in which the countries had not yet been affected by two World Wars.

All the books had children's names in them, you could read the Hornbeam history as well in the schoolroom as on the family tree in the library. The oldest books of all had been used by little boys with loose nankeen trousers buttoned on to their shirts and little girls with sashes and short sleeves, learning their geography from

Nelson's victories and Wellington's battles overseas. There was an
algebra book which had belonged to Colonel Sir George Hornbeam, who fought at Waterloo and afterwards built the Regency
half of the house. There were quite a number of Victorian school-
books, used by his seven children; Charles, James, Rupert, Alfred,
Beatrice, Amelia and Alice, the ones in the silhouette by Augustin
Edouart in the Yellow Drawing-room; Henrietta and her brother
used to call them the Black Children. The second Lord Hornbeam
had torn the pages of his Latin Grammar in a rage; Edward, his
son, Henrietta's father, the third Baron, had inscribed his "Little
Arthur's History of England" with the jingle, *Edward Hornbeam,
Fountain Court, Wilchester, Loamshire, England, the World*. It
gave his daughter quite a shock when she found it, years after
his death.

The wild-flower books by Ann Pratt had his sister's name in
them, Harriet Hornbeam, the plain queer aunt who had quarrelled with her beautiful mother, years ago. After helping to run
the Fountain Court hospital all through the Kaiser's war, Aunt
Harriet had gone off to be a real hospital nurse. She was very
capable, like most Hornbeam women and now had her own nursing home in the North of England; Henrietta had not seen her
aunt for years. The newest school-books of all dated from the
twins' childhood in the twenties; they were scribbled all over with
"H" and "H" in various ornamental scripts and adorned by Harry's
drawings. Grace Thorn, their governess, had inked-in the Ver-
sailles boundaries on the older maps, for economy's sake, when
their grandmother had grumbled about the cost of the twins' education; saying hopefully, "The rivers and cities are all the same
and the new boundaries may not last."

Grace Thorn was a kind of family relic, like much else at Fountain Court. She had been the daughter of a poor Wilchester doctor
and in her youth had taught there at the High School. She had
first come to the Court in 1914, as quartermaster of the local Red
Cross detachment. At that time the big rooms in the Waterloo

wing had been turned into wards, with beds in neat rows and young starched nurses fluttering about like a flock of white pigeons. Patients in hospital blue clumped across the terrace in plasters, on crutches; doctors in uniform came and went, the marble Octagon Parlour was used as an operating theatre and ambulances were drawn up in the courtyard; the long passages smelt of iodoform, carbolic and ether. Lady Hornbeam used to drift about in white linen robes, with a ruby cross at her throat; and Grace Thorn spent four years in the corner of the Library, doing the accounts, checking sheets and blankets, pillow cases and towels, indenting for kitchen and medical stores. In the war-photograph of doctors, nurses and patients, which still hung over the schoolroom chimney piece, Lady Hornbeam and Matron had the places of honour in the middle of the front steps; and Grace was the one in the corner out of focus.

When the war was over everybody else went away, but Grace Thorn was much too useful to be spared. She adored Lady Hornbeam and asked for nothing better than to serve her daily; she kept her wartime bedroom on the top floor, in the old servants' quarters, behind the balustrade and was called Lady Hornbeam's secretary. She wrote letters, arranged flowers, listened to her Lady's stories of the court of King Edward the Seventh, bore with her tantrums, played backgammon or piquet with her in the evenings and effaced herself when there were visitors in the house.

Grace was the one who most vividly remembered how young Lord Hornbeam, unlucky Edward, came back from the war, changed from a shy boy to a silent young man, with a touch of gas in one lung. Edward had been a throw-back to some bookish ancestor on the Wilchester side; no true Hornbeam ever opened a book to please himself. He had done well at Winchester and had won a New College scholarship but the war had interrupted all that; when he came home again, after a Swiss sanatorium had finished with him, he took no more interest in anything. His mother ran the house and an agent at that time managed the estate; he left later after the last of the farms was sold. Edward was only asked to get well and to enjoy himself, he was not encouraged to interfere with his mother's arrangements. He pottered about for a couple of years, would not hunt or shoot, hid in bushes and behind trees, watching birds; he came to be called Poor Edward and was written off as a war-casualty. Grace Thorn used to feel dreadfully sorry for him. She was a sentimental soul not more than five years older than Edward and she had had her romantic dreams of catching his eye, but this never came to anything. Edward went about in a daze, and took no notice of her. "Such a pity my son has no interest in girls," his mother would say to her friends; but she never put any in his way. She was too fond of her position as the dowager queen of Fountain Court.

Nobody was more astonished than his mother when Edward fell in love at twenty-seven with a girl as silent as himself; Sylvia, youngest daughter of Canon Kingswood, Rector of St. Blaizey's Church, Wilchester, that was how she figured in *The Times'* announcement. "I was there when your father and mother met, dear," Grace used to tell Henrietta in the schoolroom. "He fell in love with her at first sight, when he saw her dressed up as Sabrina in *Comus*. They did the play in the Rectory garden in 1922 to make money for Yeoman's Hospital. Everybody in Wilchester took tickets, it lasted for three days and your dear father went every single day just to look at her. I went myself; your grandmother took me, it really was a very good performance. All the boys from the Choir School were dressed up in green, with animal faces; my sister's two boys were in it, I remember, one was a pig, the other was a dog, and they ran about shrieking; great fun they had. One of the curates from St. Blaizey's was Comus, they dressed him up in a lion-skin from the Waterloo staircase here, Sir Alfred Hornbeam had shot it, in Rhodesia I believe; he was a very handsome young man, with a wreath of grapes on his head, he spoke the words beautifully. Miss Jones from the High School was the Lady; she sat in a chair and they made speeches round her. Of course you couldn't hear much of what they said, you never can at these outdoor performances, but it all looked very pretty." "It sounds ghastly to me," Henrietta used to say as a schoolgirl when invited to listen to these reminiscences by Thorney, as the twins called their governess.

"No, dear, it wasn't; it was a great success," Grace Thorn would tell her rebellious pupil. "Your mother looked lovely. She came up out of a hole the gardener dug in the ground, in front of a grotto with ivy hanging over it. She was just eighteen. She wore a green dress made of butter-muslin with a wreath of water-lilies and her hair hung down her back. Masses of hair she had, so long she could sit on it and so fair it was nearly white. She used to do it in snail-shells over her ears. When everybody else began cutting off their hair she wanted to cut her own because she was tired of brushing it; but your dear father wouldn't hear of it. He always said he'd fallen in love with her 'amber-dropping hair'." So Thorney would finish her story triumphantly, while Henrietta gazed dumbly at a schoolroom photograph of the mother who had died when she and her twin brother were born. The photograph looked back at her, a head with masses of hair and white shoulders draped in chiffon, large frightened eyes and parted lips, faintly tinted. "Looks as if she were saying 'Where are my clothes?'" Henrietta had once exclaimed in a temper; and Thorney had protested, "It was the fashion then, dear; all the photographs were taken that way. I was so pleased when she gave me this one. It was an excellent likeness taken by Keturah Collins. She was quite lovely." Once when Henrietta burst out, "Granny talks about her as if she'd been some sort of a white mouse," Thorney had been really shocked. "Don't ever think that, dear, it simply isn't true. She was sweet and your father adored her; two people were never so happy as they were. She wasn't much of a talker, perhaps, but then she didn't need to be. He wanted a quiet one, after all he'd been through. Nothing ever put her out, she was always gentle and kind and bore with your grandmother's ways like an angel. Oh! it was such a shame your father and she had such a short time together. He married her three months after he saw her first and she was dead in a year." And with a heavy sigh Thorney would lament, "He never really got over it."

3

After Sylvia's death Lady Hornbeam returned from London and took her old place as the mistress of Fountain Court; it had never had another since. Edward drifted about like a lost soul, with shabby clothes and an unbrushed look; he pottered about the place, gave a few orders for the look of the thing and then went off by himself to the woods. He let his mother do exactly what she liked with the house and the estate. The children were in Nanny's hands at first; later Grace Thorn became their governess, that was one of Lady Hornbeam's economies. It did not answer too badly; Grace was a twittering foolish creature, but she was kind and patient. She adored the children, who teased her and called her Thorney; she did quite well while they were little. When Harry was nine his father insisted on sending him away to a preparatory school, afterwards he went to Winchester; the son and heir, the future fourth Lord Hornbeam, could do no less. Harry was never much of a scholar, but he played cricket extremely well and scored fifty-six in his last year in the Eton match.

Henrietta had no money wasted upon her education; she remained in the schoolroom with Thorney, learning little and missing her twin brother dreadfully. Her father put books in her way, but she was no reader; he used to do sums and play chess with her, take her out with him on his walks round the gardens, fields and woods, set her down in his office and make her help him with his accounts. In this way she learnt a great deal about the way the dwindling estate was being mismanaged; before she was twelve she used to help him keep his books in order, she had a head for figures and became very good at accounts. The shy anxious man used to talk about his troubles, more to himself than to her; once she heard him say, "I don't see how we can manage, do you, if your grandmother goes on spending money like this?" It made the little girl feel quite grown up for the moment, it confirmed her in an enormous dislike of her grandmother.

She had at that time all sorts of youthful fancies about how she and Harry would help their father when they were older; but it all came to nothing, for poor Edward met with a fatal shooting accident when the twins were fourteen. He had gone out into the woods, that November afternoon with a gun, a thing he rarely did, for since the war he liked watching birds better than he did shooting them; but he wanted to get a shot at a hawk which was killing young chickens and his gun must have got caught in a branch, as he was climbing over a fence at the top of Hen-and-Chicken Wood. He was found at the foot of a slippery clay bank, he had been dead for a couple of hours, but nobody had missed him; he was always going off into the woods to get away from people. He had asked Henrietta to come with him, but the girl had got out of it; she wanted to clean all the rabbit hutches in the disused stable, with Harry at Winchester they took a great deal of her time. She was actually still at work when they brought her dead father home. She heard feet trampling on the cobbles, and men shouting, so she looked out of the window and four of the labourers were carrying something on a hurdle into the yard. A dead calf or colt, she thought, under the sack; there was a lot of blood, but she did not mind that until she saw that one of the young keepers was there, carrying her father's hat and gun. Then she left the door of the hutch open and ran out into the yard; three of the white Angoras got out afterwards and the dogs killed them. Old Furze the head-keeper was stamping and swearing. "I always told his Lordship from a boy that he'd come to a bad end if he didn't take his cartridges out before getting over a fence; but he never would take the trouble. Always wool-gathering, never kept his mind on what he was doing and now he's finished hisself. Goes all through the war without a scratch and shoots hisself climbing a fence in his own woods." He was purple in the face with fury, he did not see Henrietta come up behind him. The maids ran out of the kitchen and one of them screeched out "Oh! the poor master; he's killed, he's killed" flung her apron over her head and began crying. That was how Henrietta knew that her father was dead.

4

Nanny had a lot of trouble with Henrietta afterwards; she was sick for days together, had nightmares for weeks, kept waking up and crying. Harry came home for the funeral, because he was now Lord Hornbeam; but he went back afterwards and in January Henrietta was packed away to a boarding school. Thorney then left Fountain Court and settled down in a cottage at the gates, but she spent most of her days running up to do what she could for Lady Hornbeam. You never knew when you would not run into her at some corner of a long passage, carrying a flower-vase, a bunch of letters or a teacup on a tray. "Thorney's always under foot," Henrietta used to complain to her brother when she first came back from school. "I get sick of the way she fusses round Granny. Hasn't she anything else to do but come up here and venerate the Hornbeams?" but Harry, a sunny-tempered boy, would only drawl, "Poor Thorney, we can't turn her out after all these years." So Thorney remained, all through the Second World War, while Henrietta was working on the land and Harry was in the Army; by the time that the war came to an end it was far too late to do anything about getting rid of her. She had very little to do nowadays for the old lady, except sit by her bedside and listen to her chatter; but she had transferred her affections to Henrietta and was always running round offering to arrange the State rooms. She would dust the library books, wash all the china in the cabinets, clean the glass chandeliers piece by piece, even sponge the gilt frames and rub up the fine furniture; it was true that none of these tasks could be safely left to the various cleaning-women who came up irregularly from the village. On visiting days Thorney would take tickets, give change, show people round; and twice a week she did all the vases. This was her most useful occupation. She liked to come up early on a show-day, bring in a haystack of flowers and spend about two hours in the old schoolroom, making arrangements according to the season. She did huge trophies for the empty fireplaces, filled china baskets with roses and sweet-peas for the tops of the drawing-room cabinets, crammed the Sèvres centrepiece on the dining-room table and made tight little Victorian posies of short-stemmed flowers to adorn the three State bedrooms.

She took endless trouble to match or contrast the flowers with the colours of the different rooms; Henrietta used sometimes to imitate her to Charles. " '*White* for the Red Dining-room', she says; 'or at any rate gold or yellow; it's not only the wallpaper, it's the turquoise border of the dinner-service that makes that room so difficult. *Blue* is best for the Drawing-room, it brings out the canary colour in the draperies; fortunately there's always plenty of blue in this garden. The Library is so dark, with all those books; I have to *brighten* it'," Henrietta would simper, imitating Thorney's way of smoothing her black satin apron and patting her netted hair. " 'I use all the vivid colours I can find, snapdragons, marigolds, nasturtiums, golden-rod and of course all the dear berries.' She drives me raving mad with her nonsense," Henrietta would cry out impatiently. "I sometimes wish to God I hadn't let her start this flower-business. Nobody notices her vases and the stuff all has to be thrown out before the next show-day; it's just a waste of time." Charles had surprised her once by objecting, "*I* notice them for one and the customers love them. I often hear them say, 'Just look at all those roses.' The old girl does them beautifully, they cheer the place up and nobody else has time for the job." "Oh! Thorney has all the time in the world," Henrietta told him crossly. "She hasn't had a thing to do for thirty years except come up here and play she's a Hornbeam."

She was hard at work when Henrietta put her head round the door after breakfast, on the way to the kitchen; poking away at a haystack of fading blossoms, picking out a big dahlia and snipping off the stem. "After this wet summer, nothing lasts," she bleated mournfully. "This jolly fellow will drop to-morrow." "I came to ask you for an extra bowl for the table in the Octagon Room," Henrietta told her and she brightened immediately. "I'll do you a basket of spindleberries," she promised, "with just one or two of these big short-stemmed chaps. I always think the Octagon Room needs cheerful colours; such a lot of *marble*. And I hear you have a very important lunch-party, so we must have everything at its best, mustn't we?" She looked coy and meaning. Henrietta went out and the door banged after her.

III

ROOTE THE gardener, hobbling and stooping, was at the back door before ten with Joe the garden-boy, taking the vegetables out of the boy's basket with his earthy old hands and dumping them on the flagstones. He had brought leathery potatoes full of eyes, misshapen artichokes, bunched carrots and turnips, papery brown onions and half-a-dozen cabbages like green footballs, sopping with dew. "I don't call that lot company veges," said the fat cook, Mrs. Peppercorn, old as he, waddling across the kitchen and turning the pile over with her foot. "Ain't you got no celery yet, Mr. Roote? We've company to lunch."

"Well, if these ain't good enough, I dunno what I can do for 'ee," mumbled Roote. "Celery; you didn't orter dig celery till you've 'ad a frost to put a bone in it. This autumn 'tis all drip, drip, drip; celery's all drawed up an' stalky, 'tain't rightly fit to send to table. Shall I send young Joey back to gather 'ee a dish of sprouts?" "Brusselses ain't company veges neither, to my mind," said she. "Not without you dress 'em up some way with chestnuts or a sugar-glaze. Do you run across to the green'ouses, Joe, an' fetch me four pounds of mushrooms an' I'll make do." She poured water from the hissing kettle into a waiting teapot and set it on the corner of the table. "There's your tea, Mr. Roote," said she, banging a mug down beside it and pushing the sugar basin over. "You'll excuse my gettin' on with my work, I'm sure; we're pressed for time 'smornin'."

She sat with her knees wide, plucking the cock-pheasant in her lap with incredible speed; her fat fingers dropped tufts of orange and copper feathers, pluck, pluck, pluck, on the newspaper at her

feet; the imperial head dangled at her knee with eyes closed, like
a dead Chinese emperor. Roote sugared his tea lavishly, blew on
it, drank and continued to decry the weather. "Outlandish I calls
it; All Saint's Day to-morrow an' no frost yet. Sky was like a red
apple last night, but it rained again at daybreak; dunno what's
come to the world these days." "Never bin right since they started
lettin' off these atom-bombs," agreed Mrs. Peppercorn mechanically, as one who recites the due platitude for the occasion; with
more interest she told the kitchen-maid, "Hurry up with them
breakfast things, Gladys, my girl; it's past nine an' the dishes not
washed." "I just done 'em," pouted Gladys Moss, pushing the last
plate into the rack. "Then fetch me that pair of rabbits from the
larder, an' that snipe. Skin 'em an' cut 'em up quick an' we'll pop
'em in the pressure cooker for a start. Mushrooms," she said with
her finger at her lip, "we'll 'ave plenty; do me some potherbs an'
one or two onions for fryin'. There's the last of the mutton an' half
a hare; it'll all do to help out the gravy. Game-pie, that's what
we'll give 'em; gentlemen always likes it."

"Who you got comin'?" asked Roote, supping up his tea, wiping
his grey-bristled lips with the back of his gnarled hand. "It's Miss
Henrietta's rich American gentleman," the kitchen-maid offered
eagerly, "an' a dealer from London, coming down to buy the big
picture in the Drawing-room." "Your tongue's hung loose, that's
what's the matter with you," the cook said, scattering feathers as
she rose to her feet. "If you was as quick with yer fingers as you
is with yer tongue we'd get on better. Never did see such a girl
to dawdle." The sink tap was turned on vigorously, drowning her
old voice with splashing and drumming; Gladys tugged and
chopped angrily at the rabbit on the draining board, grumbling
to herself. "Well if you've got a party, I'd best be on me way,"
said Roote peaceably, getting to his feet and easing his back cau-
tiously. "Lord! 'ow me bones do ache; there's more rain coming, I
don't doubt." He went out of the back door, they heard his nailed
boots scraping on the flagstones and his old voice talking to the

kitchen cat. "Party," said Mrs. Peppercorn scornfully, "two gentle-men droppin' in to lunch, that ain't a party. In the old days we'd 'ave 'ad twenty to lunch an' no fuss made. There'd be a dozen pans simmerin' away on top of the range an' the oven cram-full of pies or cakes; game an' fowls turnin' round on spits before the fire an' a couple of quarts of jam cookin' on the corner; an' all our old cook'd say to me would be, 'Next time you go by, Mary, give the jam a stir.' We lived on the fat of the land then; there was plenty for everyone. The larder was full of game, you could smell it half-way down the passage; I wouldn't have had to make do with half a hare and an old cock-pheasant for company in those days, nor they wouldn't've touched rabbit in the dining-room. We had anythin' we fancied, we was never short of servants then. The girls come in off the estate to get their trainin' against the time they married; there was kitchen-maids and scullery-maids and under-housemaids; they had to work properly. If one of 'em didn't give satisfaction off she went and we got in another. There was plenty of willin' girls to choose from, they all wanted to come up here. The boys worked in the gardens and the stables, the handy civil ones came indoors; why we'd sit down twenty in the servants' hall then, without visitors. It was like one big family. We lived on the fat of the land, the young men all made up to the girls; there'd be half a dozen of 'em after one girl, great handsome six-foot chaps in blue liveries with their hair in powder, matched like carriage horses. I wonder what's become of 'em all? They had to mind their manners at meals. The butler sat at one end of the table and the housekeeper she sat at the other, to see that everything was done proper; but once the puddin' came in the upper servants all took their plates and went up to the housekeeper's room, Pug's Parlour, we called it; and then the fun and games began. Those were the days, you never saw nothin' like it, never will again, I suppose, not in a private house. I don't know why I stop on," she brooded darkly, "I ought to be getting my ten pounds a week in a hotel, with my experience; but there it is, I'm too old to change."

Gladys Moss wielded a chopper vigorously. "They did ought to give you more notice when there's people coming," she offered. "But the American boys are all the same, never let you know they're on their way, turn up on the doorstep and expect to find you ready and waiting with your hair curled and all." She brought a colander full of reeking fragments and offered it to the cook muttering, "Nasty things, I wouldn't eat rabbit anyhow, with all this myxo-what-you-call-it about. Roads is covered with 'em round the base, all squashed an' lying about, and if you go up by the quarry of a evening you can see a dozen, sitting there with their eyes bunged up, waiting to be knocked on the head. It's no joke." "These is tame ones," said Mrs. Peppercorn briefly. "They don't get it. You're a Londoner, you don't know what's what. Pheasant's an old bird, too. They'll eat well enough though, done up with mushrooms an' hare gravy. Open a bottle of tomatoes, child, they'll help to soften the bird. I don't know where we'd be in this house if the Commander weren't such a useful shot. He keeps us in game all autumn." "Don't know how he does it, with his one arm," said Gladys. "Oh! he's got that little light gun, had it made for him, like the old Kaiser, he always shot one-handed." "That was before my time," said Gladys, drying her hands, patting her black curls at the cracked glass above the sink. "You get on with your pot-herbs," the cook advised her, setting bacon fat to sizzle above the fire.

2

Gladys scraped and scrubbed with her red hands in the dirty water, a strong odour of earth and root-vegetables filled the kitchen. "Don't see the sense of all this dirty veg. work," she grumbled, rinsing. "Why can't you open a tin or two if you're in such a hurry? Our Mum buys carrots in tins when she wants 'em; not that she wants 'em often. None of us eats carrots. We wouldn't be bothered with all this cutting and scraping. Look at the waste there is with it." She dumped the peelings into a bucket. " 'Tain't waste," the cook said, poking bits of pheasant and onion about in the stewpan. "Such nonsense you do talk. Feeds the hens for one thing, don't it? We've never bin short of eggs in this kitchen, not even in the War. Caramel custard, I'll make, or a cheese soufflé; that'd be better, about all this mouse-trap cheese is fit for." A savoury smell rose from the pan. "Hurry up with them carrots, can't you?" said Cook. "Such nonsense I never did hear. You can't hope to make a stew proper unless you fry onions and potherbs first, it draws the flavour. I'm sorry for your husband, if ever you get one, Gladys Moss, with nothin' to put in his stomach but rubbish out of tins."

"I'm not marrying any of the boys round here," said Gladys, tossing her black curls out of her eyes, peeling and slicing, with onion-tears running down her face. "I'm off to America if I get the chance. They got lovely houses there, everything done for you by the electricity, all the food out of tins and packages, none of this slaving and scrubbing." "You mind what you're about," the cook advised her. "Wouldn't have too much to do with the Yanks if I were you." She added joints of pheasant to her stew and turned them about in the bottom of the pan.

"You don't know nothin' about 'em," Gladys protested, opening her eyes very wide. "Lovely boys, they are, Mrs. Peppercorn; all the girls round here are wild to get a date with a Yank. So easy and natural they are, not stiff and stupid like our boys, always nicely behaved." "There's some that is and some that isn't," said Mrs. Peppercorn darkly, picking up the little black corpse of a snipe by one leg and dropping it into the stew. "This is coming along nicely, I'll shut it up in a minute. You better go easy with those Yanks of yours, my girl." "But they give you a lovely time," Gladys wailed. "They've got so much money and they're so free with it. Why, there's one I met last Saturday night at the dance hall in Wilchester, promised me three pairs of nylons; ever so attractive he was, shouldn't wonder if he proposed." "So long as it's marriage he proposes," said Mrs. Peppercorn unconvinced. She tipped hare-gravy into the pressure-cooker and fastened down the lid, almost at once a sinister hissing filled the kitchen. "I'm terrified of them things," observed Gladys, gazing fascinated. "Then I suppose you won't want one for a weddin'-present," retorted Cook. She pulled the raving thing to the back of the stove and it subsided, purring gently and rhythmically; then she glanced at the clock. "Potatoes, plenty of 'em," she commanded; and reverting to pressure-cookers, "They're all right if you understand 'em, like some other things as I could name. Why can't you let the Yanks alone, Gladys? I thought you was going steady with my nephew Sid." She took down a basin, a bag of flour, a lump of butter and the rolling pin; all went on one end of the table, where the marble top of an old washstand did for pastry-board.

"He's got another think coming, if that's what he says," Gladys declared. "Fancy wanting me to go and start married life in the Brook Cottage, with the rain comin' through the roof, no water, no drains; we 'ad better than that in Whitechapel." She was one of a family of evacuees who had come to the village when the air-raids began and stayed on after peace was signed. Her father had a job bus-driving, her brothers had gone on the land; there were twenty pounds a week in wages coming into their Council house. The Moss boys kept greyhounds and were proper poachers, the younger children spent their free time outside the village shop, sucking ice-cream and toffee apples; the whole family went to the pictures twice a week and took coach rides on summer Sundays. Gladys was an idle slut, not much use to Mrs. Peppercorn, who declared "She don't know what work is. All she wants is a boy to take her to the pictures and she ain't too partic'lar who she goes with. I do pity the man that marries her." Kneading and turning her pastry, she only lent half an ear to Gladys at the sink, grumbling, "Jealous, you are, that's what I told 'im, can't afford to take me out and treat me proper. Why don't you chuck the farm,

Sid, and get a job at the base? I said. They wants a steady young chap to drive that bus of theirs, up and down the airfield and into Wilchester at nights; better pay than you get for going out on the tractor in all weathers."

"Sid won't work for the Yanks," said Mrs. Peppercorn, flapping the dough together and slapping it on to a plate. "Savages, that's what he says they are. Take 'em into Wilchester, an' they all comes back at midnight, roaring drunk; they broke the last driver's head for him, as well you know, that's why the job's going. Let 'em go back, Sid says, where they belong; we don't want none of 'em 'ere. You've got a good steady chap, Gladys, don't you go putting no ideas into him about changing his job. The Yanks they comes and they goes; next year or the year after they'll go home and good riddance; but the land's always there and Sid'll do best to stick to what he knows. I've no patience with you, Gladys," she concluded, dusting the flour off her fat pink hands. "Proper sort of housewife you'll make when your time comes, if ever it does. Never open the windows, never shake out the rugs, never sweep under the bed; pull the blankets up over an' call it making. Let the frying fat splash on the wall an' the pans burn at the bottom while you curls yer hair at the glass an' listens to the wireless. When it comes to dinner time slice up a meat loaf, open a tin of peas, mix up a soup-packet, put a dab of jam an' some stale cake in a sundae glass an' call it trifle; where's the use of that to a hungry man? I know your sort, Gladys Moss, you're no wife for a working man. Once you're married you'll never wash yer face or curl yer hair again. Bone-idle, that's what you are, my nephew'll be well rid of you. Wish I was."

"Then you can be any time, Mrs. Peppercorn," retorted Gladys. "I can get a better job than this one any day; place wants a bomb dropped on it to wake it up, all thinking yerselves too good for the rest of the world, talking about the good old days; I've 'ad enough of it. You can take my notice today, Mrs. Peppercorn. I'll put in for a good job at the Base canteen, or in Woolworth's."

"You won't get any such, not with the reference you'll have from me," Mrs. Peppercorn retorted. "They pays good money, they can pick an' choose. Now put this pastry by the larder-window till I'm ready for it an' take those peelin's out to the pig-pail. This rate, we'll never get done."

They had a similar exchange most mornings. It meant nothing in particular, but it helped the work along; there was plenty for two pairs of hands to do, even without a party. "Give that there cat a drop of the breakfast milk before it goes away," Cook concluded, "an' here's a tiddy-bit of hare for you, my beauty-boy," she said to Boffin. "Eat it up quick an' get out from under m'feet; I'm too busy for you 'smorning."

3

In the Second World War there had been two aerodromes close together in the valley near Tadpole Brook; Lambscot first and after it a secondary establishment at Nether Barton, used for training glider pilots. After the war the two joined together and in 1952 it was all taken over by the American Air Force, who called it Wilchester. It was now an enormous dun-coloured waste, crisscrossed by concrete runways, the biggest two miles long, and guarded by searchlights and barbed wire defences. There were twice as many hangars and buildings as before, lines of pylons and signal-lights converged upon the place, two roads which had traversed it had been shut up, dividing Lambscot from Littlefold and a new village of bungalows, huts and shops had sprung up at the gates. Here by day huge multi-engined bombers roared and circled, heaved themselves into the air and soared off, past the spire of Lambscot church, which now had a red light fixed upon it at night like a star. They trailed foul clouds of black smoke behind them, dirtying the sky; the weathercock on the steeple used to turn its head after them as they went by. On one particularly

active day, when seventeen of them went away to Texas, going
off every six minutes like trains in the sky, half the ceilings in
Littlefold dropped plaster and the suck of air drew out a willow
in the policeman's garden like a corkscrew by the roots; it crashed
into the brook and took his telephone wire with it. That year they
filled the sky with their talking, droning round hour after hour in
the summer weather, describing black-and-white circles in the air.
Men working in the fields, women and children picking blackber-
ries or mushrooms, would look up and see a plane above them like
a great fish with the dumb gape of a shark. The noise of the engines had a life of its own; after the first roar had gone over like
thunder, a high shrill whine and rumble, its echoes flapped about
and proliferated, returning from unexpected points of the com-
pass, growing louder as the plane itself became smaller and flew
away.

At night there seemed to be lights in every field, the planes
went round and round, winking red and white eyes, making a
path before them with a searchlight as they came in to land, blot-
ting out the stars with the glare from the airfield. At sunrise and
sunset they made lovely intricate trails of gold in the upper air.
When the wind suited them they would put down a smoke-screen
for practice, burning paraffin to windward; it drifted over Littlefold village, staining the brightness of the summer morning, dirtying the washing on the Monday lines, making an iridescent scum
on the village pond. "You can taste it on your tongue," the older
women would say. "Nasty oily stuff; might as well live in London."
Richer people, without ties in the neighbourhood, began to talk of
going away, only to find that the value of the larger houses had
dropped almost overnight; it appeared in 1954 that nobody was
going to buy anything on the edge of an aerodrome. "The place is
ruined," they told each other, "since the planes came. It isn't
proper country any more": and somebody said, "The price of
peace."

And the Americans swarmed into the villages, hulking pasty-faced young men, affable and noisy, in checked shirts and fur-lined jackets, with their hands in their pockets, very free with their money, always grumbling at the weather, always saying how much better life was at home. They drove big cars too fast round corners, crowded you into the ditch in the narrow lanes, ran over dogs and cats, made children scamper; four of them coming back to the base after an evening's drinking in Wilchester ran into the baker at his own door on a foggy evening and broke his arm and his leg; they said that he had been standing in front of his tail-light, emptying the van, but the villagers were very angry about it. "Should've kept a better look out," they said. "Poor Jim's in Yeo-man's Hospital, won't be out of bed for six weeks, nor fit to work for three months and where's our bread to come from?"

Presently the wives arrived, soft sleek young women most of them, with astonishing clothes, always grumbling about the cold and damp of English winters, keeping house in quite a different fashion from the village women. "That little Mrs. Hickory," you would hear them decide, "she's nice enough, but she's no use, her mother never taught her nothing. Hours she'll spend dolling up little sandwiches and biscuits for a party, with anchovies and tunny and hard-boiled eggs; but never a proper joint-and-veg. or a nice rice-pudding. The husband he pays six guineas a week for that rathole next the pub. Roof leaks, damp rises in the walls, chimneys all smoke; properly done, they been, I reckon. Nice bit of garden behind, but they don't never puts a spade in it, it's just full of weeds, high as your waist. They never eats fresh vegetables, has everything out of tins; puts their empties out of the back door when they've finished and thinks no more of 'em. My hens has a rare time scratching about, the paper and cardboard blows half-way down the lane. She says there's a spring under the kitchen flagstones, mice in the larder and rats in the roof; there's a gap under the scullery door you can put two fingers in, no wonder she can't keep the place warm. Went into Wilchester, she did, and brought back six paraffin stoves and four big electric fires. She burns 'em night and day. Gallons and gallons of paraffin they takes a week from the van, as well as all the current they burns; no wonder he says they can't live on their pay." In this way the old civilisation criticised the young one.

With all the extra electricity that the Americans used in their cottages the grid broke down and workmen were up and down the street for a week, putting extra wires on the poles. "One good thing they've brought in," the village said, "they'd never 'ave done it for us." Some of the local men got work on the base, some of the girls were employed at the canteen, the older women did charing and baby-sitting; most of their talk at the butcher's and in the post-office was about their American employers. "You never seen the way mine goes on; bone-idle, I calls 'er, puts me in mind of them evacuee women in the war." "Mine don't do no cleaning, never buys me so much as a floor-cloth or a tin of polish 'less I asks 'er twice; just strips the beds in the morning and covers 'em up again at night; never darns 'er nylons, just ladders 'em an' throws 'em away." "Mine don't keep no reg'lar hours for meals, 'Just go to the ice-box and help yourself, love,' she says to that little boy of 'ers. Everything that poor child eats comes out of a tin; even the milk's dried. Goes round in a peaky cap an' a quilted jacket an' trousers, with ear-muffs on, bundled up as if 'e was at the North Pole. Great doorsteps of bread and butter she gives 'im, spread thick with shrimps an' a bar of choc-ice-cream on top of it; stands to reason 'e's sick after. Weedy cross-eyed little chap 'e is, always whining for this an' that, like a puppy; she never corrects 'im, lets 'im do just whatever 'e 'as a mind to. Fact is, the poor child's lonely, so 'e gets into mischief. 'Smorning 'e comes in with his dirty shoes all over the clean floor in her kitchen just after I'd done scrubbing it. 'E takes 'is little toy fire-engine and scratches it up and down the wall till 'e gets the paper loose; then 'e tears it down in strips, like, and all 'is Mum says to me is, 'Ain't he cute?' 'If you was my boy', I says to 'im, 'I'd soon teach you better manners. Your Dad'll 'ave to pay for all new paper by the time he goes back to America. You get off my clean floor, I says and go and wipe your boots.' I can't bear to see a child get into bad ways. 'E minds me now, I told 'im off proper; if I stays there I'll teach 'im how to behave. Elmer, she calls 'im, now don't you think that's a silly name?'"

"They does a lot of damage to people's houses," her friend said. "Don't know that I'd want 'em in mine, for all the rent they pays."

"What's good money to us is chicken-feed to them," a third said. "Mine gives three-and-six an hour and never grumbles. She's never had much help before, says where she lives in America nobody will go out and do housework, think it's beneath 'em. Generous with her stuff she is, too; gives me tins of sweet-corn and lard, what she calls shortening, and fruit and that, all from the PX, that's what they call their shop at the Base. Once I got a prefab-cake in a packet, you only need put water to it and it comes up lovely. Then there's all sorts of soup in tinfoil, mushroom and noodles and such, she don't keep no stockpot; and every morning we sits down together to a cupper in the kitchen. She's a nice woman, I likes her."

"I likes working for Mrs. 'Ickory;" the first summed up, "only trouble is, the hours is getting too long. All them two wants is, to go on up to the base, nights, and dance till midnight or after; they'd stay till two or three in the morning if I'd let them. Well, they're young. She'll pay me overtime to sit in for 'er, in case that little Elmer was to wake up and get a fright; or set the house on fire, more likely. I 'as that great big telly of 'ers to look in at and I gets on with Ted's socks; it's all very well for two or three nights a week, but Ted don't like it, 'specially Saturdays. Says I ought to stay at home with 'im.'"

The strange young men played their part in the villages for a time, spending freely, giving presents of nylons and scent, drinking the small inns dry in turn, taking the local girls in their big cars to Wilchester for dancing and the pictures. Some were merely friendly and lonely, but you heard more about the wild ones, who got girls into trouble, smashed up cars in ditches, had fights in public-houses at the end of the evening and had to be fetched

away by their own police. In the second winter they all went away
for a time while the runways were repaired and relaid; the wet
ground of the Tadpole Brook Valley had sunk under the weight of
the big machines. It was dull in the villages while the Americans
were away, though older people were glad of the quiet nights.
"I couldn't sleep, could you?" they said to each other, "with those
great machines going round and round till three and four in the
morning. It was too much like the war." That was the real trouble;
in this countryside, which had once been lonely and quiet, every
one associated the Americans with another war. They had the
mushroom cloud behind them, blowing up out of the Arizona desert; they were a nation of strangers, though they seemed to speak
the same language; people made them feel unwelcome, resented,
shut out. At the beginning there had been attempts to be friendly,
but none of these came to very much; shyness and envy changed
to mutual dislike. The Americans were snubbed, overcharged, ignored; presently they withdrew into their own small world of the
base and were no more seen. They came and went in batches for
ninety-day courses in dirty-weather flying; they spent money less
freely, did not take out the English girls so often, gave fewer
parties. The English told each other hopefully, "They'll soon be
leaving; they've only got another year to finish, after that our own
Air Force is taking over;" the Americans said openly, "We're dead
sick of this lousy place, only putting in time till we're posted
home."

4

Henrietta Hornbeam's American was not actually from the base.
She had found him one morning in the village church, which stood
quite close to Fountain Court, in the corner of the field called
Leisure Ground, where Royalist troops had encamped in the
Civil War. It was a little plain church like a barn with neither

tower nor steeple, dedicated first to Saint George, later to King Charles the Martyr. It had no architectural features except a carving in the tympanum of the south doorway, representing Apollo, or Sagittarius, or Saint George himself, in the guise of a centaur, transfixing the dragon of darkness with an arrow of sunshine; the Wilchester archæological society usually inspected this when they had a field-day near by. Within the church had become a mausoleum for the Hornbeam family. Their effigies made a stone congregation in it on week-days. Elizabethan and Jacobean Hornbeams in stone ruffs and trunk-hose reclined upon their elbows in niches, like sea-sick passengers on a Channel boat; a Georgian admiral was lamented by puffing cherubs in marble flourishing pistols, sextants and other marine stage-properties; there was an urn erected to the memory of Lavinia, wife of General Sir George Hornbeam ('her conversation was amiable, her genius innocently sprightly'). An immense tomb and epitaph commemorated the first Lord Hornbeam, the Victorian statesman; an inscription recorded the campaigns of General Sir Alfred Hornbeam, Governor of the Unfriendly Islands; there were discreet memorials in black and white marble to twentieth century Hornbeams, including that to Henrietta's father, Edward, the third Baron, killed by the accidental discharge of a gun when out shooting. Latest of all was the wooden cross for Henry, fourth Lord Hornbeam, her lost brother Harry, whose bones were somewhere in a Dutch dyke. It hung above the family pew and Henrietta used to sit under it every Sunday.

All these monuments, however, were overshadowed for the tourist by the life-size alabaster effigy of the Cavalier captain, Mad Harry Hornbeam, in gilded armour, stretching out his hand in a gesture of command. He occupied the small north transept, at the end of the family pew; generations of Hornbeam children had got themselves through sermon-time by admiring his hawk-face, his curls, his lace collar, his mailed corselet and gloves, the wrinkles in his spurred knee-boots, the pistols in his tasselled sash.

Henrietta had found her American staring at Harry. He was a big broad-shouldered well-tailored man in his middle thirties, rather puffy and pale in the face, as most of them seemed to be; he looked like an athlete beginning to run to seed from lack of exercise. His face was pale in the cold indoor light. He stared at Henrietta, coming out of the vestry with a vase in each hand, in a sacking apron over an old coat, with a garden hat on her head. She noted the bruised look of the flesh on his cheek-bones and thought for a moment that he had been weeping; then crossly decided that he had probably made a late night of it.

He spoke to her immediately; they always did that. "I was wondering about this young soldier, maybe you can tell me who he was." Then he took the spindling narrow-necked brass vases from her and said, "You want these on the altar, I guess." They contained rigid bunches of roses; Henrietta never had the patience to do flowers properly and had only been obliged on that summer Saturday to deputise for Thorney, who had a cold. When her stranger came back down the chancel steps she was ready to tell him, "That was Captain Harry Hornbeam, my ancestor. He fought for King Charles in our Civil War, he was killed at the first Battle of Newbury." "I should know that name," the stranger said. "We have an airfield near by, I believe; my young brother was there at one time. I didn't know you British had had a battle there." "Two," said Henrietta briefly, disliking his intent look; he seemed not to be able to take his eyes off her. "Then your name's Hornbeam, I take it," said he, glancing about the little sanctuary. "There seem to be several Hornbeams buried here; those seasick gentlemen, for instance, I had a look at them. Is this your family chapel?"

She said, "No, it's the parish church, but nobody comes much nowadays. We do seem rather to have taken it over." She gave him one or two names and dates, translated Mad Harry's Latin inscription politely, thinking that he was wrecking her morning; then said briskly, "Well, I must be getting back. If you're interested in the family, come round the house this afternoon. It's one of the days when we're open to the public. We show Wednesdays and Saturdays; half-a-crown for the house, a shilling extra for the gardens; that's how we keep the roof on the place." She was always a little tart about this part of the business, did not much like luring in travellers to inspect the present decay of the Hornbeams, but her American took it all in good part. "I'd've appreciated that," said he weightily, "but I'm afraid I have to catch a two-o'clock train back to London. I only came down for . . . well, I suppose you'd call it the funeral; not that there was much left of the poor boys to bury." He looked hard at her and again she saw the strains round his eyelids; no doubt about it, he had been weeping.

"My young brother, Willy," said he, hesitating a little on the name. "He was in that crash they had on Tuesday. Coming in to land, it was very foggy; the pilot touched down a fraction too soon and stood the machine up on its nose, I believe. There were three killed and Willy was one of them. I daresay you heard the noise. The whole thing went up in flames, there was nothing to be done except wait till it burnt itself out and scrape up the bits." He added patiently, "I've heard it said they do teach the boys to land a bit too far up the runway; there isn't any room to spare, it's one of your little airfields; they've taken in as much ground as they can already. Every so often one of 'em misjudges it and that's the end of him. I wouldn't know much about that, I'm not a flying man myself."

Henrietta said immediately, in a different voice, "I'm frightfully sorry," and he admitted, "Yes, it's tough. Willy was only just turned twenty-two, the youngest of the family. Of course, it's all part of the set-up, boys getting smashed and killed before they've had time to do anything; but somehow you think more of it in peace-time." He turned his head as if away from some sight unwelcome to him, fixing his eyes on the wooden cross. "You have another Henry Hornbeam there," said he, as if trying to escape from his own thoughts. "Killed in the last war, at twenty-one; some relative,

I suppose." Henrietta said, "My brother," and with relief he muttered, "Then you know how it feels without my having to tell you." She answered briefly, "Yes, I know."

So after that she could not send him back to the aerodrome and his train without a little more talk, a walk up through the famous gardens, then at their midsummer best, and a midday bite of bread and cheese and a bottle of beer with herself and Cousin Charles in the old breakfast-room, where they usually took their meals. Charles was particularly helpful. You could always rely on him in any difficult situation. She let the two men exchange war-experiences, they were both in their middle-thirties and ten years back had been at sea. "They let me play I was a sailor for a year or two," the stranger said smiling, "but I was on the beach most of the time, didn't get further than Honolulu, never saw any action." Charles who had been torpedoed in the Atlantic, spent two days in an open boat, lost an arm and an eye, said sincerely, "Oh! bad luck." He appeared to understand the initials which garnished the stranger's vague tale of his war-services. "I wouldn't want you to think I was a fighting man," said he earnestly, looking from one Hornbeam face to the other. "I'm only a civilian really. They sent me back to the States in the end. My father died and they seemed to think I'd be better employed running the family business. Raincoats, we make," said he, brightening; "jackets, leggings, overalls, and such;" and Charles said agreeably, "Nothing more useful in a war."

The stranger's name, it seemed, was John Cornell. "Just come over on a business trip," said he, "when this must happen; so they got me down as next-of-kin. I'll have to be round this way again next week anyhow," he told Henrietta at parting, holding her hand for rather longer than she had expected. "If I may I'll call in, it'd be great to see you again, you've been wonderful to me." She said, "Oh! I'm always here," but did not really expect to see him; they always talked like that, they meant nothing by it. He shook her hand and went away.

Charles was inclined to tease her about her stranger afterwards, saying, "Well, we've certainly done our bit for Anglo-American friendship today, Penny; nice fellow, don't wonder you asked him in, wish there were more like him. Maybe he'll ask us out to dinner in Wilchester next time, he said he was coming back to the Woolpack. He called it a fine old English tavern and said he liked their food." "I don't suppose we shall ever see him again," said Henrietta crossly. Charles then gave her one of his Nelson-looks, round the corner, turning his head aside to use his good right eye. "Wouldn't be too sure of that," said he. "Fancy the chap's got the same taste as I have," and when she did not understand told her slyly, "Likes red hair." Henrietta had the most beautiful head of hair, a burning gold, like ripe asparagus fern or bracken, curling low behind her ears and springing away from her temples like flame. This Hornbeam hair was her chief beauty, but she took no trouble about it and it was usually wind-blown and unkempt. Charles had teased her from childhood about not brushing her hair. "Needs brushing now," he told her, smiling at her as if she were still twelve years old. "He never looked at it," said Henrietta tartly. "You never do either, if it comes to that." "I study it constantly," said Charles in his gentle voice. Henrietta then went out and shut the door hard behind her.

That had been at the beginning of July. Now it was the end of October and John Cornell was still in England. He had been over to Sweden and Germany, but each time he had turned up again at Fountain Court, as Charles said, like a bad penny, in search of Henrietta. At first his excuse was that it lay on his road to the Midlands, where he had business; then he found a better one, in seeking to purchase the Lawrence portrait in the Yellow Drawing-room. This heirloom, an agreeable half-length of General "Waterloo" Hornbeam's wife, was exactly what he said he wanted for his house in New England; and on this October Saturday he was bringing down a Bond Street dealer to value the picture.

5

Now that the Red Dining-room was kept all summer for show Henrietta and Charles were apt to take their casual meals in the old breakfast-room, which served Henrietta for her daily use. Any meal at which visitors were present was given in the Octagon Parlour. This domed but windowless imitation of a classical temple, with its four niches, its eight Corinthian pillars of yellow scagliola, its stucco decoration of honeysuckle and key-pattern, its frieze of rams' skulls, had been built as an Italian toy by Sir Charles, "Sensibility", Hornbeam, to house the finest of the bronzes and marbles brought back from his Grand Tour in 1775; the rest were disposed about the gardens. His portrait hung above the fireplace, opposite the door as you entered, a slender sheep-faced youth in an ash-grey satin coat and primrose knee-breeches, with his legs elegantly crossed. He leant upon a porphyry pedestal and behind his powdered head a curtain was looped up to disclose a view of the Eternal City. The artist had been generous here, throwing in the Colosseum, the dome of St. Peter's, several columns and churches, a distant lake, a cypress grove, some azure mountains and about a mile of aqueduct for good measure; no expense had been spared to remind the English milord of his travels.

In this classic retreat, which was fortunately behind the Library, on the way to the kitchens, Leaf the butler had laid the circular table for four, hobbling round like a jerky wooden puppet on his flat feet, fiddling with glass and silver under the reproachful eyes of four chaste marble nymphs. "Make it as pretty as you can, Mr. Leaf," urged Nanny, popping her grey head round the door on her way to take the dust-sheets off the State rooms. "We want to put our best foot foremost today, don't we?" She advanced into the little parlour and glanced round her with approval. There was a brisk wood fire in the marble cave of the hearth, the chill of the black-and-white pavement was mitigated by a thick, though worn, red Turkey carpet. Grace Thorn's bowl of dahlias and spindleberries did its duty on the table and there were plenty of bottles on the sideboard; the autumn sun streamed down from the shallow glass dome upon the last of the green Worcester service. Leaf had brought it out together with some of the Waterford glass and had carefully polished up the worn silver; each spoon and fork bore the maker's marks of Peter and Anne Bateman and the date-letter 1793 and was adorned by the Hornbeam crest, a serrated leaf with the motto *Viresco*. Leaf was very slow nowadays, but he knew his work.

"It does look lovely, Mr. Leaf," said Nanny, prowling round the table like an old grey cat. "I've done my best," admitted Leaf, straightening his bent shoulders. "A man can't do more." He added grudgingly, "It's good enough for them that's coming." "Times are changed, Mr. Leaf," Nanny reminded him, but he only grumbled, "I can see that for myself, Mrs. Branch; no need to remind me. A Jew tradesman wouldn't have sat down to table here in the old days, even if he did have a shop in St. James's and called himself an art-expert. Miss Henrietta need not have asked him to lunch. Tea would have been considered sufficient." He moved a dented silver mustard-pot half-an-inch to the right. "It's a long drive from London," Nanny pleaded, "and there's her American gentleman coming as well. She'd want everything nice for him, just to show what we can do." "He's been here often enough these last few weeks to know the way we live now," Leaf said. "No need to put on airs for the likes of him."

The two old servants exchanged glances. "He fancies that picture over the drawing-room mantelpiece, I hear," Leaf said. "An ugly great thing to my mind, though they tell me it's valuable. The family have had their work cut out getting leave from the trustees to sell it at all, but he wouldn't take no for an answer; says he'll give Miss Henrietta a good price for it. The room won't look the same without it, but there's plenty prettier pictures up and down the house; however he's set his heart on that woman with the bird in her hand."

"He's set his heart on more than that, if you ask me," Nanny said darkly. The old butler screwed up his face as if he were tasting corked wine and nodded mournfully. "On Miss Henrietta," he pronounced. "More's the pity. Has she spoken to you about him, Mrs. Branch?"

"Not a word," said Nanny, shaking her grey head. "When he first came about the place I own I was hopeful. She was like her old self, laughing and joking and making fun, just as she used to do before Mr. Harry was killed; but lately she's gone right back into herself. Very difficult she's been, you can't do nothing right for her. Mrs. Peppercorn said the same to me this very morning; 'what's the matter with our young lady?' she asked me; 'cross as two sticks, she is.' Of course I said nothing. I know my place better than to ask any questions. She'll tell me in her own good time, Henrietta will," the old nurse boasted. "She knows I love her as well as if she'd been my own child; but you've more opportunities to watch 'em than I have nowadays, Mr. Leaf. She doesn't bring him up to me. Does he seem serious about her?"

"Never takes his eyes off her," the butler pronounced. "Listens to every word she says, takes no notice of anybody else when she's in the room, follows her about from pillar to post. As clear a case as ever I saw; if she wants him she's only got to hold up her finger."

"Ah! but will she do it? that's the question," Nanny demanded, coming close and peering in the old man's face. "Come, Mr. Leaf, you and I have been in service here all our days; we're part of the family, as you may say, by this time. Will she have him if he asks her?" but the old man would not help her. "I hope to God," said he sternly, "that our Miss Henrietta wouldn't do anything so unsuitable. Why, what would become of this place if she left us? Mr. Charles is well enough, he does what he can, but he's not the owner; her Ladyship can't last much longer and his little Lordship, he's only a child. Everything depends on Miss Henrietta for the time being. This American gentleman, if you can call him that," said Leaf, working himself up, "a man that has a factory and makes raincoats; he may be in a good way of business, but is he a fit husband for her? He's rich and he's kind and he's head over ears in love with her; but you can't get away from it, Mrs. Branch, she has a right to expect something better. In the old days he would never have been thought fit to marry into the family. Would she be happy if she went off with him to live in that United States, where everything's strange to her?"

"What kind of a life will she have if she doesn't take him?" the old woman retorted. "What's to become of her? There's nobody left for her to marry round here, all the young men she was brought up with were killed in the war, or they've married or gone off to earn their livings in foreign countries. The old days you talk about are finished, dead and done with; if my Henrietta stays here, mark my words, she'll die an old maid. I see it coming. She's got too much on her shoulders, she hasn't any time to think of herself. I've brought her up from a baby, I love her as if she were my own daughter. I want her to have a home of her own and a loving husband and children," said Nanny. "I want to see it before I die."

There were tears in her faded blue eyes, but the old man only spread his hands in a gesture of despair. "If Miss Henrietta were to go away," he declared, "they might as well sell up the place and be done with it. There's nobody can keep things straight but her."

IV

THE PINES arrived from Stafford before eleven and got Leaf into a
fluster, the old man hardly knew where to put them. He was still
fussing about his table in the Octagon Room, after that he would
have to put the Red Dining-room in order for the afternoon and
Nanny was still taking off the dust-sheets in the Yellow Drawing-
room. The gentleman seemed in such a hurry, stamping about the
marble hall. He was persuaded with difficulty to part with his hat
and coat and kept talking about getting back to Stafford before
midday; he upset everybody. Mrs. Pine, young Lady Hornbeam
that had been, was quite worried and little Lord Hornbeam did
not know where to look. "Always the same with these jumped-up
people," thought Leaf resentfully. "Don't know how to behave in a
gentleman's house. He's nothing but a builder for all his airs. In the
old days he'd have come to the side door with his book and his
pencil and tape-measure and seen the agent about mending the
roof and putting the drains in order." So he put the little boy's
suitcases under the stairs, showed them into the breakfast-room
and said that he would fetch Miss Henrietta.

"Lord, what a place!" said red-faced Bob Pine, spreading his
bulk before the remains of the fire, looking with pardonable disgust at the discoloured walls covered with photographs, the old
mahogany chairs with cracked leather seats, the shelves of dusty
books. "I thought you said it was such a grand house, Maureen;
tip-top rooms stuffed full of art treasures and all. Don't see any of
that here." The little dark-eyed creature he had married did what
she could to soothe him. "It used to be lovely, Bob, when I first
stayed here, there was miles and miles of grand rooms; that's what

they show to the public nowadays." "Then why don't they show it to me?" demanded Mr. Pine. "Aren't I good enough to see the State rooms you talk about unless I pay my half-crown?" He was working himself up into one of his tempers. Mrs. Pine glanced anxiously at the door. "He said they hadn't got the rooms ready yet," she whispered. "It isn't half-past ten, scarcely; you would make such an early start. She'd've given us lunch, I'm sure, if we'd asked." "Well, we've got no time to waste," he grumbled. "Got to get back to Stafford by one. Don't know why they couldn't've fetched the boy themselves. I only came to please you, because you wanted to fuss over him up to the very last minute." They talked in undertones, while Victor stood with his back to them, looking out into the glossy leaves of a bay-tree. He was nine and small for his age, dark and silent, no Hornbeam, his mother's boy all over. "Always wool-gathering," his new stepfather would complain. "Doesn't listen to a word you say. I can't make head or tail of him."

His mother sat on the club fender, stretching out a thin hand to the fire. She was a plaintive pink-and-white little woman, pretty but commonplace, with a pair of huge dark Welsh eyes and a pointed face; she sat huddled into a beaver coat, too heavy for the day, sighing "It's always cold in these old places. When I stay here, I'm frozen, keep my coat on all day." "Not enough fire," said Mr. Pine severely. "No coal, just a lot of damp logs out of the woods; place is thoroughly run down, of course, haven't got a penny to bless themselves with. Wish somebody would come; you'd think we weren't even expected. If this Miss Hornbeam doesn't show up inside five minutes, I'm going." She tried to soothe him down, while the boy stared out of the window. Henrietta did not come a moment too soon. She had been down the garden, she said, tidying up the herbaceous border. She kissed her nephew and his mother, offered tea or coffee and a walk through the State rooms, but could not persuade Mr. Pine to abandon his grievance. "I got no time to spare," was his ungracious answer to everything. "We're

late as it is. We got to get back to Stafford. There's a man coming
to see me about a conversion-job." Inside ten minutes he had them
all out under the pillared portico and had started up a car with a
snout like a mouth-organ; his new wife was kneeling on the black
and white marble flagstones, with her fur coat spread round her,
kissing goodbye to her son. As they drove away she looked back
and saw him, standing by his tall aunt. He raised his hand in a
timid farewell and his mother's eyes filled with tears; after this
morning he would never really be her boy any more.

2

Bouncing through the lanes on their way to the Wilchester by-
pass, she scarcely listened to her new husband giving his opinion
of Fountain Court. "What a ruin! I can tell you, Maureen, I
wouldn't have the job of putting it to rights, not for five thousand
pounds I wouldn't. I know these old barracks, water in the cellars,
worm in the beams, rotten floorboards, cracked plaster-work, and
a roof like a sieve. All the outside woodwork's cracked for want of
painting. I bet the whole place wants rewiring, I don't suppose
they've bothered with the drains since Queen Victoria. Once you
touch a place like that, you bring it all down about your ears. Only
fit for burning, I'd say, pity they didn't get a bomb on it in the war.
I'm sorry for that boy of yours having such a millstone round his
neck. What'll they do with him, when he grows up?"

Maureen was not certain, murmured vaguely, "They did say he
was to go into the regular Army for a bit, like his father, all the
Hornbeams does that; and then I suppose just come and live here."
Bob Pine exploded, "Where's the sense in that? If he must go into
one of the Services, the Air Force is the place for him. The Army's
no catch nowadays, if they want him to lead a gentleman's life
that's not the place to find it. Blessed if I know what's to become
of him, Maureen; the gentleman's jobs are all played out, no future

in any of 'em. Who wants to be a doctor, f'rinstance, rushed to
death filling up forms. It's a dog's life to be parson or teach school,
there's not enough work to go round for the lawyers and the ar-
chitects; the civil service is well enough for them that likes it, but
there's no money in it. No, my dear, all the bright boys are coming
into industry. You're the boy's mother, it was for you to settle it,
but you shouldn't've given him back, to my mind. I could've done
more for him than his own stuck-up family ever will! 'Stead of this
snob-school of theirs, where he won't learn nothing useful, I'd've
put him into the yard at fifteen, let him start at the bottom as I
did and work his way up; by the time he was grown he'd've been
ready for a proper job. I'd've looked after him," he told her with
rough kindness, "just the same as if he was my own; you could've
trusted me for that." She only whispered, "Yes, I know, but I had
to let him go back to them, I promised his father."

They drove a mile or so in silence, along the narrow curving
lanes, between golden beeches consuming in the fires of autumn.
Then he asked her suddenly and jealously, "What was the chap
like?"

She had been in a dream from which she returned with difficulty, of Victor looking very small at the top of those twelve steps,
under those six huge apricot-coloured pillars. She vexed her new
husband by saying stupidly, "What chap?" and he roared at her,
"Why, *him*, of course, Lord Hornbeam, the boy's father;" then,
less violently, "You've never told me properly, Maureen."

She honestly tried to remember but could not, it was all more
than ten years back, she had known so little of young Harry. He
had been killed only a few weeks after their stolen marriage, they
had never had time to make any life together. She fell back on
externals. "Why, just like *her*, the one you saw, his twin sister. It
always gives me a turn when I see her again. They were like as
two peas, dress her in his clothes and you'd scarcely know the
difference." "Sissy, was he?" demanded Bob, but she shook her
head vigorously. "No, tough as they come, couldn't've done his

job else; but tall, pale, red-headed, held up his chin and looked at you as if you was dirt, sometimes; I can't explain."

"*She* does that," said Bob Pine resentfully, taking a corner too fast. "Thinks no end of herself, looks down her nose at you, got nothing to say to people like us; we're not good enough for her. I still don't see how this young Lord Hornbeam ever came to take up with you."

Maureen had never really understood herself. "The boys used to come into the ice-cream parlour every night," said she, "from the training-camp. It was funny how fond they was of ice-cream, just like a lot of kids. I used to serve behind the counter and they'd sit and talk to me. Harry got talking and then we went to the pictures together on my night off; that was how it all began. There wasn't much for any of 'em to do outside the camp."

"Yes, but to go and marry you, Maureen," he insisted, looking sideways at her. "It was a pretty queer thing for him to do. I can tell that now, when I've seen the place he came from." She did not know, could never understand herself quite why Harry had been so mad for love of her. She knew perfectly well that if he had come back safe from the war their marriage could never have lasted. All she could tell her new husband was what she used to tell herself after Harry had been killed. "I didn't ought to have let him, but he wouldn't take no for an answer. They was all waiting to go overseas, I think he knew he was going to be killed. He used to say he wanted to leave a son behind him to inherit the place." Bob scowled and drove faster, as he swung the car out into the by-pass and turned north she heard him mutter, "Hornbeams must've wished it had been a girl. Were they kind to you when you went there, or did they frighten you?" He would have liked, she knew, to console himself by thinking that the Hornbeams had treated her badly, but she could only falter, "They was all kind, I was ashamed how kind they was. Nobody frightened me except the old lady; she was very grand, something like Queen Mary. I was terrified of her, couldn't find anything to say, didn't belong,

I was always glad to get away; but it'll be different for Victor. He'll belong," said she, "and I'll be happy with you."

3

Under the portico, meanwhile, Henrietta had said, "Now we must go in and say good morning to Granny and then you shall go into the garden and see Cousin Charles cut down the Jubilee Tree."

Victor never much liked this beginning to a Fountain Court visit. You went up the Waterloo staircase and along the upstairs passage, past one closed door after another; Granny's room was at the far end of a second passage, in the south-west corner of the Victorian wing. Its windows looked one way south to the terrace, the other way west to the woods; the old woman got all the sun. She lay in a high bed with many lace-trimmed pillows, under an embroidered coverlet, among blue-and-white curtains hung from a gilded coronet; a little fretful old woman, a Duke's daughter, who looked to him exactly like a sick monkey. She wore a night-cap this morning, a trifle of lace and rosebuds, fit for a bride; she never troubled to wear her ginger wig or put in her teeth in the mornings unless a visitor or the doctor were expected. Her little hands were like monkey's paws, curled and dark, her face was all nose and chin, her voice shrill and plaintive. "Is that the boy?" she demanded. "Come here, child, and kiss me."

Victor did not care for this performance, but he advanced politely and touched his lips to the soft withered cheek; the old woman smelt to him sweet and mawkish, like dying roses. He stepped back a pace and saw her great dark eyes staring at him out of her painted face. "*You're* not much like your father," she complained in her cracked voice. "You don't look to me as if you'd grown at all since last summer. That mother of yours can't have been feeding you properly. Is she coming up to see me?" He said, bewildered, "They've gone back to Stafford," but did not make himself heard; Lady Hornbeam was now growing rather deaf. His aunt said something behind him, the old woman turned herself irritably in her bed, shook her head and listened to neither of them. "She might have had the manners to come up and see me before she went. Nobody has any manners nowadays; well, I didn't want to see her, I've no use for her, I'm sure. Why did Harry want to go and marry a shop-girl?" She chattered her toothless lips together, exactly like a monkey in the Zoo, Victor thought; then fixed those magnificent terrifying eyes upon him and said, as if he were not there, "What are we going to do to amuse the child? Would he like a ride on the pony, boys usually do? Cole can take him out, I suppose." Cole was only a name to Victor, a coachman dead these thirty years. There was no pony in the empty stable, he knew, nothing but a bridle hung up in the harness room and a little old saddle on which his father had learnt to ride. "Charles will look after Victor this morning," his aunt said. "I'm rather busy myself, the house is on show this afternoon and lunch is early. Mr. Cornell is bringing his dealer to value Lavinia." "I don't know what you're talking about," the old woman said crossly. "You mumble so, I can't hear a word you say. Oh! the Lawrence in the drawing-room; well, I hope you get a good price for it from this American of yours—I never liked it, an ugly face. I'm sure the woman must have been a mulatto; she has such great staring black eyes. The drawing-room will look much better without her." Victor did not know just what they were talking about, he looked from his aunt to his grandmother. "Then you really don't mind if she's sold?" his aunt said in her clear polite voice and his grandmother shook her little head. "I said I'd give my consent," she croaked, "and I do give my consent. I don't care for the picture. All I say is, you and Charles must be managing very badly if you have to keep selling heirlooms. First it was the Holbein and then it was the two Gainsborough drawings and now it's your great-great-grandmother's portrait. By the time Victor inherits there'll be nothing left." She lifted her forefinger and beckoned his aunt closer. "I can't hear what you say when you stand so far off," she complained and when Henrietta stood by her pillow muttered angrily, "Now mind you bring this young man to the point today. You're wasting time."

"He'll take the picture, I really do think, if this dealer will let him," said Henrietta in a loud cheerful voice which only made the old woman put her hands to her ears. "I'm not deaf," said Lady Hornbeam. "You needn't shout at me. I'm not talking about the picture, you know that perfectly well, I'm talking about the young man's intentions. You don't know your own business, Henrietta, you never give your mind to things properly, you'll die an old maid like your Aunt Harriet. When I was your age I'd have had this American on his knees to me by this time, writing notes, sending flowers, buying me expensive presents, following me round from one party to another." She gasped a little and beat her hand fretfully on her chest. Henrietta coloured up as if she were vexed, but said lightly, "All I want him to do, Granny, is to give me a good price for old Lav."

Victor wished himself elsewhere, he tried to shut his ears to their jangling voices. He gazed desperately at one photograph after another, set out in rows on the table beside him; the handsome dead women in their Court trains and feathers, the dead men in uniforms, in diplomatic gold lace, in shooting jackets, in frock coats; a whole vanished generation of unknown faces, lean, handsome, distinguished, stout, clever, even faintly common, with their full beards and drooping moustaches, their funny collars and hats. All by himself in front, in a gilt frame with a crown on top, was old King Edward the Seventh, in the full uniform of a field-marshal, looking as big as a barrel and holding a plumed helmet under his arm. Victor fixed his eyes upon the monarch and tried not to listen to what was not meant for him. "How long will the price of one picture last us?" the old woman demanded. "You ought to marry the man, Henrietta, while you've got the chance.

I don't care for these Americans myself, all so noisy and the women so over-dressed and over-jewelled; but His Majesty encouraged them, they amused him, they always gave wonderful parties and I'm told the men make very good husbands." Her voice trailed away as if she were getting tired. "Come, now, Granny, you don't want me to go off to America," said Henrietta with false cheerfulness. "How would you all get on here without me, I'd like to know?"

Staring at the old King's picture, Victor began to feel dreadfully confused and frightened. He wished the venomous old woman would stop scolding his aunt, but she went on, "You'll never get a husband at all, Henrietta, if you go about all day long in your old clothes, looking as if you'd just come in from the stables. Your mother was just the same, never had any idea how to dress herself; she went about like a ragbag, always looked as if she'd bought her clothes at a jumble sale. I remember I was horrified when poor Edward first brought her here to see me; a regular parson's daughter, long pale face, long nose, long bony hands and feet and her mouth always hanging half-open like a village idiot. She had no figure at all, just straight up and down, five-foot-ten if she was an inch, with her waist round her hips and her skirt down to her ankles. A dowdy broomstick, with nothing in the world to say for herself, I can't think what Edward ever saw in her. When I was that age I had a twenty-inch waist and I took fours in gloves and threes in shoes."

"But you were a beauty, Granny," Henrietta said wearily. "All the men ran after you and I don't wonder. You must have been a charmer. Now you must let us go away, or Victor will miss seeing Charles cut down the big hornbeam tree." The little boy felt her hand on his shoulder, she gave him a friendly unexpected squeeze which was some comfort to him.

"Go away, go away," his grandmother exclaimed. "I'm tired, I've talked too much; you all come in here and bother me. It doesn't matter, nothing matters to me now; you can do what you like, I shall never come downstairs again to see what a mess you've made of the place. I'm so old . . . so old; I shall soon be dead and buried." She caught at her throat with her fine hand and gasped, "Maria . . ."

Her Swiss maid came in then through the open dressing-room door, a small woman in a black dress and apron, darting fierce looks at the visitors. Victor was always frightened of her, she made him think of a quick little spider running out of a hole in the wall. She advanced to the bedside, lifted the old woman up on to her pillows, poured some brown sticky drops into a glass of water and offered it to Lady Hornbeam's pale lips; then soothed and tidied her, all without haste and in a disapproving silence. Victor watched open-mouthed, his aunt stood by the bed letting Maria do what she chose, not offering to interfere. In a moment the old woman pushed the maid away, exclaiming fretfully, "That's enough; let me alone, do, you fuss over me day and night. Go away, go away; I'm tired of you all."

Victor was thankful to be on the other side of the door, trotting down the passage with his aunt, digesting what he had seen and heard. He peeped up at Henrietta slyly, to see why the old woman had scolded her so for being untidy; but she looked just the same as she always did, tall, pale, with red-gold Hornbeam hair, in corduroy slacks and a white wool sweater, with a thick collar coming right up to her ears. She walked fast and easily, with a sort of swagger which pleased him. It was the first time that he had ever considered her particularly; he found that he liked her looks. "I say, Aunt Henrietta," he burst out uncontrollably, "you aren't really going away to America, are you?"

She glanced down at him, laughed a little and said in her pleasant off-hand way, "You don't need to listen to everything Granny says, Victor. She's a very old lady now and she forgets things. Let's go down the garden and find Cousin Charles. He promised he wouldn't cut down the tree till you came. It's the Jubilee tree at the end of the lawn and it's going to make a tremendous crash."

4

So Victor and his aunt went down the neglected garden together. On that last morning of October it was looking its best, but
there was nothing rare left in it. Roote had little time or strength
left for getting round the borders and Henrietta took more interest
in the vegetable garden, though she sometimes made an onslaught
on the big border nearest the house. Here there was now a wild
autumnal jungle of Michaelmas daisies, cream and wine, violet
and a sharp electric blue, with mop-headed crimson and yellow
dahlias sticking up between the clumps, enormous sunflowers like
brown velvet soup-plates, destined for the chicken-run, and pale
towers of the Vatican Salvia which smelt like tom-cats when you
brushed against it. All down the path between the box-edging
were Victorian iron arches, covered with late roses, red, white
and yellow, which the next gale would scatter everywhere. The
Virginia creeper burnt on the wall like fire, the arch over the faded
turquoise-blue door into the kitchen garden, had a red vine on it
bearing masses of little hard grapes which seldom ripened. The
grapes were a disappointment to Victor; but the apples were
bright as flowers on the old neglected trees in the orchard and the
mulberries had dropped like rain on the carpet of yellow leaves
under the big corner tree. Victor made a mental note to come back
in the afternoon and eat mulberries by himself.

Peacock butterflies, drunk with juice, were opening and shutting their wings on fallen fruit. The goldfish had come up to bask
in the layer of warm water on top of their fountain, where a stone
boy from Italy wrestled eternally with a dolphin as big as himself;
they all dived with a flick under the lilypads as Victor's shadow
fell upon them. He promised himself a hunt later for the toad
which lived in a hole under the statue, a fat one with a tight
leathery mouth; he marked the grey squirrel which ran up a tree
as they came near it. So they went down the path and crossed the

lawns where the old tennis courts used to be, Henrietta pacing
bare-headed in the sun, like a young queen, Victor looking over
his shoulder to admire the trail of their footsteps in the white furry
dew which yet lingered on the grass.

The hornbeam tree which was to come down stood at the end
of the tennis-lawns, beyond the cedar of Lebanon; its fluted grey
trunk rose quite seventy feet in the air. It was the largest of several
others planted about the grounds; the first Lord Hornbeam, the
Victorian statesman, had set it in earth in 1887, on a golden day of
flag-flying and bell-ringing, before the assembled villagers, to com-
memorate Her Majesty's Jubilee. Now it was past its prime and
stag-headed, with dead grey branches poking out of its golden
foliage; its time had come to die. The men had been at it all
morning; Roote, grey-haired and stooping, Tim, the Irish labourer
who worked in the vegetable garden, Joey Moss, the garden-boy,
and Cousin Charles. He looked more like a pirate than ever that
morning, thought Victor, in a violently black-and-red check flannel
shirt and his oldest corduroys, both exceedingly dirty, with his
black patch over his lost eye and the stump of his arm hanging out
of his rolled-up sleeve. He was brown as leather from being always out of doors. Victor admired him enormously, secretly
thought him like the Red Knight in *Alice through the Looking-
Glass* which his aunt had read aloud; artful, provoking, three-
cornered, rather impish, terribly brave; just a little alarming when
anything went wrong. "Sure, the Commander's got a terrible twist
to his tongue," Tim would say, winking. "Skin you alive, he will,
if you vex him." Cousin Charles did not, however, lose his temper
often; he lived cheerfully here in the very middle of England,
worked like a black in the greenhouses, never saw the sea. Everybody liked him, but nobody saw much of him, he was too busy
with the garden, the only thing that paid at Fountain Court. Henrietta and he were great allies.

This morning he seemed uncommonly cheerful, standing under
the tree, waving his one arm to Henrietta and Victor as they came

up, shouting "Come on, look alive; just in time for the fun, only
one more branch to take off before we bring her down." Roote
passed his gnarled fingers over the smooth bark in a gesture like
a caress. "Should've been felled ten years back," he pronounced,
"if there'd been anybody here to do it. You won't get much heart-
wood out of she, sir."

"I'll get enough to pay for the labour of felling the thing," said
Charles, sticking out his underlip in a way he had. "Lovely silky
white wood, Roote, close and fine, grand for turning, with a grain
in it like a mackerel sky. I don't know why it isn't in more demand
for cabinet-work. It's tougher than oak, smooth as beech, or better;
stain it black and you can't tell it from ebony." "'Tis cross-grained,
all hornbeams is cross-grained," said Roote. "That's why folk don't
plant 'em, 'tis hard to work and hard to handle, not worth growing
for timber, only fit for a hedge. A fine strong hedge it do make,
I grant you that, sir; keeps out cattle and gives good shelter and
it holds its leaves in the hardest winter; but nobody wants hornbeams now. This tree's been let grow too tall, we'll be better off
in this corner without her." He sounded as if he were pronouncing
an elegy. "Where shall you throw her, sir?" They consulted together, while the Irishman felt the teeth of the big cross-cut saw
and Joey the garden-boy made a face at Victor.

"Take off that one more big branch first," said Cousin Charles
suddenly. "After that we'll get her down in no time; just here." He
struck his heel into the turf; then without warning he was going
up the tree like a monkey in spite of his one arm. He disappeared
among the leaves, then you saw him walking about the tree as if
he were on the ground, balancing easily on one foot, passing his
rope round the trunk, tying a knot one-handed. Then he shouted
down for the saw and a coil of rope dropped through the leaves
and writhed at Victor's feet like a snake. He jumped back; but
Joey the garden-boy made the handle of the saw fast and it went
up wriggling and swaying like a live thing. Cousin Charles
worked furiously, a shower of sawdust and leaves came pattering

down, Roote said sharply, "Stand clear now," and the boys ran backwards. Then a branch creaked, swayed and came tumbling down upon the grass; it looked much larger there than it had done on the tree. A gap like a window appeared in the foliage with Cousin Charles sitting in it, astride a stump, in his red-and-black check shirt, grinning and kicking one foot in the air. Then he slid down the rope to earth again, grumbling, "Don't like working up there with the leaves still hanging on, can't see what I'm doing. Let's get going on the trunk."

Henrietta went off, but Victor remained, enchanted, running about picking up sticks with Joey, sitting with his knees up to his chin, watching the men take turns at the big cross-cut saw. They had got half-way through the foot of the naked grey trunk before Henrietta came back again. Charles and the Irishman were knocking in wedges, Roote was near by, leaning on his spade, the two boys were perched like squirrels in one of the fallen branches; they were all ready to watch the death of the tree. "Just in time," said Charles to his cousin. The men all turned to stare at her and Victor perceived obscurely that she was looking handsomer than usual; or perhaps it merely was that she had just put on, for a public appearance that afternoon before strangers, a tidier frock than he had yet seen her in. It was a clean lavender silk, falling in straight lines like a classical tunic and her hair was exactly the colour of the dead asparagus fern in the kitchen garden, a ginger-gold, curling round her head.

"Why can't you ever keep an eye on the clock, Charles?" she demanded. "It's struck twelve. The men want their dinners and we've these people coming to lunch at one to look at the picture. You'll have to stop work. I came out to get Victor and take him up to Nanny." Victor recognised the note of authority and began to scramble out of his perch, but Cousin Charles only grinned. "Can't leave off now, my dear," said he impudently, with his head on one side. "We're three parts of the way through. If the wind got up while we were indoors, that tree might come down and kill some-

body. Take the boy out of the way and go and stand over by the
hedge and keep your nice frock clean, Penny. We've enough for
the rope without women and children, we shan't want you."

She stood for a moment uncertain and the colour came up into
her face; Victor waited, not quite knowing his part in all this.
Then she took him by the hand and the pair of them went obediently across to the path by the yew hedge. "Will it make a *very*
big noise when it comes down?" Victor asked her rather anxiously,
but she did not reply. He noticed that she held his fingers very
tightly. The men and Joey had all got hold of the rope from the
trunk together and were walking away with it across the lawn.
"I do want to see it come down. Don't you, Aunt Henrietta?"
Victor persisted, more to reassure himself than because he expected any answer. His eyes were on the rope, which was taut
now and stretched down at an angle through the branches. The
men began to strain at it and he scarcely heard his aunt mutter,
"No, I don't." Then the Jubilee hornbeam began to sway in a
rhythmic fashion. "All together now," shouted Cousin Charles.
"We've got her." All of a sudden they tossed the rope away and
ran off sideways, ducking and stooping. The tree tottered like a
man struck with apoplexy, then crashed down and buried its head
in the ground. Fragments of wood jumped up and rained down
about it and a new piece of sky appeared where its golden tower
had been. Victor screamed with excitement, "Lovely . . . lovely
. . ." but Henrietta never stirred. Cousin Charles came up, rubbing his single hand against his hip, repeating, "Just in time. I'm
glad you saw it, Penny."

"I didn't want to see it," said she. "I liked it where it was. I
don't enjoy seeing a tree come down." Victor noted that she was
quite pale. Charles merely laughed and took her by the elbow
saying, "Well, anyhow it was fun for Victor." They walked to
where the fallen tree lay, holding up its stiff arms. Victor saw the
pale concentric rings of nearly ninety years' growth visible in the
pale outer section of the trunk, but the whole centre was black

and rotten. Charles knelt beside it like a surgeon, plunging in his hand, scraping out wet fragments and shaking them off his fingers on to the ground with a gesture of disgust. "Rotten at the heart," he complained and Victor heard his aunt say under her breath, "Just like us."

He did not know what she meant and stared up into her face. Charles shrugged his shoulders and turned to the men as they came up. "You go and get your dinners," said he, with an effort. "It's past twelve. Shan't want you again, Roote, or the boy either; it's Visitors' Day. Monday we'll get on with sawing up the top and lop and Tim and I will split the trunk. I shall get enough of the sound wood for the job I want and we'll burn the rest in the winter." The men went off and the three Hornbeams walked back together across the amber-green lawns towards the old house. Victor did not want to leave the tree, he kept looking back over his shoulder, wishing that he could see it still standing. Half-way he heard Charles say, "You know, it did have to come down, Penny," and his aunt replied quite submissively, "Yes, I know." It occurred to the little boy that they spoke to each other as husband and wife might, apologising without words for some neglect or offence.

Charles kicked a fallen horse-chestnut aside, looked round and up at the sky and grumbled, "Wish these two chaps weren't coming. I shall lose a couple of hours one way and another, messing about after them and then all the half-crowners will be here before we can turn round." Henrietta merely said, "You promised to back me up," and he retorted, "All right, all right; I'm coming, aren't I? I just don't like strangers about the place and as for that Yank of yours, I grudge him any of our heirlooms. I don't want him to go off with Lav's picture; or anything else about the place, as far as that goes." Henrietta looked straight before her and did not reply.

They passed the goldfish pond and Victor eyed the red school of basking fish eagerly; he did wish he could have stayed out of doors. All of a sudden he heard his aunt say, "Victor's filthy, covered with sawdust and grass-cutting. He's going to have his lunch with Nanny to-day and she can clean him up, I haven't time. As for you, Charles, I wish you'd put that check shirt on Roote's bonfire. It makes you look like a Yank yourself." "It's on its last legs," said Cousin Charles stubbornly, "but it's quite good enough to cut down trees in." "Well I hope you mean to change into a decent suit before lunch," said Henrietta. They all three walked in silence after that under the red, white and yellow rose-arches towards the stable yard and again Victor made the startled observation that his two relatives had sounded like husband and wife.

V

THE CLOCK struck half-past twelve as they came into the stable yard. Henrietta instructed Victor, "You go up to Nanny for your lunch when it strikes one," and implored Charles, "Do make yourself decent;" then she disappeared into the house by the back door, like a cuckoo going into a clock. Victor caught the twinkling single eye of Cousin Charles and found that he had received a message. "All in a flap, poor girl," said the little man. "You keep out of her way till this party's over. I've got to go to it, worse luck." He darted away up his outside staircase as if he had a train to catch and Victor looked about him for entertainment.

Boffin, the kitchen cat, lolled on the scullery window-sill, a young tabby striped like a tiger. The sill was so narrow that his paws dangled abjectly, while the slinking black stable cat and her two stiff-tailed kittens gambolled below him on the flagstones in the sun. He was fat as butter and his winter coat glistened like satin. The black cat and her kittens were wild as hawks and they darted off as Victor approached, but Boffin did not disturb himself. Even when Victor touched him timidly under the chin he only squirmed over a little further on to his back, exposing his furry stomach more completely to the autumn sunshine. He uncurled one paw, expanded its five black claws like a starfish, yawned enormously and closed his eyes. The purring in his throat went on by itself like a little engine.

Roote the gardener came out of the kitchen wiping his mouth and talked to the cat as if it were a human being. "Ah! you bad boy, been out on the tiles all night, I lay; why don't you catch more mice? The women feeds you too high, that's wot 'tis; don't have to work for your living like the rest of us." He gave Victor a slow surprising wink. "Milk an' fish an' all kept for this cat in the fridge," said he, rubbing Boffin's fur the wrong way with his old hand. "When I was a boy the women didn't 'ave no fridges to fuss over. Ice-'ouse, that was the way of it, in a big place like this. Down the bottom of the woods you'll find it," he instructed Victor. "Little round-'ouse like a cheese, sticking out of a bank; best part of it was under ground. Come January, when the ice was thick on the lake, two of us'd be told off to cut great blocks out of it. 'Aul 'em on sledges, stick 'em in the ice-'ouse, cover it all up safe with two foot o' sawdust from the saw-mill; then come summertide, when they wanted their ice for the larder an' such, we'd cut it out for 'em as and when they ast fer it. Fridge," said Roote again and spat.

"But suppose it *didn't* freeze," objected Victor, fascinated by this legend. "Suppose it rained all winter long?" "Always froze when I was a boy," Roote insisted. "Skating parties, they 'ad on the big lake at Wilchester Castle reg'lar every winter. Eighteen ninety-five, that was the best year of all, skated right on till the middle of March they did. There was bonfires every night, with 'ot coffee, 'ot grog, roasted chestnuts; everybody went sliding and skating. The ladies all turned out, in their long skirts and their fur jackets, with their 'ands in them little muffs; like swans they looked sailing about," said Roote, turning poetical. "The Old Lady upstairs, she was a beautiful skater when she was a girl. You never seen nothin' like it. Don't get the weather for it nowadays, that's a fact, my lord. It's the atom bomb, upset everything; nothin's been right since they let off the nasty thing. Well, I must get off to me dinner."

He went away to his cottage, in the corner of the kitchen garden, and Victor found himself alone in the courtyard, stroking Boffin's hot fur.

Then round the corner came Joey Moss, the garden-boy, of whom he was rather in awe. "Let's go up the Tower and hunt jackdaws," said Joey. "I'm done for the day, Sat-day. Our Mum's gone into Wilchester, bus don't get back till after one, but I got a piece in my pocket." He pointed when Victor stared. "Up the Abbot's Tower, that's what they calls it. Cram-full of jackdaws it is. Too late for young birds now, but we can pull down the nests. Power of harm, daws does, eats peas and beans and young seedlings; old Tower ought to be cleared up, Mr. Roote says. Can we go up? Of course we can, softy. I been up scores of times, I keeps candles up there 'n matches 'n all, my gang meets there. You don't know y'r own house," said he with scorn. "Fancy never gone up the Tower, it's the best place there is, 'specially in spring time. Then you can smash the eggs 'n wring the young birds' necks 'n throw 'em down the staircase." He grinned agreeably.

2

The Tower stood beside the ruined Chapel, square and disused, with a rag of wall clinging to its northern side. It had never been a belfry, merely some unidentified part of the monastic buildings; every so often the County Archæological Society would come and argue about its use. Its walls of mixed chalk, brickwork and apricot-coloured local stone had been patched up and slapped together with cement by the second Lord Hornbeam, in the early nineteen-twenties, when there was still some money for repairs. Since then nothing had been done to preserve the fabric, and a good many stones had fallen from the battlements; but it was still reasonably safe. Victor felt sure that his Aunt Henrietta would have told him not to climb it, but he did not dare say so to Joey, who was grinning and putting out his tongue, saying, "Stop down below if you ain't got the nerve to go up y'r own Tower." So he went inside.

It was quite ordinary at the bottom, just an eight-sided stone-vaulted room with a corner fireplace, heaped with a mass of

dead sticks, birds' bones, old rags and feathers; the floor was trod-
den earth and the whole place smelt mouldy. Roote had put a
bar across the doorway to keep out cattle, but the boys ducked
under that. From this room you went up a spiral staircase, down
which the jackdaws had dropped more sticks. The treads were all
worn hollow and in some places there was no step at all. The
stones of the newel-post were beautifully carved and fitted; dead
hands had polished them until they shone like yellow marble.
Every so often there was a loophole to the outer air, but many of
these were blocked by old nests. Once there was a queer hollow
in the outer wall, a cupboard perhaps to hide things in, for it had
a neat stone shelf in it. The children were safer climbing the stair
than grown-ups would have been, because they went upon hands
and knees and the steps were just the right height for that, if you
put your hands two steps higher than your feet; but every so often
you came to an opening looking down into the hollow of the tower
and then Victor felt quite giddy, for the iron bar across, waist-high
for a man, was no help to children. He soon grew tired of scram-
bling up after Joey. His knees ached dreadfully and there was a
cold wind blowing down the staircase, it seemed to push him back.
There was green slime on the wall beside him and the stairs were
dirty with birds' droppings; all the time, up above, in the bird-city,
the jackdaws were crying and complaining with an angry monoto-
nous rhythm, they sounded like waves on a beach. There seemed
to be words in the noise they made, "Go 'way . . . 'way . . . 'way
. . ." they told the children. Victor began to wish with all his heart
that he had never come.

The top was the worst of all, because there was an oaken trap-
door at the head of the stairs and a short ladder to it; you had to
draw the big iron bolts and hold up the door as you scrambled
through on to the leads. It was all very well for Joey, but rather
too heavy for Victor, who only just got through and snatched his
fingers clear before it dropped. However once they got out on to
the leads he had to admit that it was lovely. "Like being up in a

plane. See down on everything," Joey said. The midday shadows had all gone small under the buildings, the big chimney-stacks of the Court stood up like dolls' houses above the grey, blue and red roofs, the garden was laid out like a map, the hayricks and corn-stacks, cows and tractors in the fields, were like so many toys; there were even one or two people queerly foreshortened, mov-ing about to animate the scene, a man digging in the vegetable garden, a young woman on a bicycle in the drive, a woman looking out of a window. "Smashing hideout," Joey said. "Nobody knows we got our eye on 'em" and he made a face at the windows of the Court.

There was a narrow walk or gutter round the top of the Tower, within the flaking stone battlements and a leaded slope behind it, rising to a central peak. Here the boys sat down together in the sun, and inspected the contents of each other's pockets. Victor had a grubby handkerchief, a bit of string and a bar of dusty milk-chocolate which they divided; Joey had some boiled sweets in a screw of paper, a couple of keys and a pink plastic revolver from a toyshop. "That's my atomic space gun," he explained. "When I point it at you, you're dead," and he thrust it at Victor, who gig-gled uneasily. There were also half-a-dozen dried and shrivelled horse-chestnuts, which they lobbed over the battlements, after Joey had explained, "I don't play conkers no more, only kids plays conkers. These got left over, don't know why I keep 'em." Victor pleaded "Give them to me," but Joey told him, "You get y'r own; there's thousands and millions in the avenue." He shied the last chestnut at a perching jackdaw, which flew off with an indignant squawk and said, "Come on, we got to crawl all round the gutter before we go down."

3

Victor did not like the sound of this and looked about for better entertainment. He found it under his hand, the outline of a boot drawn in the warm lead. The County archæologists would have told him from the pointed shape that a sentry in the Civil War, bored with his idle watch, had put up his foot against the slope and scratched round the outline of the sole with the point of his pike. "Somebody drawing feet," said Victor vaguely, but sharp Joey got the point as quickly as any expert. "Soldier, I reckon; soldiers will draw anything to amuse themselves. There's two more round the corner, one's much smaller than this; drummer-boy, maybe."

"There *were* soldiers here once upon a time," Victor boasted. "Aunt Henrietta said so. They slept in the attics, dozens of them, the big one is called the Barracks still. The Queen came and fetched them all away to fight for King Charles. That's how the big gold statue of Mad Harry got put up in the church. He was my ancestor." He was rather proud of this, but Joey said instantly, "Silly old King, 'ad him in school last week. Got 'is 'ead off an' serve 'im right. My Dad says when I'm a man there won't be no more Kings and Queens, they'll all be done away with. Out-of-date, that's what they are, just an expense to the country." Victor, profoundly shocked, said, "We'll still have Queen Elizabeth then, won't we? Why, she's only just been crowned;" but Joey seemed doubtful. "Coronation was somethin' like," he admitted. "You did ought to've been 'ere for that. We all got off school for the day an' there was a TV set laid on for the grown-ups in the Institute. There was a fancy dress parade, I wore my cow-boy rig, I got second prize. Then we 'ad a feast in the school, 'am sandwiches 'n cakes 'n jellies and the grown-ups had a supper in the Tithe Barn, 'n after there was a bonfire an' fireworks. Everybody said it was better than the Peace bonfire. You never seen nothin' like it."

Victor indeed never had. "I was in London," he offered. "We didn't go to the procession because Mum doesn't like crowds; but we did see the film of it." "I seen that too," Joey retorted, not to be out-done. "It come to Wilchester the week after, to the Regal an' we all went. Dad took us, said there never mightn't be another Coro-nation, so we'd better see it to remember it. The girl that did the Queen, she was smashing." Victor, quite bewildered, said, "That *was* the Queen," but Joe insisted, "It's never *them*, in a film, it's their stand-in. You are a proper fool; everybody knows a flick is only actin'."

He jumped up and stretched himself. "I got to go," he said. "Dinner-time . . . Saturday . . . got to go out with the gang after. You can't come . . . you don't belong; I shan't tell you where we're going, it's a secret."

"I've got to be here anyhow," said Victor trying to keep his end up. "People come on Saturdays to see the house." "I know, my Mum come once with the Institute," Joey retorted. "Can't think why anybody wants to pay to go round your silly house. I wouldn't come if you asked me." He looked round the corner at Victor, trying to see how far he could go. "Rotten stupid old barrack," said he. "Nobody in it that's any use nowadays, only women an' birds. Wants a bomb dropped on it to wake it up. When I'm flyin' about in my plane I'll drop one on it, see if I don't." "You won't be allowed," stammered Victor and when Joey swaggered, "Who's to stop me?" doubled his fists absurdly and vowed, "I'll stop you." "Like to see you try," Joey told him. "Your family won't be 'ere, any'ow, you'll all be sold up before then. My Dad says so. You 'Ornbeams ain't got enough money to keep your place up; time you're grown-up, this place'll be a school or a hospital or a Gov'-ment office, or it'll be fallen down. You won't never live here, they all says that in the village." His piggy eyes sparkled with pleasure. "I shall . . . I shall . . . It's my house," Victor asserted, but Joey merely laughed loudly. Then he suddenly darted off and disap-peared round the angle of the roof. Victor heard the trap-door bang down, but did not realise that he might be a prisoner until, reluctantly following, he found that he could not lift the heavy timber alone. He wrestled with it for some minutes, but as soon as he got it up a little way it slipped from his weak fingers and came down again with a crash.

4

Baffled and angry, he walked round the top of the Tower, peering down helplessly from its angles, wondering what to do next. It was an enormous relief, after some four or five minutes, to see Cousin Charles, in a tidy blue suit, come running down his outside staircase and make across the yard towards the house. Victor uttered a thin scream like a snared rabbit and the sailor looked up and round immediately; Victor screamed again, waved his arms and was seen. Charles waved back and shouted "What are you doing up there, you little idiot?" When Victor piped, as loud as he could, "Stu-uck," he heard his cousin groan, "Lord! All right, stop where you are, I'll come and get you." He disappeared into the lee of the Tower and was to be imagined running nimbly up the circular staircase; presently he burst the trap-door open and sprang out like a jack-in-the-box, pretending to be angry. "Nice sort of chap you are to have about the place! Couldn't you open the trap for yourself?"

"It kept slipping," faltered Victor. "It's too heavy for me to lift." When Cousin Charles grumbled, "Then how did you get it up in the first place?" he had to confess vaguely, "Joey was here then, we did it together. He showed me the way up, he comes here after jackdaws' eggs. We both pushed but then he went off and I couldn't manage it by myself." He did not mention the quarrel, that was not for grown-ups. "I see," said Cousin Charles. "All right, I'll talk to young Joey; skylarking idiot. If he brought you up, he should have seen you down safely. Now listen to me, young man, before I let you down, you've got to give me your promise that you'll never come out here again without a grown-up. No sense in killing yourself till you're asked." Victor gulped and promised. "And that goes for all the roofs, mind," Cousin Charles said severely. "I've other things to do than coming up three flights of stairs to rescue miserable boys. Not but what I see your point," he added with one of his lightning changes. "It's a nice place for a lookout, I must come here again myself." He walked to the angle of the Tower, leant over the edge, looked round, across and down with his single eye, came back and grinned at Victor. "Old house looks well from here," said he as man to man, waving his hand. "Got quite an air about it." Victor emboldened, enquired, "Didn't you ever come up before, Cousin Charles?"

The sailor shook his head. "Never in my life. Your father now and your aunt, they were devils for climbing roofs and such, when they were your age. I remember Penny broke her wrist once, falling off the kitchen-garden wall, when I was here on leave. Your grandmother made a devil of a fuss about it, Penny didn't live it down for months." "What do you call her Penny for?" murmured Victor, fascinated by this glimpse into the past, wanting to prolong it; but Charles was not to be diverted. "Lord, I don't know," said he, "I can't remember; everybody did when she was a little girl. It was a fairy story, I think, some joke they had in the nursery. *Cocky-Locky said to Henny-Penny, the sky's falling. We must go and tell the King.* Nanny will remember; everybody's dropped it but me. I don't like calling the girl Henrietta, too starchy." He cocked his single eye at Victor and said very seriously, "Now do try not to be a worry to her while you're here. She's got a lot on her shoulders, I can tell you. I don't want her bothered."

Victor blushed and murmured, "I will try," but he felt himself quite at a loss in this strange world. "Well, come on down now for God's sake," snapped Cousin Charles, "or I shall be late for her damned lunch-party. I was just starting over when I heard you yelling for help." He dropped into the open trap-door and stood holding it up with his shoulder, grinning at Victor. "Sit on the edge now," said he briskly, "dangle your feet into the hole and feel for the top rung of the ladder. Don't panic now; I've got you." His one arm was as strong as a rock; he held Victor with it and eased the trap-door down with his shoulder till it shut with a bump. Then they went down the ladder and the spiral staircase, with Cousin Charles going first. It was much better than coming up, Victor did not mind it at all.

Going across the stable yard in the sunshine, Cousin Charles said sarcastically, "When you get upstairs, young man, you'd better have a good wash. Your hands are filthy and you've got cobwebs in your ears; you're a disgrace to the family. Don't let the visitors see you." Victor giggled, "I'm going to have lunch with Nanny upstairs," and Cousin Charles said, "Wish I was! Tell the old girl she might have invited me too." At the foot of the scrubbed wooden nursery stairs he concluded, "Look, Victor, if you're bored this afternoon you can go down to the glass-houses and help my landgirl plant bulb-bowls; tell her I sent you. There's a couple of hundred to be done this week-end. Each bowl gets two Roman hyacinths and a tulip in fibre, a nice clean job; it would be a real help to me and Jean will look after you. She offered to do a bit of overtime for a special order. It's a bore for you it's show-day, but it can't be helped; we shall all be too busy to do much about you. If you keep out of mischief, Victor, I'll take you on the pond to-morrow. Not in the morning because it's All Saints' and I've got to read the lessons in church; but in the afternoon we'll row over to the island for a picnic, just you and me and Penny if she'll come. We'll make a family party of it, we'll light a fire and roast potatoes; it's a date." He grinned, executed a mock-salute and went away very fast down the passage; Victor climbed the stairs with weary knees and thought bewildered, "What a funny man! But a picnic will be lovely."

5

John Cornell and his dealer had arrived a little before one and were already drinking sherry with Henrietta in the library. Lunch was served punctually in the Octagon Parlour. Leaf, the butler, had seen the big pale American before often enough, and was more interested in Mr. Birnbaum, who had turned out to be quite different from what he expected. Instead of a bearded stout Hebrew he proved to be a neat smart man in his thirties, who looked like a Treasury official in his black coat and pin-striped trousers. He wore a grey silk tie and little side-whiskers, had a neat bony head, showed very good teeth in a frequent smile and talked in a clipped voice, like a cavalry officer in the old days. As he unfolded his darned napkin Leaf heard him try what was obviously a prepared opening. "Your brother and I were both at Winchester I believe, Miss Hornbeam. Same house, but of course we didn't overlap, I was about ten years before his time. We did meet though in rather an odd place, some time in the late struggle; I remember we had a few minutes talk about the old school." Leaf, handing round the soup-plates, could have told him that this was no way to ingratiate himself with Miss Henrietta; she would never talk about her dead brother. She gave Mr. Birnbaum what Leaf recognised as one of her keep-off looks and said, "Harry never told us much about what he was doing."

"Well, it was all rather hush-hush," admitted Mr. Birnbaum, turning on a flashing smile. "Cloak-and-dagger stuff, you know; sort of thing one really can't discuss even now, might be wanted again some time, you never know. When people ask you what you did in the late war you have to mislead them a little. Of course they stuck me into Intelligence because I happen to be rather knowledgeable about some of the odd corners of Europe, I'd travelled about a bit in happier days. That was how I came to be behind the outfit who were interested in your brother. No harm

now just to mention that we were planning to drop him somewhere, but the other show came first. A bad business, Arnhem,"
Mr. Birnbaum told his American. "Funny thing, isn't it? how we
English always talk most about our defeats." Henrietta sat like a
woman carved in stone; Leaf bent over the visitor's shoulder and
said, "Burgundy, sir;" and Charles struck in, "You must try this,
sir; my own discovery. I was grubbing about in one of our cellars
and I found a whole bin of it stuck away behind a great wardrobe.
We're drinking it up while it lasts."

The dealer sipped meditatively and said, "A nice wine. Queer
what'll turn up in odd corners, in old houses." He lifted his glass to
Charles, drank and looked round the room with appreciation, trying another tack. "Very charming; about 1780, I take it, a little
late of its kind, but quite classical." Leaf, handing the game pie
and taking round the vegetable dishes, heard Charles giving him
the tourists' facts about Sensibility Hornbeam and the Grand
Tour. "The old boy brought back no end of stuff," rattled Charles,
"there are busts in the library and statues all over the grounds;
you know the kind of thing." "And had himself painted in Rome,
I see, sir," approved Mr. Birnbaum. "Not a Zoffany? no, I didn't
think it could be, one knows more or less where all the Zoffanies
are; but Rome then was full of ingenious fellows who knew just
what would please the English milord. Dear me! what fun the
young gentlemen did have in the old days, rushing about the
Continent with their pockets full of guineas, picking up all the
foreign nonsense that appealed to them, knowing there was a nice
big family house waiting to absorb all the souvenirs when they
got home again. Life's so difficult nowadays," he told Henrietta,
"all one's friends are living in service flats; nobody's got anywhere
to *put* anything. You can't sell the big stuff any longer however
good it is; even Royalty have got as much as they can manage."
He spread out his hands and looked for the moment much more
like Leaf's notion of a dealer.

"I should have thought hard times made trade though," said

Charles dryly. "People like us, you know; we turn out our cupboards, we take down our pictures, we get our spare silver out of the bank to turn an honest penny. All that must be helpful to you." He smiled agreeably at Mr. Birnbaum. Henrietta said nothing, but her American joined in pleasantly, "Where I come from, we're still covering our walls and filling our cupboards, we're glad to get hold of some of your beautiful things. My father had been collecting for fifteen years before he died. Duveen used to buy for him. I'd like to show you some of my pictures," he said directly to Henrietta, trying to make her look at him, but not succeeding. Leaf could not think what was the matter with Miss Henrietta today. She sat there in a kind of daze, quite white in the face, letting the party slide, just when she ought to have been doing her best to keep things going. It could not be that she minded so much having to sell that ugly picture in the drawing-room, something behind the scenes must have upset her. Perhaps old Lady Hornbeam had made one of her rows. Mr. Charles kept watching Miss Henrietta sideways and the American gentleman looked quite bothered.

His dealer tried to cheer him up, flattering him about his pictures, talking about the great collections they had over in the United States. "All the good stuff is going there nowadays," said he, waving his hands. "After the First World War the landslide started everywhere; old families being driven from one country to another, estates sold up, good stuff coming into the market cheap, property confiscated, buildings pulled down and carted away. The Second World War was even worse. All the treasures are on their way westward, everybody's trying to unload heirlooms, quite soon there'll be nothing left here worth exporting." Was he having a dig at his unwelcoming hostess? Leaf wondered. At least the colour came up in her face. She said dryly to Mr. Cornell, "So when Europe's been converted into a mass of radioactive rubble it won't really matter to you. There'll be no need to cross the Atlantic any more, you'll have all the art-treasures you need on view at home."

Her American didn't like it, any more than the dealer did; Mr. Charles had to strike in, saying in his pleasant way, "I'm afraid you're in a dying trade, Mr. Birnbaum, sawing off the branch you're sitting on." The dealer laughed, shrugged his shoulders, nodded his head and recovered his temper admirably. "Oh! we all recognise that," said he. "Let's hope Europe will last our time."

After that awkward corner the conversation became a little easier. Leaf changed the plates and handed round the cheese soufflé, while the three men talked to one another, coming round from sale-room anecdotes to the subject of country houses being open to the public. "Poor Chatsworth," sighed Mr. Birnbaum, as mournfully as if he had been a Cavendish relative, "it makes you weep when you think what it was in the old days. Longleat and Wilton and Althorp and Knole and Blenheim if it comes to that; there's a fresh one each year going the way of the rest. People rush from one to the other like sheep. They go tramping round the State Apartments in their muddy gumboots quite literally thousands at a time, they throw paper in the flowerbeds and cigarettes in the fountains; one doesn't know where it's going to stop."

Henrietta said nothing to encourage him, but Charles kept things going. "Well, it's got as far as us, thank God!" said he pleasantly. "We show two days a week and uncommonly helpful it is. Of course we aren't in the first flight, we don't count our visitors in thousands, like the big places. We haven't got a Birth-room, or a Skylon or even a paddling pool for the kiddies, but our friends are very good about bringing their week-end visitors. We have to rely on the gardens and natural curiosity." "Quite, quite;" agreed Mr. Birnbaum. "People often like to see a small inhabited house better than a great barrack like a museum, but it's tricky, I grant you. I've always wondered how many visitors a house like this would get. Four or five hundred a year, I suppose?" He showed his admirable teeth in what passed for a smile, but Charles was equal to him, merely saying vaguely, "Oh! it varies a good deal, you know; it depends on the weather mostly. This year you couldn't expect anybody to want to sit out in the gardens, could you? It has to be fine for us. When the sun shines we make an object for a walk, or a drive, we fill up a Saturday afternoon." The American turned his blank face from one man to the other, as if he were watching a fast men's single at Wimbledon. "You get quite generous allowances, I gather, for this sort of thing from the Treasury," suggested Mr. Birnbaum. "You have a rough and tumble with your income-tax man; you put in for keeping up the garden and repairing the roof and rewiring the electric light supply. You remind him about telephone calls, and postage and advertising; you point out how heavy your insurance premiums have to be. You pay yourselves guides' wages, on paper, you don't necessarily give in a full return of all your takings . . ." He sounded quite pleading. Charles merely laughed and said, "Oh! we're a bit more amateur than that; Henrietta hasn't started paying me for my time yet. Overtime for thirty Saturdays in the year would add up to something. I really think she should. Look, my dear," he called across to her, "Don't you think we ought to make a move? Time's getting on; the customers will be coming, we have to open the doors at two-thirty and we can't keep them waiting. Don't you think we ought to have coffee in the drawing-room, so that these gentlemen can take a look at Lavinia?"

VI

THE YELLOW DRAWING-ROOM was the finest of the rooms which
Colonel George Hornbeam had added to the house in 1820, after
he married his West Indian heiress. It was a formal apartment,
most imposing, sixty feet by thirty, with chimney pieces of yellow
Sienese marble at either end, a pair of double doorways in the
long wall, framed in classical mouldings and five tall windows opposite. They overlooked a lawn planted with cedars of Lebanon
and a mile-long vista down the lime-avenue; but their eastern as-
pect made the room cold, it only got the sun in the mornings.
The walls were covered with a flock paper, soft as velvet to the
touch, branched with acanthus leaves, a whole autumn wood of
them. The windows were draped with yellow brocade, disposed
in loops and swags upon massive curtain-poles; the pelmets were
adorned with military trophies of helmets and spears and so was
the ceiling, where they appeared in light and formal plaster-work.
Similar designs had been woven into the Aubusson carpet, which
had a centre-piece of cuirasses, guns and flags in the French taste;
Colonel George had had it made in Paris when he was there on
Wellington's staff after Waterloo.

Upon this warlike carpet stood black lacquer chairs, inlaid with
mother-of-pearl and love-seats arranged in groups for tea-drink-
ing, cards and conversation. There were also two sofas as big as
beds and a pair of Empire couches with lion-feet and hard bol-
sters. All were upholstered in the same yellow damask. When the
room was first furnished the effect must have been dazzling; but
all that kingcup colour had been faded to primrose and cowslip
by a century of summer suns. Nobody sat in the Drawing-room

much nowadays. There was an old piano at one end, never tuned or played upon, with one or two lyre-shaped music-stands arranged beside it and a harp with broken strings in the corner, as if waiting for the family to play trios and quartettes. The walls were chiefly adorned by mild ladies' water colours and silhouettes; there was an oval drawing by George Richmond of the first Lady Hornbeam and her children and a glossy Sargent of Lady Hornbeam in a trailing gown, with a fichu and a picture hat, carrying a sheaf of white daisies. In the corner were recesses for china, but there was nothing of value in them, only cracked and riveted tea-sets, Oriental vases turned best side foremost, Chelsea and Staffordshire figures, shepherds and shepherdesses mostly in green bowers, lacking hands or heads. There was, however, a bright crackling fire on the marble hearth for the sake of the visitors and Henrietta sat down like one of her ancestresses upon the sofa with the coffee tray before her, while the three men gathered on the hearth-rug, stirred their cups and surveyed the Lawrence portrait at their leisure.

It hung above the mantelpiece, a three-quarter length, rather below life-size, and represented a tall woman with a high colour and commanding eye, sitting in white classical draperies against a white wall. The painting had been executed with marvellous dexterity in every tone of curds and cream, the only colour being in the heavy gold bracelets which encircled the woman's arms, the few close curls of auburn hair which escaped from under her gauze turban and the crimson cheeks and gold-tipped wings of a tame finch perched upon her left hand. This hand with its bright new wedding-ring was spread upon her breast; the goldfinch with outspread wings seemed about to fly away, the woman stared down at you from under her heavy lids like a Byzantine empress. "Hard-faced bitch, I always think," said Cousin Charles cheerfully, cocking his head sideways and surveying the picture with his one good eye, while Henrietta murmured dryly from the sofa, "I'm supposed to look like her."

Her American peered owlishly through his horn-rimmed glasses. "I don't get that," he complained. "No, I don't get it at all. The hair's the same colour, of course, what you can see of it for the muslin bandage she's wearing, but that's about all. She looks mighty proud, mighty bad-tempered, I'd have been terrified of her." He turned and studied Henrietta frankly, while she drew up her head on its slender neck and looked sulky, like her ancestress. "Old Lavinia had the family temper all right," said Charles mischievously. "It goes with the hair, sir, all the women have it. I wouldn't have cared to be married to Lavinia myself, with her temper and her money she'd have ruled the roost. I wouldn't have taken her on at any price. Still, she has a right to look proud. She might have been Queen of England."

Mr. Birnbaum turned from his stare at the portrait, he had a puzzled air. "You tell him that legend you told me about your ancestress," John Cornell urged them. "You ought to hear it, sir, it's fascinating." He beamed at Henrietta who shrugged her shoulders. "It's just a family story," she told the dealer, "you can believe it or not as you like. We always have to tell the tourists about it. She was supposed to have had an offer of marriage from William the Fourth."

Charles took up the tale in his light tenor voice, as if he and his cousin were performing a duet, so often repeated that each knew the other's part. "She was a great heiress, one of the West India cousins. We had an earlier ancestor who'd been transported after Sedgemoor; he came up at the Bloody Assize for supporting Monmouth and Judge Jeffreys sent him to Barbados. He made good there and married his master's daughter; his descendants had a big sugar-plantation and any God's quantity of black slaves. I believe there are some of them out there still. Lavinia Hornbeam came over after the Napoleonic wars, with bags of money, husband-hunting. Prince William was looking for a rich wife just about then. He was old George the Third's fourth son, Nelson's friend, the one they sent into the Navy to get rid of him. Nobody expected him to come to the throne. He was running about England that summer looking for heiresses, but the girls all turned him down; he was supposed to be a bit touched in the head, like his father. Lavinia quite bowled him over, she always swore he'd made her a firm offer at Bath and she'd accepted him. She spent five hundred pounds on a Court dress to wear at a State Ball at Brighton Pavilion; the engagement was to be given out that night, she thought, but she never got her invitation. Old Queen Charlotte and the Prince Regent put a spoke in her wheel; they found a German princess for William and Lavinia was left in the lurch."

Mr. Birnbaum smiled gently but made no comment; John Cornell said, "Well, well, quite a story, isn't it? Wallis Simpson had nothing on her. It must have been a considerable disappointment for the poor lady." "She never shed a tear for Prince William," Henrietta contradicted him, glancing up at the portrait. "She had other strings to her bow. She was rich enough to pick and choose, but she didn't waste any time. She came straight down here to visit her English relatives, and inside three months she'd married her Cousin George."

"We've got his portrait in the library," Charles contributed, unconsciously hitching up his empty sleeve. "A Cosway miniature; he was on Wellington's staff in the Peninsula and lost an arm at Waterloo. Told the surgeon his knife wanted sharpening and insisted on waiting till they got another. He was a fearfully handsome chap, wild as they come, a regular Regency rake, he made ducks and drakes of his money, gambling, betting, cock-fighting, you know the form. He was a younger son and hadn't expected to come into the property, so when Lavinia accepted him it must have been a gift from Heaven."

"She made him leave the Army," Henrietta said. "They did up the house in style and added this Waterloo front, he hunted the Wilchester hounds. Lavinia never would go to Court again after King William came to the throne, she said Queen Adelaide had made everything too dull. They were great people in the county, they fairly made the money fly, though the Barbados estates didn't bring in so much after slavery was abolished. I believe she led George Hornbeam a cat-and-dog life," concluded Henrietta in rather a breathless childish fashion, as she found the three men all staring at her. "She had just the one son, who was my great-grandfather; he became the first Lord Hornbeam, the Victorian statesman, our most distinguished ancestor. Then she went into a decline and died; we always suppose she couldn't stand the Midland winters after Barbados. George married again quite quickly. He picked another heiress, a nice dull girl whose father owned a colliery in Yorkshire and they had six more children, so that was all right. Charles is descended from one of what we used to call the Black Children." And she pointed to the silhouette by Augustin Edouart of an Early Victorian family, hanging beside the chimney piece; a group of delicate black figures with little impertinent noses. The mother was seated on a spindle-legged chair, with an infant on her lap, the father had a newspaper in his hand; the children were charmingly grouped about them, the boys with kites, whips and hoops, the girls with dolls and posies. "Charles, first Lord Hornbeam," said Cousin Charles, grinning; "James the Indian judge, Rupert, the Colonial bishop, Beatrice, Alice, Amelia and General Sir Alfred Hornbeam K.C.B., Governor of the Unfriendly Islands, the one with the bow and arrow. I'm descended from him, we show his bedroom upstairs. He was a very dreary old devil, one of those Mid-Victorian soldiers who served all over the world and shot big game when he wasn't exterminating native tribes. The house is full of his trophies."

The American turned his large pale face from one mocking cousin to the other, bewildered by their careless familiarity with the centuries. "Well, I'm truly sorry Miss Lavinia didn't get to be Queen of England," said he gravely shaking his head. "I guess she'd have adorned the position."

2

They were talking for talking's sake, while the dealer was peering at the portrait from all angles, with a dissatisfied air which might have been put on for effect. He got as close as he could, standing at the side of the marble hearth, trying to avoid the fire; then he produced a little electric torch, flashed it here and there, scratched very delicately at one corner, used a magnifying glass and shook his head doubtfully. "Painted soon after her marriage," said Charles helpfully. "Lawrence's best period, they tell us. I believe there's a copy in Detroit, but I don't know anything about that." "Never exhibited, I think," snapped Mr. Birnbaum, and when Henrietta murmured, "Granny wouldn't let it out of the house; she said it might get damaged," retorted, "A pity. It always makes a difference to the price if the experts have seen the picture. Still, we know about this portrait, it is documented. I have looked it up. It was commissioned by her in June 1817 before her marriage, but not sent home until October 1821; there were a good many sittings needed and they were given at long intervals. Lawrence was always a slow finisher. He used to sketch in the head, you know, that amused him; he was very clever at a likeness. The difficulty was to keep him up to the collar. He'd lose interest in one sitter and start on the next. Of course he always had far more commissions on hand than he could get through; he was *the* fashionable painter of the time, he could charge what he liked. He went off to Aix-la-Chapelle in October, 1817, to paint all those official portraits for the Waterloo Chamber at Windsor Castle, and he didn't settle in London again for quite eighteen months. He was P.R.A. by that time, at the very top of his fame, he didn't need to worry much about one unimportant sitter. He must have finished off Mrs. Hornbeam all in a hurry, or got one of his assistants to do it for him, more likely, polish off the dull bits, you know, the background, the drapery; you understand me? once he'd knocked off the head and the bird." He plucked at the air with a long brown forefinger. "They all do it," said he. "This picture looks to me as if it had been, shall we say? a little assisted."

"I think it's a lovely picture," the American burst out. "It's just what I want." Henrietta tapped her foot and looked sulky, while the dealer was obviously distressed by so much innocent enthusiasm. He reproved his client. "We have to remember, sir, that Lawrence doesn't fetch the prices he did. This Regency vogue has gone on for a long time, but it's petering out. There's a tendency nowadays to think Sir Thomas a little glossy, a little meretricious and careless, rather too fond of theatrical poses. No, the market for Lawrences isn't what it was."

He arched his eyebrows at the cousins. Charles told him bluntly, "You've got to crab the thing, of course; that's what you're here for. We quite understand that," and Henrietta flung off, "If you don't want it you needn't take it. I don't know that we're all that keen on selling." The dealer smiled gently. "Well, we shall be sorry if we've made our journey for nothing," he murmured. "If you did want to sell, Miss Hornbeam, what would the figure be?"

She seemed to choke, did not get out any answer. Charles came to her rescue, saying, "Well, it's insured for a thousand pounds." The dealer smiled, shrugged his shoulders, spread out his hands, went through a whole pantomime of admiration, amusement, doubt, refusal. "It's always as well to be properly covered. Still, a thousand pounds is a lot of money nowadays, Miss Hornbeam; I'd say it was more than this particular picture was worth." He addressed himself to his client, turning his shoulder to the cousins. "You're sure you really want this thing, sir? If it's just a good Lawrence you're after, I can get you half-a-dozen better examples of his work. The sitter isn't a particularly handsome woman after all, it's a bad-tempered face, to my mind; if you hang it on your wall you may get tired of looking at it day after day. We mustn't be in too much of a hurry, we must get you the best value we can for your money. The family set a high value on the picture, naturally, because of the associations; but you and I must ask ourselves, what is it worth in the open market?" He shot Henrietta an apologetic look.

"I want this very picture, Mr. Birnbaum," the American insisted. "I've set my heart on it. I like it and I can pay for it. I'm re-building myself a house up in Maine and I mean to have a parlour in it exactly like this room, with the same sort of furniture in it and that lady hanging over the mantelpiece. It's my notion and I don't intend to change it. All I want you to tell me is just what the picture's worth." The dealer bowed submissively. "Then I must have it down and out of its frame," said he briskly, turning on the Hornbeams.

Henrietta in her ignorance had not expected this; she murmured, "I don't know . . . if we can manage that." Charles reacted better, saying, "None of us very able-bodied here, sir, I'm afraid." Nevertheless he produced within a few minutes shaky old Leaf and a step ladder. The dealer ran up this like a lamp-lighter; among them they got the big portrait down. It was enthroned on two chairs and he walked round it, knelt down behind it, rubbed the dust from the back of the canvas, scowled at the brushwork, shook his head again, while they all tried not to look at him. Charles cocked his one eye at the dusty square on the wall and said to nobody in particular, "Makes a gap, doesn't she? We shall have to hang somebody else over the patch if she goes." "I'll have a copy made for you if you'd like it," the American told Henrietta eagerly. "I believe that's often done in these cases." He looked all round him and admitted, "I certainly can't imagine this room without the portrait." Henrietta took no notice of him; she had stood up and was staring intently and anxiously at the dealer. He rose to his feet, dusted the knees of his elegant trousers with his hand, sighed and said to his client, "Well, sir, I cannot recommend you to buy this picture. It is not by Lawrence at all."

3

Henrietta turned so pale that her freckles showed strongly; she opened her mouth but no sound came out of it. The American complained, "I don't get you," at the same time that Charles protested, "But we all know the chap painted it. You said so yourself. Lavinia sat to him, we've got the correspondence between them in the library, we've got his own receipt for the money. Five hundred pounds, Lavinia and Colonel George paid him for the thing. I looked the papers out yesterday myself, I was going to give them to you with the portrait, if we made a sale." All three men were suddenly talking together while Henrietta, standing, felt for the arm of a Regency day-bed and leant upon it. The dealer's voice concluded the argument. "I don't dispute the documents, *they're* genuine enough, I'm sure; but they refer to the original picture. This is a copy."

In the shocked pause that followed he laid his hand upon the ornate gilt corner of the dusty frame. "I was worried about it from the first," said he with evident satisfaction. "It never looked right to me. Now that I've examined it I've no doubt about it at all. It's a copy; not even a contemporary piece of work, but a completely modern copy. A very clever one, I admit; if it had been done on an old canvas it might have deceived me." He smiled again in triumph. "Get any other West End dealer to look at it," said he. "They'll all tell you the same. It's not fifty years old."

"You mean we're trying to sell you a fake?" demanded Charles, clenching his one hand. "Just because Cornell's a rich man who doesn't know much about pictures." Mr. Birnbaum shrugged, John Cornell said hastily, "Now, now, we don't want any of that kinda talk. This is as much a shock to the family as it is to me, I'm sure. I can't really believe it." They all turned to pale Henrietta who said, in a small voice like the mew of a kitten, "Please, Charles, stop talking. He's perfectly right. It *is* a copy."

Charles began, "Oh! my dear girl . . ." then checked himself; the dealer looked at the floor, the American said, staring, "There's something here I don't get the hang of." "I'd better explain," said Henrietta in a surprisingly steady voice. "Granny told me all about it this very morning. She says my grandfather sold it in 1900, to pay her debts. She'd run up bills all over the place and lost a lot of money at baccarat; she couldn't settle up. He didn't want a scandal, so he sent the Lawrence away to be cleaned; that was his story, but of course it never came back. There were two other pictures went at the same time," she said aside to Charles; "that thing of Mad Harry that we've always thought so much of and the Henrietta Maria, up in the Queen's Bedroom. They were all copied and the originals sold privately. The buyer promised not to exhibit them anywhere in Granny's lifetime, of course he never expected her to live to be over eighty. He was an American who wanted to found a collection. She told me his name, she says he lives in Detroit." She added to Mr. Birnbaum with a good deal of dignity, "My grandmother is a very old lady and we can't believe everything she says nowadays. So I waited to see what your opinion of the picture would be; but if you say it's a modern copy I'm afraid that does bear her out." "Old girl's as mad as a hatter," Charles was heard to murmur. "Doesn't know what she's talking about half the time, if you ask me; makes up these stories just to be annoying." But he was shaken and rubbed the side of his face unconsciously, as if he had received a knockdown blow. "She was very clear about it all, that's why she was so against our selling," Henrietta told him. "She was afraid it would all come out." The American was saying something meanwhile to his dealer about another opinion. "No offence to you, I'm sure you think you're right." "Oh! you'll find I'm right enough," said Mr. Birnbaum carelessly; then glanced at his wrist-watch and said something about catching an earlier train. "If that's all you want from me, I could catch the two-forty-five from Honeybake Junction; it runs non-stop to Oxford, it would get me up to town quicker than we could

do it by car." "Sure I'll drop you," the American said. "I don't know
that I need go up to-night, necessarily. I'm at the Fleece in Wilchester." He glanced at Henrietta, but did not catch her eye.
Charles said, "It's five miles, you'll have to hurry," and they
quitted the Yellow Drawing-room.

Passing through the Red Dining-room, Mr. Birnbaum glanced
with approval at the sporting pictures. "That's a nice little Stubbs
you've got there, Commander," said he to Charles who was attending upon him. "If you ever want to part with that, I'd be glad
to have the first offer. I'm often down this way, I can look in any
time if you've something to show me. I'm not interested in rubbish,
you know, but I'm always ready to take a good picture. The Americans all come to me," said he in Charles's ear; "they know I can
find them what they want. My real line is finding good stuff in
the small country houses and passing it on for export." He produced a card and insisted on Charles taking it. Then turning back
to Henrietta, still babbling tactfully of time and trains, he had
them all out on the steps and was taking his leave under the pillared portico. Obviously he had written off Fountain Court for the
time being. "I'll come back later, maybe, if you'll let me," the
American said anxiously, with eyes for nobody but Henrietta. He
held her hand earnestly, but got no reply. "We're open this afternoon, sir," Charles excused her. "We may have rather a rush on.
We've a bus-load coming at two-thirty. It's our last day this year,
so we may be busy up to six." "Well, maybe I'll wander in," said
John Cornell. The dealer fretted, "We haven't too much time, sir,"
and they drove off.

4

The two cousins were left on the top of the steps under the portico side by side, looking out at an empty circle of dry white gravel
and a ring of statues, each in its clipped alcove in a circle of yew.

Henrietta stared at them, Charles looked sideways, only at her. "Well, Miss Henrietta," said he at last, "you're a nice one, aren't you?"

It was an echo of her childhood, when he used to spend his leaves at Fountain Court; Nanny Branch always said it to her when she came in wet through from hunting or tore her dress and skinned her knees tree-climbing; or on the famous occasion when she fell off the garden wall and came in pale as ashes, holding her broken wrist.

He had hoped to make his cousin smile, but she stood there as mute as one of the stone women by the yew hedge and never turned her head. "You might have briefed me," he grumbled. "I didn't know what line to take, you kept me in the dark and then you sprung all this tale on me without any warning. I can tell you, Penny, you made me look a pretty fool. That dealer thought we were in it together, to do his Yank down; not that I care about him. I say, when did the old girl come out with it all? Do open up."

"Just before lunch," said Henrietta, in a sleep-walking sort of voice. "I went into her room on my way down while you were changing and told her the expert had just arrived and she said with quite a cheerful giggle, 'Let's hope he doesn't find out the picture's a fake'. I thought she was in one of her muddles; she was sitting there eating up her lunch, with a half bottle of champagne on the tray, but she was perfectly bright and sensible. She came out with it all, names, dates, everything. I really think she'd been saving it up to spite us, I wouldn't put it past her. Then I came down and they were both in the hall and Leaf said lunch was ready. So I thought I wouldn't say anything about it till that frightful expert had finished."

Charles shook his head. "That fellow was too clever," said he, "knew his stuff all right. If you ask me, he spotted the picture for a fake right away. I daresay it's obvious to any skilled man, only nobody of that sort has been here for years. One sees why she never would let it go for exhibition. No, she's fooled us all, the old devil!" Henrietta sighed. "It would have been easy except for the dealer. Poor old John doesn't know the first thing about art, he only wants a nice picture. If it hadn't been for Mr. Birnbaum we'd have got our thousand pounds quite easily, but it would have been too much like taking candy from a baby." And as Charles stared at her she burst out, "I wish to God Granny had held her tongue!"

Charles would have liked to put his one arm round her and console her, but he simply did not dare. "Oh! well," she sighed, rubbing her hands over her face, "It would all have come out sooner or later, I suppose. Poor John would have taken his wonderful beautiful Lavinia off to the States and shown her to all his friends and somebody who knows a bit more about pictures than he does would have pointed out to him that his dear British friends had cheated him. Then we should have had to offer him his money back and that wouldn't have been so funny. It's a great handicap in this world, isn't it, to have been brought up to be honest?"

"Often found it so," agreed Charles pleasantly, but he was still puzzled by his cousin's distracted look. "Poor old Penny," he thought, "she's beginning to let this business about the house get on top of her. It's all too much for a girl, I suppose. If I had any sense, I'd be persuading her to throw in her hand and go off to the States;" and in spite of himself he asked her suddenly, "Look, dear, are you going to marry that chap?"

She turned her long grey eyes upon him and he saw that the lids were heavy and swollen, as if she had not slept for a week. "Need we go into all that?" she protested. He shifted his stump a little as if it pained him, a habit which had grown upon him lately. "Well, perhaps we'd better not," he admitted. He stared round the empty sunlit courtyard, when he looked back at his cousin she seemed to have turned into a stranger. For the first time in his life he could not guess what she was thinking. "I tell you one thing, Penny," he said. "We can cut out the insurance on that damned picture," and he added with forced cheerfulness, "Every little helps."

"Nothing helps," said Henrietta under her breath. She turned on her heel and walked away from him into the dark door of the house. As he went down the steps and across the gravel sweep towards the stables, the melancholy thought remained with Charles, "She'll take that Yank in the end, I shouldn't wonder."

VII

THIS GREAT ENTRANCE to Fountain Court had been one of 'Sensibility' Hornbeam's notions. Returning from the Grand Tour in 1780 and remembering Roman gardens, he had planted a ring of yews round a circle of gravel, cut embrasures in the hedge for ten antique statues and called the place the Grove of the Muses. Apollo Musagetes, himself, was mounted upon a high pedestal in the centre of the gravel, striking his lyre. Colonel "Waterloo" Hornbeam half a century later had respected these arrangements, which included a pair of wrought-iron gates and an imposing portico, approached by a double flight of steps. His Waterloo wing ran down the east side of the old house, fronting the rose-garden; but here on the north front there was no colour, only a sober effect of dark green and apricot-coloured stone, like an eighteenth-century print. The yew hedge in two centuries had grown up to a height of thirty feet and was supposed to be the second finest in England, but it had so over-shadowed the courtyard that Apollo never saw the sun. His Nine Muses were shabby and neglected old maids, with lichen-spotted tunics and broken noses. Clio had lost her book and Erato her Lydian flute, buskined Thalia had only half an actor's mask. Terpsichore, dancing, held up stumps instead of arms, Urania brooded upon a shattered globe. The white gravel was weedy nowadays, the great hedge itself ragged and badly clipped, going brown in patches.

Inside the hall it was cold as a church. Harry Leaf the butler fumbled with his old fingers as he pottered about after lunch, setting out his little table, with tickets, cash-box, visitors' book, printed guides and picture postcards. Victor, coming down from the nursery on his way to the glass-houses, inspected these, but found them dull; half-a-dozen views of the north portico, the serried white sash windows and green tin veranda of the Waterloo wing, the balustrades and urns of the south terrace and the massive Victorian front behind it, the tombs in the Dogs' Cemetery, the Abbot's Tower reflected in the pond. He would, however, have selected the one with his own window in it to send to his mother, who liked picture postcards; but Leaf said gloomily, "Now if you please, m'lord, we'll open the doors and let in a bit of warm air from the outside. Temperature's the same today as it was on August Bank Holiday, it said on the wireless; that might bring us a few extra visitors. We can't reckon on many this time of year, it's a wonder they come at all."

He always called Victor "m'lord," in his cracked old voice; it made the little boy feel flattered and embarrassed. They set the two heavy white painted doors wide and the afternoon air flowed in like tepid water above the black-and-white chess-board squares of the marble pavement, where no sun ever came. "Ought to have had a fire by rights," grumbled Leaf, rubbing his knuckles. "Still, 'tain't hardly worth it for the last afternoon, we've got to save fuel." He came out to stand by Victor under the portico and watch for the first arrivals.

People had been coming and going there for centuries. Coaches and carriages, black, scarlet and yellow, had swung round the circle, and drawn up at the steps, powdered footmen had banged the knocker, ladiers had descended in their silken gowns to pay calls, drink tea, dine or dance; young gentlemen had ridden up on horseback, family brides had run down the steps through showers of rice and rose-petals, coffins had come out unsteadily on the shoulders of mutes, and been pushed into wagon or hearse. Visitors had come and gone, leaving a crop of family stories; how Mr. Pitt in a fit of the gout, had stayed for three nights on his way to Bath, how the Duchess of Kent and little Princess Victoria had broken their journey to Anglesey, how Dr. Jenner had ridden over from Berkeley in his brass-buttoned blue coat to vaccinate the whole household, how Miss Jane Austen, slender and silent, unnoticed by anybody in the company, had once been brought over to tea by her rich relations from Stoneleigh Abbey. The Iron Duke had ridden up once to inspect a volunteer parade in the park, Lord Beaconsfield had addressed a Conservative fête, King Edward the Seventh had driven up in the first Daimler ever to crunch the gravel. All through the comfortable nineteenth-century visitors had come and gone, arriving in flocks for cricket matches, for flower shows, for archery and tennis tournaments, for shooting parties, for Hunt balls. "Hounds used to meet out there every winter when I was a boy, m'lord," Leaf told Victor, sighing a little. "The old Duke always brought the bitches from Wilchester, twice in the season; a pretty sight it was, all the gentlemen in their pink coats on their fine horses. The ladies rode side-saddle then, they wore top hats with veils tied over them and a rose in the buttonhole, maybe. Her Ladyship, upstairs, she used to look wonderful on horseback. We had to carry round trays," said Leaf, "with glasses of port and Madeira, there used to be gingerbread and cherry brandy. I was only a boy then. Her Ladyship was very particular in these days about the hedge being kept clipped proper. My grandfather was second gardener then and he always cut the top into figures, he was a rare hand with the clippers. A string of hounds he made her, all round the top and the fox in front of 'em, going away past the stables. A pity your Lordship never saw that, it was a pretty fancy. There's nobody here could do it nowadays, hedge ain't even clipped right; Roote, he don't much care about going up a ladder at his time of life and the rest of 'em are too busy with the market gardening. You need two men by rights, one on each side up a ladder and the long clippers between." Victor gazed at the empty courtyard. He had a blurred Christmas calendar picture in his mind, of scarlet coats and black velvet caps, hounds flowing in like a river from the lane, dappled backs and waving sterns, but he could not fill in the details; he had no notion of how handsome the old white-haired Duke of Wilchester used to look when he was Master, or how elegantly his bed-ridden great-grandmother would have bent from the saddle in those days, raising her tightly-knotted veil to sip from her glass and greet a friend. He wished that he could have seen the long-legged green creatures galloping round the top of the Muses' hedge, that must have been comical and charming. "When I'm grown-up," he decided, "I'll have them cut again."

"Down there," said the old man, jerking his thumb, broad with rubbing silver for a lifetime, "that's where they used to take the photographs, m'lord;" and when Victor, baffled, asked timidly, "What photographs?" said impatiently, "All of 'em. There's books full of 'em in the library, with signatures and such; everything that happened since cameras was invented. House-parties, cricket-elevens, wedding groups, comings-of-age, all the distinguished visitors coming and going. The ladies sat on chairs down in front and the rest stood behind on the steps. Why we've had Royalty here, when I was a young footman. Old King Edward the Seventh he came down for the shooting, they said he was very fond of her Ladyship. We ran out the red carpet and flew the Royal Standard while he was with us. They sat His Majesty down in the middle, I saw him as plain as I see you now, m'lord; a great stout smiling man in his thick tweeds, with his deerstalker hat on one side, lolling in his armchair very bored with it all; having his picture took was no treat to him. They had to hurry the photographer in the end. Her Ladyship sat on his right hand, pretty as a picture in those days, talking to him to make him laugh; she could always do that. The whole house-party was there, with their spats and their shooting sticks and a dog or two; it was a cold morning, I remember. The women all had their furs round their shoulders and we had to bring out a rug or two and put under their feet. The housemaids were peeping out of the windows and the stablemen hanging round the gate, they all wanted a peep at His Majesty. That was in 1903," said Leaf, straightening his bent shoulders. "I

was just twenty then. The photograph's in the library still." He
smiled faintly, remembering the old days; then raised his head
and listened. Down the lane came the sound of wheels, a horn
was blown and a big red motor-coach turned in at the gates. "Here
comes somebody," said old Harry, looking pleased. "That'll be the
Women's Institute from Wilchester; they booked a party. We can
get them done early. You run off into the garden, m'lord; they
haven't paid to see you." So Victor went off to the glass-houses,
where he spent an enjoyable afternoon with Jean the landgirl, fitting hyacinth bulbs into bowls, stuffing fibre round them, spilling
the water-can over the floor, dirty and happy.

2

Parties going round Fountain Court were met in the marble
hall by Leaf or sometimes by Mrs. Plane the parson's wife, or Mr.
Bush the retired village schoolmaster, who gave them tickets and
change, separated them on wet days from their dripping um-
brellas and plastic mackintoshes, and encouraged departing visitors to buy picture postcards and put tips in the guides' box.
Those who wanted to visit the Queen's Room could pay an extra
sixpence and go straight up by the kitchen passage and the
Chestnut Staircase to the landing where Grace Thorn waited,
like a spider in a dusty web. Every half-hour or so a tour started
round the Waterloo wing. Charles, Henrietta or Leaf took turns
to guide their flock through the Red Dining-room, the Yellow
Drawing-room, the Green Boudoir in the Chinese taste and the
Library. They returned by way of the Victorian ballroom, added
by the first Lord Hornbeam in the eighties, an echoing tomb with
nothing remarkable about it except an expanse of parquet, a
minstrels' gallery, two heavy glass chandeliers and a distinct smell
of dry rot. After the ballroom people were directed up the Waterloo Staircase and Nanny displayed three bedrooms in the Victorian

taste; then on a fine day most of the visitors went out to get the
rest of their money's worth in the gardens.

Charles took the first turn this afternoon, coping cheerfully with
some thirty members of the Women's Institute from Wilchester.
Old and young, stout and thin, sour and sweet, they all liked his
debonair off-hand manner, his accustomed jokes. He had got his
tour of the faded saloons down to a system, he never seemed to
hurry anybody, but he did not let them waste any time; he prided
himself on getting round the five rooms under the half-hour.
After five years he knew just what the visitors liked, could tell
what they would say about each family picture. They were bored
with a dim Elizabethan widow, in black cypress with a veil and
ruff; they admired a buxom Lely beauty falling out of her clothes;
they gazed dumbly at the two portraits of the first Lord Hornbeam which ornamented the ballroom. G. F. Watts had painted
him, head and shoulders, in a suffused golden autumnal glow,
looking conscientious and obstinate; a local artist of no particular
note had done him later at full-length, in billows of Garter-blue
velvet, which most of the half-crown tourists preferred.

"Born 1821, died 1887," Charles would gabble, "First Baron
Hornbeam, Knight of the Garter, Privy Councillor, three times
member for Wilchester, Lord Lieutenant of the County, under-
secretary for Foreign Affairs, Chancellor of the Duchy of Lancas-
ter, Lord-in-Waiting to Queen Victoria." Everybody had always
heard of him and his merits. They were usually bored with the
Lawrence portrait and would say to each other, "What a disagreeable face!" They admired a handsome Hornbeam younger son,
painted absurdly in Roman armour with bare knees and gilded
boots, or a pretty Hornbeam daughter laced into a brocade gown,
with her hair in powder and her fan spread. They liked to see velvet latticed with pearls, the gleam of pink satin, the fall of lace
over a plump hand; what they chiefly looked for were portraits of
children or animals. The Red Dining-room, with its sporting
pictures, was always popular; the favourite picture of all was one

in the Green Boudoir of a little girl in a muslin dress, with a pet mouse on her finger. This drew ecstatic cries of "Little love" and "Pretty thing," which always amused Charles and he would wait beside the Alfred Chalons group of the first Lord Hornbeam's children for the inevitable comments, "Pretty dears, how sweet they look! how nicely those muslin frocks are got up! what darling curls the little thing has got!" or sometimes, more crossly, "Fancy dressing up boys in that silly way, all in pink and blue satin, only to have their pictures taken! Fancy letting the girls wear low necks in the daytime out of doors under trees, enough to give them all their deaths of cold! Stupid, I call it, asking for trouble." There was a little picture of a baby, swaddled on a quilted cushion, which was always liked. People would ask, "Who is it *of?* who is it *by?*" with the most lively interest; they were always disappointed when Charles had to admit, "We haven't the least idea. It's very early eighteenth-century; of course we'd like it to be a Hogarth, but it isn't," and he would add, "It would be pretty valuable if it was." They always liked to be told about prices; their highest praise was, "That must be worth big money; somebody must have paid a lot for that; it would fetch a good price if it was sold, I reckon." Henrietta used to say they were like vultures, peering about for a bit of meat, and was rather short with the ones who asked her how much anything was worth; but Charles thought it quite reasonable and would turn off an envious comment cheerfully. "Oh! Lord, yes, there's plenty of money about the place if we could get at it, but you see it's all tied up. We aren't allowed to sell any of these heirlooms, worse luck! they have to go down from father to son." It usually satisfied what he called the customers and sent them away feeling superior and cheerful.

The pictures, he found, were always a draw; the furniture was unfamiliar and less appreciated, though he could get even quite uninstructed people to admire a Persian rug for its bloom and colour, an ivory-and-tortoiseshell cabinet for the complication of its drawers and recesses, a Venetian mirror for its great size. Tourists always enjoyed the stuffed pug in the ballroom passage and he had another object in reserve, a large circular drawing-room table in mosaic work, brought back by 'Sensibility' Hornbeam from Italy. Its glossy surface was covered with birds, flowers and foliage, all inlaid in coloured marbles on a black ground. "Every flower's different," Charles would point out guilefully and watch the women gather round the shining object, pointing out favourites to each other. "There's a tiger-lily, sort-of; there's a stripy tulip, there's a columbine; that's one of them old-fashioned auriculas that Granny used to grow in earth from mole-hills; I didn't know they had *them* in Italy. There's a butterfly on a peach, oh! how sweet and there's a bullfinch eating a caterpillar. Look, Mary, Mother will lift you up and you can see this caterpillar." The table was Charles's show-piece and he always kept it to the last, letting people linger about it while the slow-coaches caught up, before he marched them back through the ballroom to the foot of the Waterloo staircase and packed them off to Nanny. "Took a chap five years to make," he used to say of his table, though really he had not the least idea and had only made his figure up.

Charles believed in giving value for money and only wished he had a ghost-story to tell, or a haunted room to show, for these were frequently expected and it was disappointing to confess that all the Hornbeams seemed to be sleeping well in their undistinguished graves. "We might have footsteps, perhaps," he would sometimes suggest to his cousin. "Just one or two, you know, on stormy nights. Mad Harry galloping back from the war and his wife sitting by an open window, wringing her hands, listening for his horse's hoofs. Or a monk; don't you think, Penny, we might have the gliding form of the last Abbot, up to his knees where the old floor used to be? The customers would appreciate a monk," he would plead, trying to make her see the funny side of a task which nowadays she resented.

3

Americans came in all shapes and sizes. Large men with expensive tailoring and horn-rimmed glasses; neat chattering women in beautifully-ironed silk dresses, always looking as if they had just stepped out of a cellophane package; pretty wild girls with their hair tied up in pony-tails, who tried to flirt with Charles; College boys with crew-cuts and linen suits, bored airmen off-duty from the base; they all moved, a little bewildered and discontented, through the faded State apartments of Fountain Court. Americans were usually in a hurry, he had long ago decided. They never kept you back, as the loafing English tourist did, by enthusiasm for a particular object; they simply wanted to see the best things and see them quickly. "What's so specially good here?" they would demand openly. "What *ought* we to see?" and quite often would add, "We haven't any time to waste." When he had spoken his piece there was usually some woman to tell him politely, "That sounds just *won'erful*. I can't tell you what it means to us, to see all these lovely old homes. We've nothing like this, back in the States," but now and then you got the other sort, who would not admit that anything in Europe was admirable. "I don't know why they come here," Henrietta would say, "if they hate it all so much;" and Charles could only surmise, "They have us on their list. They feel they mustn't miss anything."

He had two of them this afternoon, apparently travelling companions, an amiable white-haired old lady in black and a younger one in flowered yellow silk, with a little white hat like a sea-shell clinging to her smooth head. "This is a very elegant room you have here," the elder one said kindly to Charles, in the Yellow Drawing-room; but the younger complained, "This isn't so special, this is just like one of the old plantation houses down in the South; they all have columns outside on the porch and great big rooms inside that need dozens of black servants to keep 'em clean. My aunt bought one of them for a winter residence; it's outside Charleston. It's all of two hundred years old, it has rooms in it every bit as good as this and columns on the porch too; of course she's had it all done over and air-conditioned and she only goes there in the winter months. The summers are so hot in the south." She gazed resentfully at Lavinia's portrait over the mantelpiece and said suddenly, "That woman looks kind of coloured to me."

Her elder companion instructed Charles kindly, "Yes, we do have some fine houses in the States. Last summer I visited the Jefferson home at Monticello. That was built to his own design, about the time of the French Revolution, I guess; it's a national monument now, people come to see it from all over. I daresay you've heard of Jefferson, he was one of our early presidents, he drafted our Declaration of Independence; but maybe I shouldn't talk about that to you," said she archly. "If ever you go to the States, you really should visit Monticello; Williamsburg, too. That's a town no traveller ought to miss. They've done all the houses over, the way they used to be. You can walk right into them. They have people going around in costume in the streets in visiting hours, all dressed up in silks and satins, with buckled shoes and white wigs on, riding in coaches and sedan-chairs, just like in the olden days; and at the taverns they serve you old Southern dishes. You've nothing like it over here," she assured him. "You should go to Williamsburg if ever you get the opportunity, but I don't suppose you ever felt you had any call to go to the States." Charles said pleasantly, "Well, I was wrecked there about ten years ago," and found himself obliged to enlarge a little. "Oh! we were on convoy-duty, you know, and we got hit. I was one of the lucky ones, I was pulled into a boat and we were picked up next day. They took us into Charleston. I was in hospital for a bit, everybody was very kind to me." She blushed at that, smiled at him very sweetly and just touched his empty sleeve. "You must let an old woman say Thank you," she murmured and turned away. He shrugged out of his mind the intruding recollection of the crowded boat climbing a grey hill of water with its load of dying men, the great swinging roll of the Atlantic under them, the increasing torment of his wounds, the clouds driving over the empty sky. He never let himself think of that episode if he could help it. He gathered his party together briskly. "If you have seen all you want to see in this room, ladies and gentlemen, shall we go into the library?" As he waited by the door, counting them through, running his eye over the small valuables he had to check, he heard the younger woman talking to her friend. "Yes, it can be tiresome when you do too much sight-seeing. In September, when I took the girls on a culture-tour round Italy, we all nearly died. My, my, how bored we got with palaces and galleries and all those statues and Madonnas! The girls were just sweet, they looked at everything the guide told them. 'You don't want to miss anything that's got a star in Baedeker,' I'd say to them; 'you may never come here again.' But every night they'd go dancing till two or three and could I get them up next day in time for an early start? No, I could not, dear. All my life I've wanted to visit Italy but sometimes I wish I'd gone there alone. Yes, we're through with Europe now, dear, I'm thankful to say. I join the girls and their father in London tomorrow and we're flying over to Ireland. We plan to have twenty-four hours in Dublin and catch our plane next night from Shannon. We sort of thought we'd like to see just a little bit of old Ireland; but, dear, I can hardly wait to get home! So this is another of these old libraries," she sighed, as Charles followed her through the doorway. "My, my, you'd hardly think anybody could have time even to dust so many books, let alone *read* them."

4

Grace Thorn always showed the Queen's Bedroom, where Henrietta Maria had slept in 1643 on her way south from Yorkshire, going to join her husband. "It's just the job for poor old Thorney," Henrietta had told her cousin three years back after the first few weeks of showing the house. "She's always had this thing about the visit, says it's so romantic, goes all tearful about the dear Martyr King and Mad Harry Hornbeam and his Cavalier troop; I remember how she used to rave about him when Harry and I were doing lessons. You could side-track her for hours on the Civil War, I always did when I hadn't done my prep. If I wanted to tease her I used to start a hare and say that Cromwell was a noble fellow. Thorney would be frightfully hurt if anybody else was to show the Queen's Room." "And then, you know," said Charles, rubbing his sound eye in a way he had when he was bothered, "the old girl does want to lend a hand, but she isn't much use. She's getting deaf, poor old soul, and doesn't always hear what the customers ask her; and I can't get her to harry them along fast enough. This afternoon she kept a whole crowd of them up in the Queen's Room for half an hour, yarning." "And it's right off the beat from the regular round," Henrietta agreed. "People have to go up the Chestnut Staircase and down again; they don't all want to be bothered and it'd be hell for us guides, on a busy afternoon, having to keep trotting up and down that extra flight. Suppose we make the Queen's Bedroom an extra sixpence, put all the Stuart relics into it together and shove old Thorney up there out of our way? People can take it before the Waterloo wing, or after; then go out by the gunroom into the garden. We can put up red arrows to show the route and Thorney will be frightfully pleased; she'll get to think the Bedroom belongs to her."

And so Grace Thorn did, pluming herself on her post, growing more and more long-winded in her stories about the Cavaliers, turning jealous if it was ever suggested that she might change with Nanny or the butler for an afternoon. "Oh! I hardly think that would do, dear. Nanny is a good soul, but she doesn't know the history of the Queen's Room inside out as I do and I'm sure

Leaf would be quite hurt if he wasn't allowed to show the dining-room after he'd taken so much trouble to set the table nicely. Much better for each one of us to know our place and keep it." She used to dust the Queen's Room herself lovingly with a little feather brush which she hid in the secret cupboard, and she made a point of drying lavender and rose-leaves herself each summer to fill the Lowestoft bowl on the window-sill, polishing the mirrors with an old silk handkerchief, indulging a secret fantasy that she was the lady of the manor and the room was her own.

It was a dark and solemn place, heavy with melancholy, whispering of lost grandeur. Even the tourists felt that, approaching it in single file up the shining black oak staircase, turning in a square, with its balustrade of great scrolling acanthus leaves, its newel-post representing a wild man with a crown of feathers. The Bedroom itself was panelled in scented cedar wood and it had a plaster ceiling which the tourists always particularly enjoyed; between ribs of heavy laurel-foliage some unknown pargetter had amused himself by modelling a fat elephant, a butterfly, a sun-in-splendour, a dolphin and a mermaid with two tails. In the centre panel a hornbeam tree spread its branches, sheltering five nameless birds, larger than eagles and over the mantelpiece he had moulded the family coat of arms in high relief, with painted quarterings, supported by wild men.

Above the panelling was a painted frieze, so stained and decayed that the subjects could not be discerned; in the corner of the ceiling there was a great stain of damp. An equinoctial storm in wartime had washed a sparrow's nest down from under the tiles and lodged it in a rainhead, where it stuck. Black moss from the tiles, with sodden leaves and mould, had blocked the gutter behind the nest for weeks, unobserved; whenever it rained again that winter the water dammed up behind the sodden mass and leaked down between the stones and the plaster of the wall. Now there was a spreading green stain across the ceiling and a square of pargetting, adorned with a dancing cherub, fell down in a winter gale. Hastily repaired, the stain worked through again whenever the weather was damp. The whole of the Queen's Room nowadays had a musty smell of beeswax and pot-pourri mixed with damp and dry-rot, with hints of mice nesting behind the wainscot, jackdaws' droppings and rotten sticks lodged out of sight in the huge chimney, wet leaves in the gutters and mud in the moat outside. The floor was an expanse of elm-boards each the whole width of a tree-trunk, split in half, the round side down; it was uncarpeted and on wet days the visitors' shoes made damp marks on the boards for Grace to polish away, the ones from crêpe soles were the worst.

There was very little furniture nowadays. Once there had been a Mortlake tapestry, but it had been sold; now there were a few high-backed armchairs upholstered in raspberry and mulberry tones of threadbare velvet and trimmed with silver fringe, which three hundred years had tarnished and blackened. Each chair had its attendant stool and crimson guard-rope hooked from arm to arm. There was an oaken table with a faded Persian rug laid across it and a cabinet of tortoiseshell and ivory, with much of its inlay broken and missing; there was a silver-framed mirror and a workbox covered with tattered stumpwork on a table and a leather nail-studded trunk stood in one corner. Three portraits hung on the walls between silver sconces and there were a few coats of arms in the windows, which had been broken and put back wrong; they flung a coloured stain on the flooring when the sun shone. The chief treasure was the State bed, a huge four-poster, with wild men upholding the canopy and carved panels at head and foot; the curtains and valances were rags and tags of a sad green velvet, so was the bedspread and the worn cushions heaped upon it. At the corners of the canopy were ostrich-eggs with plumes of cobwebbed feathers sprouting from them; Grace Thorn was too small to dust up there without getting on a ladder.

When she heard footsteps on the stair she plunged her hand

into the bowl of lavender, stirred it up, dusted her fingers, pulled down her drab cardigan nervously and advanced to greet her little party of visitors. "This," she told them with her most gracious air, "is what we always call the Queen's Bedroom." Unconsciously she put it that way, hoping that visitors might take her for one of the family.

On this last afternoon of the season she had shown round the Women's Institute in batches, after them she had been idle for almost three-quarters of an hour. Then she had a party of six, a grey-haired elderly man who looked like a scholar, a little old American lady in black and a younger one in yellow, beautifully shod and gloved, with a white hat; a schoolgirl, Lucy Holly, in a grey flannel uniform and two countrywomen. Grace collected their sixpenny tickets, put them in the box and prepared to tell her accustomed story, but was interrupted by the elder American lady, peering about her, bright as a bird. "Your Queen Elizabeth slept here, I suppose," she remarked, taking the centre of the floor. "She slept everywhere, didn't she?" She seemed disappointed when Grace said that it had been Queen Henrietta Maria who had laid her head on the green velvet pillows. "I don't believe I ever heard of her," said the American lady, with a polite but dubious air, as if she were rejecting an unfamiliar dish in a foreign restaurant. "Queen Elizabeth the First, I know all about her, of course, and then there was Queen Anne who died and your Queen Victoria; but I expect this little girl can tell us who she was. You're last from school, honey," said she, turning with great kindness to young Lucy. "Who *was* this Henrietta Maria?"

All the tourists looked at Lucy, who blushed and murmured, "Wasn't she the wife of Charles the First?" It did not seem polite to appear quite certain, when the old lady was being so silly. "Yes, she was," said Grace Thorn, feebly attempting to reunite the party in her own charge. "She was a French princess, the daughter of Henri Quatre. That is her portrait over the mantel-piece and opposite to her is a likeness of Charles the First."

The Frenchwoman had been painted at full length, in draperies of oyster satin, looped up with knots of carnation ribbon, one white hand toyed with the huge painted pearls round her throat. She hung there staring across at the smaller portrait of her doomed husband, with his face like a death-mask, peaked, pale and frowning, in a velvet cloak, with the ribbon of the Garter and a dangling star. Neither of the Royal portraits was by any artist of repute, they seemed to be wooden copies of something better; the family were doubtful about them, but they served to furnish the room. "Yes, Charles the First; he had his head cut off," said the younger American lady, yawning slightly. "Oh! I know *him*," said the elder one with satisfaction. "After him there was King Charles the Second, with all those long black curls and little dogs; and Nell Gwyn, I certainly haven't forgotten about *her*," she declared with modest pride. "And then there was James the First, he was the Old Pretender, and James the Second, who was the Young Pretender. Isn't that right?" she demanded of the embarrassed Lucy. "You see I haven't forgotten all my history, but we don't have any Kings and Queens where I come from." She added kindly, "I don't suppose you've been taught the names of any Presidents, except Eisenhower and Roosevelt and maybe Abraham Lincoln and George Washington."

Grace decided that the nice American lady had delayed the party sufficiently. She stepped forward hastily to the foot of the bed, laid her hand on the velvet coverlet and said firmly, "This is where the Queen slept. She spent three nights in the house on her journey from York to Oxford, in June, 1643. They called her the Generalissima, she wore a black velvet habit and rode a white horse. She had more than three thousand men under her, besides guns and transport; they all camped across the moat there, in the meadow we call Leisure Ground. Lucius Hornbeam and his lady gave up this room to her, it was their own, the best room in the house. She never paid a penny for her entertainment. Mr. Hornbeam killed his sheep and oxen to feed her men, and gave her fodder for her horses; she and her officers dined each night at his table, *on carp and capons,* the story says, and they drank his cellar dry. When she went away she took all his silver spoons in her baggage and three or four pieces of plate for melting down at the King's Mint in Oxford. The eldest son of the house went with her and half-a-dozen stout young men off the estate. Harry Hornbeam took two of his father's best hunters, and a bag of gold pieces; the men were all mounted and armed with swords and pistols, three of the plough-teams were taken for the guns. Her Majesty left this riding-glove behind," said Grace, laying her hand, as she always did at this point, on the glass case on the table, "and she gave this token to be redeemed later, *when the King should enjoy his own again."*

All the visitors peered with interest at the fringed white doe-skin gauntlet, embroidered with gold and silver, the locket of crystal cut like a table diamond, enclosing a scrap of red velvet, with the filigree initials, *H.R.* "Interesting," said an elderly man, putting on his glasses. "I never happened to see one of those before. She scattered them wherever she went. It wasn't redeemed, of course." "No," sighed Grace, "and young Harry Hornbeam never came back from the war. He was one of Prince Rupert's wild riders. They said he didn't know what fear was, he was nick-named Mad Harry in the army. He was killed that very summer at the first battle of Newbury and his mother died of grief. The family lost all their estates under the Commonwealth, it wasn't till after the Restoration that Harry's son, Charles, got back the house. He set up a monument then to his father in the parish church here, a life-sized statue in gilded armour; it is in the Hornbeam chapel, behind the family pew. And that is Mad Harry's portrait on the wall."

She pointed with her thin brown hand and all the visitors turned to stare at the cavalier, hanging in the last of the autumn sunshine, in his steel corselet, his crimson sash and his falling lace collar, with his crisp auburn ringlets, his pale eyes, his haggard sidelong smile. He carried a huge white felt hat, adorned with a crimson plume and seemed to disdain the whole company. "All the women in the house ran to the windows to see their men ride away," related Grace with shining eyes, just as if she had been there. "They waved handkerchiefs and threw flowers as if it had been a wedding. Harry Hornbeam's young wife was on the steps, they had only been married a few months. As he kissed her goodbye he said to her, 'If the child's a boy call him Charles, if it's a girl call her Henrietta.' Ever since that day," related Grace solemnly, "the eldest child of the Hornbeams is supposed to take one of those names."

She always moved herself by this recital and usually moved her audience. The old American lady obediently said, "Isn't that cute?" But one of the countrywomen stifled a yawn and said to the other, "Bit silly, really. You'd think they'd have got on to some better names by this time. Charley's not so bad, our second was christened Charley after his uncle, but fancy making a girl tag round labelled Henrietta. Unchristian, I call it." "Pearl's a nice name for a girl," her neighbour said, "or Valerie or Jennifer, or one of them double names like they have on the films, Mary Lou or Sally Ann or something. No, I wouldn't want to call any child of mine Henrietta. Such a queer name for a girl. Don't they never change it?" she asked Grace.

"Well, the names have been changed, once or twice," admitted Grace, "but it usually seems to bring bad luck. There was a Sir George Hornbeam in the eighteenth century, who was killed in a duel and little Sir Arthur Hornbeam, the lame boy, who was drowned in the moat, in 1801. Then there was Miss Alice Hornbeam, a maid of honour, who ran away with a married man in the sixties; it caused a great scandal at the time. And the present baron's grandfather, he was called Edward, after King Edward the Seventh; he came to a very tragic end. He was found dead in the woods, he had an accident with his gun, climbing over the fence. I daresay some of you may remember the story. It was in all the papers at the time, it happened in 1933." The two country-women glanced at each other; they knew a different version.

"And what about the present generation?" enquired the young American crossly. "Do they keep up this old-world tradition?" Grace had to admit that the name of the Martyr King was not being used in the direct line at the moment. "Poor Edward, the third Lord Hornbeam, only had the two children; twins they were, his wife died when they were born. The girl was the elder, so he had them christened Henrietta and Harry. Miss Hornbeam lives here now, she may have shown you round the State rooms. Her brother Harry was killed at Arnhem. His little boy is the present Lord Hornbeam. We always call him Victor, because he was born on VE Day, but when he comes of age he may change his name to Charles."

The party fidgeted a little as she rambled on; Lucy Holly thought, "That's the little boy we're to have tea with." She looked round her at the dark walls, the tarnished silver sconces, the velvet-hung bed; she imagined the haggard French queen, the Little Madam, rolling her sleepless head on the pillows, staring at the flickering taper on the bed-table, waiting impatiently for cock-crow, while outside in the June night the camp-fires gleamed in Leisure Ground and the horses stamped in their lines. For the first time in her young life, history came alive for her, the an-guished queen was a real person. From the wall the melancholy smile of Harry Hornbeam spoke to her in a moment of silence. "All in vain," said Mad Harry. "I'd better have stayed at home, that June morning. The King lost his throne, in spite of all we could do to save him; my father lost everything that he had in the world and I lost my life. She cast a black spell on us, that lady, when she came riding by with her foolish little army; but that's the way of the world. I'd ride again with my Generalissima, if I had my choice."

VIII

In three years the Fountain Court guides had collected a treasury of eccentrics, who stood out from the ordinary tourists. Leaf's suspicions had twice been aroused by a visitor who took one spoon after another up from the dining-room table to examine the hall marks and did not put the last one back. Nowadays he had a very good look all round the table before he let any tour proceed to the Green Boudoir. Grace Thorn had delayed a whole party once for half an hour while she argued the justice of Charles the First's execution with an angry little man who proudly proclaimed himself a descendant of Bradshaw the regicide. Nanny had had several skirmishes with local visitors to the King's Bedroom, who wanted to talk scandal about Lady Hornbeam and Edward the Seventh, and Charles had an affectionate recollection of the lively native of Barbados, very dark in colour and much marked with the small-pox, who declared himself to be Ephraim Hornbeam the rightful owner of the estate. It seemed that his great-grandmother, a full-blooded negress of great beauty and character, according to him, had caught the eye of her master, Lavinia Hornbeam's father, and exercised influence over him for many years. In the end he had manumitted her and her children and left them large sums of money; but this was not enough for her descendants, who had persuaded themselves, on no particular evidence, that he had legally married her on his death-bed. All this had come tumbling out in the Yellow Drawing-room, under Lavinia's portrait, right in the middle of an afternoon tour, fortunately quite a small one. Charles had coped firmly with Cousin Ephraim, led him into the Library and kept him talking while Henrietta finished with the visitors; but he stayed on for hours, talking of his imagined wrongs; they had to endure several more visits before they could persuade the poor man that his claims were quite unfounded. Charles still amused himself sometimes with the notion that Fountain Court really belonged to black Cousin Ephraim, the Rightful Heir.

Henrietta's best visitor had appeared that autumn, on the day after Arnhem Day, which this year had fallen upon a Friday. She was showing the library and one of the women, eyeing the photograph of Harry on the writing table, in the silver frame, with the flowers beside it, said stupidly, "Is that the present owner?" Henrietta replied in her colourless voice, "My little nephew is the present owner. That was his father, my brother, who was killed at Arnhem." The woman was silent, one or two people looked sideways at the photograph. Some informed person said, "Ten years yesterday, it started," and then a little man drew attention to himself by saying, "Arnhem, that was a proper do, that was. I was there meself." Everybody gaped at him and he became rather red in the face, but squared his shoulders and said sheepishly, "I served with the Airborne lot, glider-boys, the red-beret chaps; we thought a lot of ourselves in those days." He observed that nobody knew what to say, spread his hands, sighed for his lost companions and said again, "It was a proper picnic. You know what you ought to do; if ever you meets a man in a pub who tells you he was at Arnhem, you ought to stand him a drink."

Two or three women tittered, an older man said, "That's right. If this was a pub, I'd see you got one." Henrietta with a heightened colour turned round and told the little man, "This isn't a pub, but you can have one with me now if you'll stay here." She marched her party into the empty ballroom and told them, "This is the last room we show down here. If anybody has a ticket for Queen Henrietta's Room, you can go up there from the hall; if you want to see the gardens, this is the side-door."

When she had got rid of them she went back to the library
and found the little man on the hearthrug with his back to the
fire. She walked to the side-table where the drinks were set out,
reached for the sherry decanter and touched a full glass to his.
He said "Thank you kindly, miss" and drank. "This gentleman
now, this brother of yours, he was a paratrooper, I take it, from
the photograph," he said: and when she nodded dumbly said,
"Ah! they dropped the Parachute Regiment at the very beginning
and the First Airborne after 'em, to hold the north end of a big
road-bridge there was, crossing over the Lower Rhine. I didn't
get over till the third day and a proper death-trap it was by that
time. It looked grand enough going over the North Sea; the whole
sky was full of aircraft, strings and strings of our gliders, with the
big machines towing us and fighters buzzing round. There was
waves and waves of us, you'd have thought we could swamp a
whole city, let alone one or two bridges, but the Jerries was wise
to us by that time. They just waited till we come low enough and
then shot us down."

"They didn't get you anyhow," said Henrietta, looking at him
earnestly and tasting the wine in her mouth like blood. He
stamped his right foot, smiling at her. "This knee's stiff; I'll walk
with a limp all my days, the doctors tell me. We was hit coming
in to land and we crashed all in a heap, that was when I crocked
me knee. I crawled out of the wreck, but I couldn't stand nor
do much fighting. All I was good for was to lie there in the mud
and fire off dead men's rifles. We was dropped much too far to
the west, miss, on the wrong side of a muddy great ditch, we
couldn't get near your brother's lot, nobody couldn't. The Guards
come up in the end and a whole crowd of Yanks, and they got
Nymegen, but it was no use; the men in Arnhem was cut off. Some
of 'em got away on the last night, swimming and floating over
the river under fire; about one in four I heard, the rest was all
killed or taken prisoner. I know I was back home again inside a
week and in hospital three months while they poked about with

this knee. A poor bargain the Army had with me. Worst week of my life, I tell you, miss; I'll never forget Arnhem, not if I live to be a hundred. It gives me a funny feeling still whenever I hear that word."

She said, "It does me too. I'm sorry about your knee;" but he shrugged that away. "Doesn't matter in my trade," said he cheerfully. "I'm an undertaker, always have to walk slow. Nice little family business, my father had it before me. Any time you want anybody buried, miss, you let me know. I'm much obliged to you for that drink."

2

This man was still the kindest of Henrietta's recollections, she liked to think of him from time to time and feel that they had given each other a friendly greeting. The man she least liked to remember was a discontented young mechanic in dirty dungarees, who had emerged on that August Bank Holiday from a tour round the State apartments, grumbling to the girl on his arm—"What did you want to bring me here for?" he was asking; "what's so special about it? You wanted to come here, I didn't, we got something better to do with our money than waste it trailing through this lousy dump. I don't want to pay out another two bob for us to see their gardens; we'll push off right away and go back to Wilchester. I don't want to see no more of these old half-crown houses."

The girl was flushed and ready to cry, she tugged at his sleeve, muttering, "Hush up, do, boy; they'll hear you." The rest of the party came straggling out and drew away from the couple; but one little man in glasses, ruffling up like a cock-sparrow, walked right up to the young man and said, "That's enough from you, spoiling everybody else's pleasure. If you don't appreciate what you've seen, so much the worse for you." Charles, coming out last, said "What's all this about?" sounding exactly like a policeman; Henrietta with a red spot in either cheek, snatched up a couple of half-crowns and held them out on her palm. "You've seen all we've got to show you," she told the young man tartly. "If you don't feel you've had your money's worth you can take these and go."

He took the money stupidly and turned it over in his hand; "No offence, miss," said he feebly, but Henrietta stared him out of countenance. He pocketed the money, said, "Come on, you," to his girl and walked out. She slipped past Henrietta at the table, bleating, "Oh! miss; I'm sorry," and ran after her young man down the steps; in a minute there was the roar of a motor-cycle starting up and going away. Henrietta stood silent at the table while the other tourists filed past her. One or two mumbled sympathy or thanks; the little man repeated, "Too many of these young swine about, if he'd stayed I'd've told him off proper." Leaf tidied up his unsteady piles of money and whispered, "Thirteen, twelve, six; miss," Charles came up and shook his head at her gently, she stood as if turned to stone. It was just six o'clock; Leaf went over and began to bolt the big doors. "Well, that's about all for today, thank God," said Charles. "Bank Holiday is always pretty frightful, but it does pay." Suddenly she burst out, "What's the use of going on at all?" Leaf was so startled that he dropped the big door key, but Charles, taking her by the elbow, merely said, "Temper, Penny. Come on, dear, you're just about done up. Walk over with me and I'll get you a drink. You'll feel better about this tomorrow." You could always rely on Charles.

3

On this October afternoon Lucy Holly came down from the Queen's Room all in a daze. She found her mother and Lady Linden waiting for her impatiently; Mrs. Plane the parson's wife had

arrived on her bicycle, late as usual, to take a turn at the cash-table
and Leaf was just starting on a tour. "Do be quick, dear," said
Lady Linden anxiously, "we're keeping everybody waiting, I'm
afraid. I didn't think you'd be so long upstairs;" and Elsa Holly
said unkindly, "Lucy always dawdles." Everybody turned round
and looked at her and Lucy became crimson in the face. She did
not see why she should be scolded, for how could she have hurried
Grace Thorn? Besides, the tour had to wait for the other five
people, who now came drifting along the passage. The American
ladies, it seemed, had already been round and were going into
the gardens, but Mrs. Plane had to give out three tickets and find
change for a pound. Altogether there was quite a little delay and
Lucy was sulky by the time she got into the Red Dining-room.

Here, however, she soon cheered up. She went round the walls
by herself, with her back to the company, ignoring Leaf and
sulkily repeating the names on the heavy gilt picture-frames; but
quite soon she decided that these unknown Hornbeams must be
a most sensible family, who had their animals painted instead of
themselves. For the pictures in the Red Dining-room were almost
all of creatures who had lived or died for the use or pleasure of
the Hornbeams. Delicate spider-legged race-horses minced along,
each in charge of a yellow-coated groom; Stubbs had painted
them in a pearly morning light on Newmarket Heath in the year
1781. Sartorius had depicted four fox-hounds standing under a
hedge, just before the kennels were moved from Fountain Court
to Wilchester Castle. Their lovely names were traced upon a
scroll in the corner of the picture, Huntsman, Hornblower, Haggard and Hotspur; in the background was a distant view of the
old south front, gabled and apricot-coloured, with the whole pack
in full cry across the valley below. John Herring, the stage-coach-
man, had taken the likeness of Sir Leoline Hornbeam's mare, Rox-
alana, in her loose-box, attended by a very small stable-boy with
a bucket. Ben Marshall had been employed to immortalise the
great black stallion, Patroclus. Landseer had painted the first

Lady Hornbeam's pet, Fidèle, a spaniel the colour of orange marmalade, with the ringlets and the lovesick air of a Victorian belle.
In the corner by the fireplace was a still-life by the same artist, a
roe deer as large as life, hanging from a larder hook among dead
hares and rabbits, pheasants and black game; all this fur and
feather was delineated with the unnatural and glossy precision of
a colour-photograph. The walls were covered with pictures to a
considerable height, three or four rows of them, all heavily framed
in gilt, as if the intention were to conceal the crimson flock wall-
paper, the colour of freshly-spilt blood. Any odd corner had been
filled up with meticulous studies of game birds and wildfowl, nesting, flying, or heaped together on larder shelves; in the corner by
the fireplace some bygone Hornbeam had found room for a portrait of his best salmon, an Irish fifty-pounder, with every glittering scale marked. There were several portraits of fighting-cocks
and even the white marble mantelpiece was carved with a hunt-
ing-scene, hounds pulling down a stag of ten points most faithfully rendered.

Lucy did not like this quite so well as the pictures and turned
away. "Beautiful workmanship," she heard the old butler say reproachfully. "Ordered from Italy by the second Lord Hornbeam,
at the same time as the group in the window; a lion attacking a
bull, cut in marble, also considered very lifelike." It was lifelike
indeed; tender-hearted Lucy could scarcely bear to look at the
maddened writhe of the bull as the lion's teeth sank into his neck
and the great claws tore at his loins. The other tourists gathered
round and stared fascinated at this eternal agony in marble, displayed on its black pedestal. "Funny thing to have about the
place," they said, as usual. "Shouldn't care to look at that every
day; not really suitable to a dining-room." "Nice bit of beef,
though," a fat man said with a wink; his wife tossed her head and
declared, "It would put me off my food." "Note the work in the
mane," Leaf insisted, pointing out the tight curls, crisp as a judge's

wig, while Lucy turned her head away and thought confusedly, "Oh! poor thing; how that must have hurt."

4

Harry Leaf, whose life had been spent laying tables, had set out this one exquisitely for the tourists, laying twenty places, as if for one of those Edwardian banquets which he could remember, fifty years earlier. The dinner service was Sèvres, each plate had a turquoise-blue border and was painted with a fairy landscape; the fruit-dishes were shaped like shells, like hearts and clubs, diamonds and spades; in the centre was a flower-vase classic temple with gilt columns and medallions of turquoise porcelain. At intervals down the table stood candlesticks, shaped like blue-robed goddesses in gilt armour, each had a candle stuck in her helmet and two more held at full stretch of her slender arms. At the foot of the table were the two leather trunks with their velvet-lined shelves and compartments in which the whole service could be packed for travelling. "Taken complete from the baggage of one of Napoleon's generals, at the battle of Waterloo, by Colonel Sir George Hornbeam who added this wing to the house." So droned Harry Leaf, shifting from one tired leg to the other, looking straight in front of him as he recited his accustomed snippets of information in his old cracked voice. "A dozen plates for each course, painted at the Sèvres factory, with views of beauty-spots in France and Italy; for the use of the General and his staff in the field."

"Trust the top brass to do themselves well," said a stout man, with a wink to the company. "It's wonderful what you can pick up on active service if you keeps your eyes open. Of course in his position the Colonel could bring back what he liked and no questions asked." A little ferrety man who might have been a dealer said, "Lovely stuff, but these big services are a drug in the market nowadays; you can't sell 'em except to a museum, we're all overstocked with such things." "Fancy having to wash and polish all them plates," the fat woman said to the thin one. "The table glass is Waterford," the butler said, with a stern eye for these interruptions. "The table silver here is all by Peter and Anne Bateman, every piece engraved with the family crest, a leaf from a hornbeam tree with the motto *Viresco*." "How beautifully you keep it all, Leaf," said Lady Linden. The old servant bent his rheumatic shoulders, jerky and stiff as a puppet and his bony hands twitched; he had been polishing that silver for fifty years. "Not a chip in the china all these years, my lady," said he proudly. "There was a young gentleman down here lately from one of those London museums. He said they'd got nothing finer up there, not even at Apsley House."

The Wilchester women stared open-mouthed at the table. "How'd you like," they asked each other, "to wash up all them plates, polish all them glasses, clean all that silver? Like something on the films," they said, "like the Guildhall banquet on the telly." "Lovely, it looks," Elsie Ashe, the youngest of them, sighed with envy. "I'd like to see it all lit up with candles and flowers in them vases," said she. She was not long married, her husband was doing well at the aluminium works. They had a bandbox of a house on a new estate, with two rooms up and two down, a good kitchen and a pram-shed outside, but no pram in it yet. Ted Ashe did not think they could manage a baby for a year or two. Elsie was very house-proud, always scrubbing and polishing the bright little room they called the lounge. They were furnishing it on the hire-purchase system, they had a three-piece moquette suite, the pride of her heart, thin flowery curtains, a folding table, four gimcrack chairs, a couple of flimsy rugs which skidded on the polished linoleum and an electric fire in the cold hearth. Wedding-present vases adorned the mantelpiece, everything in the room was brand-new. There really was hardly room to turn round in it and they always ate their meals in the kitchen because the big TV set took up so much space; it stood under the window instead of a side-board and all the chairs faced towards it as if it had been a household altar.

Elsie thought her lounge quite beautiful; but here, confronted by a scene from a vanished world, she had a sudden prick of misgiving, loyally stifled. "Lovely, it must have been," she said to Leaf, who did not hear her. With his old shaking hand he had picked up a framed menu card from the table. "This was the dinner that was served when King Edward the Seventh dined here in 1903," said he. "This menu was found underneath a dish at the back of a cupboard in the pantry and I asked Miss Hornbeam if we should have it framed and put it out to amuse our visitors." Holding the card at arm's-length to help his long-sighted old eyes, he recited the soups, the Severn salmon, the white and brown entrées, the roast, the sorbet; then, like a second dinner, the game, the sweets, the savouries with the choice wines, the fruit from the hothouses and gardens. "Three or four dishes in each course to choose from," he told the gaping circle, mildly pleased to astonish them. "A couple of hours it took to serve a dinner like that; then when the ladies had left us we cleared away all the plates and silver, rolled up the side-cloths and left the gentlemen to their wine and cigars." He slightly lifted a corner of the great table-cloth to show that it was in three parts.

Lucy's mouth watered to hear him recite the menu which had been served to the old King. She was growing like a young tree and always hungry. At school, thank goodness, you could always stuff down something to fill you up, sitting at the long table, scraping the chipped white plates, never stopping to speak until you had downed the mutton and rice-pudding; but at her mother's flat, in the holidays, there were never any regular meals. Her mother was always dieting, counting calories, living on rusks and black coffee, great salads of lettuce and tomatoes, tossed in lemon-juice, on omelettes and grape-fruit; once she lived for a week on a diet of three glasses of milk and six bananas a day. The fat char grumbled, "Yer ma don't eat enough to keep a sparrer alive." She was always dashing in and out, in a great hurry, crying over her shoulder, "I've got to fly, Sir Harry's waiting, I've a fitting, a hair-do, a film, a dinner, a play; get yourself something out of the frig, darling, just for now and tomorrow we'll go out to lunch together," but when tomorrow came she was always off again. Mother had not had a square meal, Lucy thought, since they came back from Kenya. She and the char used to lunch together most days on scraps, coffee, bread and Camembert cheese, bananas, ice-cream blocks from the dairy at the corner; by three o'clock Lucy was hungry again. She heard the thin woman now say to the fat one, "Fancy stuffing down all that rich food," and her mother saying to Lady Linden, "No wonder they all took cures at Homburg." She said to herself defiantly, "I'd have liked to go right through, eat every bit of it; I wish I could have it now. If this old man doesn't stop talking to Lady Linden we shall never get any tea." She felt in the pocket of her flannel blazer, found half a bar of nut-milk chocolate and put it furtively into her mouth; it helped a little but not much.

5

Leaf was growing garrulous under Lady Linden's mild smile. "No, the family never uses this room nowadays, we only keep the table laid for show. We haven't the staff here to look after it as it deserves. This is our last open day; on Monday I shall put it all away in the cupboards for the winter," and he sighed and con-fessed, "I always miss seeing it out. Even in the old days, m'lady, it was thought too valuable for everyday use. It was only brought out for the Hunt Ball dinner, or a wedding breakfast or a coming-of-age. Of course when King Edward was here for his visit it was used every night; that was when one of the compôtes got broken."

"Fancy your remembering that, Leaf," the old lady said. "You

must have been a very young man, in 1903." "I was twenty that
autumn, m'lady," he said, bowing his stooped shoulders. "It was
the first year they let me serve in the dining-room. Of course Mr.
Lime, the butler we had then, he wouldn't let me anywhere near
the table; but I helped fetch and carry and got inside the door
once or twice. We had all the leaves in the table for the big dinner,
we had to bring in extra chairs and use two of our longest cloths;
they sat down thirty, I remember. Every servant in the house was
on the job; we all wanted to set eyes on His Majesty. He sat here,"
said Leaf, laying his hand firmly on the back of a big armchair,
half-way down the side of the table. "A big man with a grey beard
and a twinkle in his eye, and a cigar sticking out of one corner of
his mouth; that's how I remember him."

Lucy had listened open-mouthed, now she interrupted. "Why
didn't he sit at the top of the table? I thought that was the
grandest," but Harry Leaf persisted, "No, he sat in the middle of
this side; that's the place of honour for Royalty." His glance wandered up and down the table; his mind's eye saw men long since
dead, sitting round it in pink coats and white ties, women in silks
and satins, with pearls and diamonds about their necks. In the
cold air of the disused room his old nose smelt a rich long-vanished
smell of roast meat, port and cigars; his shaking hand closed firmly
on the neck of a bottle emptied fifty years earlier. "It's the shirt-
fronts I miss most," said he mournfully. "I shall never see that
many white shirt-fronts round this table again. You were there
yourself, m'lady," he told Lady Linden suddenly. "You were a
bride, you wore your wedding dress, you sat over there beside the
fire. You looked very well, if I may say so." The bright colour
stood on his cheek-bones.

"Fancy your remembering that, Leaf," said Lady Linden, smiling. "Yes, I was there, I was terrified, I'd never been to such a big
dinner. I had to sit beside old Lord Pinecoffin because I was a
bride. He was as deaf as a post, we hadn't a word to say to each
other."

It all came back to the old woman as if it had been yesterday, how cold her hands had been, how hot her head, how tightly laced her white satin gown; she had hardly been able to breathe. Dumb and frightened, she had looked up and down the table for a comforting glance from her young soldier-husband, but the bouquets of roses and maidenhair fern, the pyramids of grapes and peaches, had hidden him from her. All she had got was a satirical smile from her hostess, sitting up in all the pride of her beauty beside the old King, hung about with jewels like an idol. "Mary Hornbeam did look so beautiful," she told Elsa Holly, "in a yellow brocade gown, with a dog-collar of emeralds and diamonds round that long neck of hers. She had yellow Paradise plumes in her hair and a big diamond tiara; I shall never forget her. She was the loveliest woman in London then, none of the others could hold a candle to her. Yes, it was a wonderful night, it was the last of the big parties, there was never another like that one."

Her eyes met the faded watery blue eyes of the old butler; she saw that he remembered as she did. That had been the year of the great scandal. Lord Hornbeam had the anonymous letter from a jealous woman while he and his wife were at Homburg, it told him how she had deceived him. They parted company, she remained abroad for the winter and next year he broke his neck at a fence out hunting; he had always been a reckless horseman. Lady Hornbeam did not come back for some little time after his death, and when she did was not much welcomed by her neighbours; but she had faced it all out. Nowadays there were very few people who troubled to remember how wild the old woman upstairs had been once upon a time, but Lady Linden and Leaf knew her story well enough, it had been part of their vanished youth. The old lady glanced up at the picture over the chimney piece, the second Lord Hornbeam, painted in hunting-kit by Maurice Greiffenhagen in 1900 and looking very gloomy. "Oh dear," she sighed, "he was a very difficult man; I don't wonder they didn't agree."

6

"All that was donkeys' years ago," said Elsa crossly behind them. "Why, it must have been before the First World War. There never were any big parties here when I was a girl. I can just remember this house being a hospital and Lady Hornbeam floating about in a white veil, with a ruby cross on her breast, doing damn-all, I'm sure. This room was one of the wards," said she looking round as if in surprise. "I was about five years old; I can remember beds down both sides and men sitting about in hospital blue, one of them gave me some chocolate." "No doubt that would be so," Leaf admitted. "I wasn't here at that time, madam." "You would have been called up," said Lady Linden, whose husband and sons had all been soldiers, and Leaf replied proudly, "Yes, m'lady, I went to sea. I was in the Royal Navy, when they found what my work had been they would make me a steward; but I was torpedoed once in the Mediterranean. I was fifteen hours in an open boat," said Leaf with modest pride. "Her Ladyship took me back into service here afterwards, I was made first footman and then butler, but times were very quiet at that time. We all hoped for better things when Mr. Edward grew up, but he was such a quiet one, all for his bird-watching and such; it was a new notion then, you didn't hear so much of it as you do nowadays. We all cheered up in the Hall when we heard he was to marry Canon Kingswood's daughter, we thought there'd be some life about the place again. The wedding was in Wilchester, of course, but there was a tenants' dinner here, and a ball and a piece of plate subscribed for; that salver on the sideboard," said he, pointing shakily. "But her young ladyship was as shy as he was, she never had a word to say for herself in company, never asked anybody inside the house and then she died, poor young creature! when the twins were born. After that it was all as quiet as the tomb here between the wars; his Lordship a widower and her old Ladyship caring for nothing but her bridge-parties. I almost forgot how to lay a big table," said he with a faint joking smile. "The best we ever had was a children's party at Christmas time. Your Ladyship would remember those, I daresay."

"*I* can remember that part of it," Elsa Holly admitted. "Of course I was too old for the parties really, but Lady Hornbeam used to ask me over to lend a hand. The twins always sat at the two ends of the table. They had a cake each, with their names iced on top and candles for their ages; they wore paper crowns out of crackers and after they'd cut their cakes every child on the estate got a slice. There were presents all round off the Christmas tree and parlour games and all that nonsense; I was bored stiff. I had quite a swing round with Charles Hornbeam at one of those parties, I remember, he was home on leave. He kissed me under the mistletoe, that wasn't in the book of the words. I remember Lady Hornbeam, very tall and stiff, in a toque like old Queen Mary, looking down her nose at us. Charles and I were both about eighteen then, we didn't bother about the children much, we went off into the conservatory instead of doing our stuff; she never asked me again. Oh! dear, how handsome Charles was in those days. I don't think I want to see him again with only half a face. Everything's changed." She sighed fretfully and moved towards the door. Lady Linden murmured, "Such a pretty sight, those Christmas parties, all the children came from miles round, they looked forward to it so much. Poor Harry was such a handsome boy." She glanced involuntarily towards the empty chair at the head of the table; behind her Leaf said, "Ah! poor young gentleman, we'd all looked forward to his coming-of-age; but Hitler spoilt that party. I shan't live to see his little Lordship grow up." He glanced round, ran his eye over the table to make sure that nothing was missing, raised his voice and said formally, "Now, ladies and gentlemen, if you've seen enough here we will proceed to the Green Boudoir and the Yellow Drawing-room." The visitors filed one by one through the door which he held open for them; as

Lady Linden went by him last of all, she said kindly, "Yes, we've had good times, Leaf, but we must try to look forward. We can't put the clock back, can we?" He spread out his shaking hands and said mournfully, "Oh! m'lady, I wish I could put it back fifty years."

IX

NANNY SHOWED the three bedrooms at the top of the Waterloo staircase. All were now disused, they were too far from that part of the house where the family lived, they faced east and you could not keep them warm in winter. Visitors had to climb two shallow flights under the oval glass dome, between walls covered with sporting trophies, now moth-eaten and dusty. Low down came snarling masks of fox and badger; higher up curved or twisted horns of antelopes and mountain sheep, the branching antlers of moose and deer. Highest of all were grinning lions and snow-leopards and elephants' tusks, one above another; there was even a leathery crocodile snout, showing all its teeth to frighten children. Most of these big-game trophies had been shot by Henrietta's great-uncle, that eminent mid-Victorian soldier and sportsman, General Sir Alfred Hornbeam, K.C.B. He had been the third son of "Waterloo" Hornbeam and his second wife; in the silhouette of the "Black Children" in the Drawing-room he was the tall one armed prophetically with a bow and arrow. The landing at the top of the Waterloo Staircase was spread with the skins of his lions and tigers. His portrait hung between the windows, a handsome old boy in full uniform, with a fine weather-beaten complexion, painted by Sir John Millais for the Royal Academy in the year when he became Governor of the Unfriendly Islands. Beneath the portrait was a masterpiece of taxidermy, a glass case in which five tiger-kittens frolicked innocently about a buffalo-skull and beside it hung the skin of a twelve-foot python, turning and rustling in the draught from the staircase with a horribly lifelike noise, as if it were gliding through dead leaves.

At the top of the staircase was the General's Bedroom where Nanny used to lurk behind the door, a little bent old woman in a grey cotton gown and a starched waistbelt, getting a whiff or two at a cigarette before pouncing out to collect each party. The room was at the north-east corner of the house and was rather dark and gloomy. It had intricate draperies of green rep at its five windows and contained innumerable trophies from his campaigns; Burmese blackwood cabinets, intricately carved, a Coromandel screen of some beauty, a good deal of Indian brassware, Chinese ivories and porcelain from the sack of the Summer Palace. His sword hung above the chimney piece and on the flowery Victorian wall-paper were cases of medals, native-weapons, African fetish-masks. There was also a delicate set of paintings on rice-paper, depicting, between the windows, the gathering of tea and in the dark corner behind the wardrobe tortures and an execution in the Chinese manner. In place of the four-poster which should have been the best piece in the room stood the General's camp-bed, in which the old widower had obstinately continued to sleep after his retirement, when he came back to end his days with his elder brother at Fountain Court.

His camp-washstand and his canvas chairs stood there too, on one of his tiger-skin rugs; Nanny used to tell her tourists, when they exclaimed over this, "The old gentleman used to like pretending he was back in the jungle." Henrietta and her Cousin Charles had amused themselves, one wet afternoon, by completing this picture of a veteran campaigner. Charles had lugged down from the attic a couple of empty tin trunks with Major-General Sir Alfred Hornbeam, K.C.B. painted on the lids and an odd-shaped canvas box with a shako inside. Henrietta had stood spurred riding-boots in the mahogany boot-rack, put a couple of polo-sticks and a solar topee in a corner, and laid a cocked plumed hat on the dressing table; finally she had hung up her great-uncle's scarlet dress-tunic on the back of a chair, as if it were waiting for his ghost to put it on. No room could have looked more military

than this one, where the red blinds had been pulled down when
the General died peacefully in his bed, in the year of the Diamond
Jubilee, at the age of seventy-seven, having survived both the
Crimean War and the Indian Mutiny, besides various lesser campaigns in Afghanistan, China and Egypt, Zululand and Burma
and many hairsbreadth escapes from lions and tigers, charging
buffaloes and elephants and lurking crocodiles. Nanny could just
remember, as a little girl, standing in the park with her mother to
see his fine funeral go down to the little church; now that she was
close on seventy herself she could understand better why the old
warrior had wanted to come home and die at Fountain Court.

The men in her parties used to enjoy the General's quarters and
crack jokes about him, "Tough as old boots, that sort's died out;
old soldiers never die, they only fade away." The women all preferred the Pink Bedroom next door. It was a period-piece and had
been furnished from Paris in the year 1896, when old Lady Hornbeam came to Fountain Court as a young bride and this part of
the house had been done up for spare-rooms. It was frivolous and
completely feminine; the chairs, the couches, the bed itself, set up
on a low dais in the French manner, were all of white-painted
wood panelled in fine cane basket-work. The walls were tapestried
in rose brocade, the curtains and cushions matched; there were
even lengths of pink satin ribbon, wide as the palm of your hand,
slotted through the hems of the fine linen sheets and the muslin
draperies of the dressing table were tied up with pink bows. Henrietta had laid out some unimportant toilet silver to brighten this
table and Nanny used to count it with her eye sharp as a robin's
as each party left; the two soft and worn old hairbrushes, the three
glass containers for powder, cream and hairpins, the hand-mirror
embossed with fat cherubs, the two candlesticks, the three vases,
the seven photograph-frames. These had all belonged to Henrietta's mother in her girlhood at the Canon's house in Wilchester
close, they were only cheap Edwardian stuff, but they seemed to
suit the room. The carpet was the best thing in it, a very delicate

Aubusson with rosy garlands on a cream ground. To protect it Charles had slung white ropes from doorway to doorway, so that the half-crown tourists jostled each other along an alley-way, like sheep going into a pen.

Nanny used to hear the women chattering together like so many jackdaws, greedy, pecking, curious, always saying the same things. "This is dainty, ever so dainty; I'd like to sleep here, wouldn't you? . . . Dull, don't you think, too much of the same colour; I like a bit of pattern, I'm all for variety . . . Why do they stick the bed up on two steps, like a lying-in-state? I call that silly . . . Looks comfortable, though; I'd love to sleep under all them muslin curtains . . . Hardly big enough for two, dear; you wouldn't get a wink of sleep. I suppose they hadn't invented twin beds then . . . Never can see the sense of a sofa in a bedroom, if you want to put your feet up why not lie down on the bed? Just look at all that ribbon, too; extravagant, I call it. Fifteen-and-six a yard, at least, if you could get the quality nowadays. Of course things were half the price, then . . . Still there's the work it makes to consider; fancy having to take out all that every wash-day and run it in again by hand; fancy having to rub up all that silver every day when you did the room! . . . Ah! but there was plenty of people to lend a helping hand, in those days and plenty of time, I reckon; they could take things easy." Nanny heard that sort of patter almost daily; it seemed like an epitaph, pronounced by an overworked generation upon vanished wealth and leisure. "They all had time to spare." "We've changed all that nowadays," somebody would be sure to conclude. "No sense in making work."

2

Nanny kept the best to the last, King Edward's Room, where the bearded monarch, seventh of his name, had snored and choked among his pillows when he came down to Fountain Court for the shooting, some fifty years earlier. The furniture here was all on the grand scale, massive wardrobes with mirrored doors and crystal knobs, huge chests of drawers, tables and chairs of pale ashwood, a double washstand as big as a sideboard. The decorations were as flowery as the carpentry was solid. Great cabbage roses sprawled in crimson and purple over the chintz-covered chairs and sofas, and on the thick carpet; they ran up the wall-paper on a green trellis, even the broad ribbon bell-pull had a garland of roses upon it. They rioted over the bedroom china, the great jugs and basins, the vases and soap-dishes, all in pairs, the huge foot-bath, the two big chamber-pots, candidly displayed. If you had been lying sick in that bed you could have counted hundreds of feverish roses.

The curtains at the five tall windows were edged with green ball-fringe, yard upon yard of it and looped back with green silk ropes, each ending in a foot-long tassel. After more than fifty summers those billowing curtains were as thin and rotten as tissue paper, you could have poked your finger through them almost anywhere. Nanny never drew or disturbed the curtains nowadays, she only pulled the red blinds down in the mornings, till the sun had worked round to the south. The female visitors were always calculating how much chintz you would want to redecorate King Edward's Room. "A hundred yards would go nowhere," they used to tell one another, "even if it were double-width and these fabrics mostly come narrow, twenty-seven or thirty inches at the most. You know how a patterned material cuts to waste, you'd have to match all them roses. You'd have to reckon seven yards at least for those big armchairs and a dozen yards for each of the sofas. Then there's five of them big windows going right up to the ceiling, besides all the valances and flounces and the walls padded to match the chairs. Oh! my dear, a hundred yards would never do it. Besides, I don't care for chintz, do you? it's that cold and slippery. If it was mine I'd do it up quite different. I never could afford the expense." They used quite to frighten one another with the contemplation of so much extravagance, even for a King's visit. "You can't wonder," these anxious housewives usually ended, "that it's never been renewed."

It was the younger visitors who talked so; their elders eyed the big bed and said, "Fancy old Edward sleeping in that bed; he liked his comforts, he made himself properly at home wherever he went. It wasn't the shooting he came for," they used to tell one another. "He knew a pretty woman when he saw one, he had a roving eye, the old man did and he liked to be amused. Lady Hornbeam was a great beauty, they say, when she was young; afraid of nobody, like all the Wilchesters. She had a sharp tongue, she could always make the King laugh. I did hear she was one of his best favourites." Nanny used to stiffen and look down her nose when they began that kind of gossip, she thought that they might have had the grace to wait till they were out of the house first. "Ah! there used to be gay times up here in the nineties," they told each other enviously. "Great goings-on, from all you hear."

3

Nanny could have told the Women's Institute plenty that they would never know. "I came into service here the summer of the Diamond Jubilee," she could have said, if you asked her. "I was just seventeen then and reckoned a pretty girl though you might not think it to look at me now. I had yellow hair and blue eyes and a bright colour; the young maids all wore blue sprigged prints here in the mornings, it was her Ladyship's fancy. I liked that, because it matched my eyes. I was one of the under-housemaids to start with, I didn't go up to the nursery till later. Rose was my name, Rosie Birch, but nobody remembers that now; I'm always Nanny to the family or Mrs. Branch to the under-servants. Yes, this wing was as busy as a beehive then, whenever there was a house-party; this was where we put the most important guests, their names were written out plain on cards and slipped into those little frames on the doors. None of you people walking round have any idea how much work we had to do in those days; up at six every morning, running up and down stairs, sweeping and dusting, rubbing and polishing; the old head-housemaid we had then was a tartar, it was all you could do to please her. Then when the visitors were here it was running up and down stairs all day long, with breakfast-trays and long tweed skirts to be brushed and shoes to be cleaned. Of course we didn't get much chance of seeing what went on in the bedrooms. The guests all brought their own maids to wait upon them and very smart they were, foreigners half of them, always dressed in black, much too grand to wear cap and apron; they used to sit at table in the servants' hall, each in her proper order, according to the rank of her mistress. Burke's Peerage was kept in the housekeeper's room for reference in case of any dispute; and at pudding-time they all went up there with her. They used to look down on us country girls. A lady's maid had a hard job in those days, for their mistresses were always changing their gowns, not like nowadays. They'd take breakfast in bed and then all come down about ten o'clock. Coats and skirts had just come in and they used to wear Harris tweeds with a starched collar and tie like a man and a Homburg hat, with a pheasant's or a blackcock's tail feather stuck in at the side. Then they'd all go out with the guns for the day, or maybe there'd be a lunch-party for twenty or thirty. In the afternoon they'd go driving in their sealskin jackets and little perched-up hats, then they'd come back and get into their frilly tea-gowns and after that they'd dress for dinner. They never seemed to wear the same gown twice, they brought great black trunks packed with clothes, it took two men to carry the luggage upstairs. I used to hide behind doors with the other maids, or hang over the banisters, to see the ladies going down to dinner. They moved like swans in those days and held up their heads like queens. They used to come gliding down the passages with their long trains rustling behind them, all in lace and velvet, with huge puffed-out sleeves, and frills and bows and great waving feathery fans. You never see such dresses nowadays, nor won't again. Some of the older ladies wore their gowns so low that it made our eyes pop out of our heads, we'd seen nothing like that before. Of course they made up for it with those long white kid gloves, eighteen-buttons, over the elbow and never worn twice and all of them had jewels such as you never saw, great collars of rubies and diamonds and ropes and ropes of pearls; it quite frightened you to look at them. Nobody was poor in those days."

"No," she would have said, quite indignantly, "I never was in this room when King Edward was in it; of course not! what business would an under-housemaid have there? The nearest I've ever been to the old gentleman was to peep at him through the crack of a door, when he was going along the passage with his gentlemen. I've smelt his cigar; he was always smoking those great Havanas. He brought his own men-servants, of course, all the visiting gentlemen did and very grand they were; the king's valet used to sit next the butler in hall, I remember. Most of the visiting servants were very stiff and disagreeable, but of course the younger ones now and again would have an eye for a pretty girl. One of them got his arm round me once," Nanny reflected with a twinkle in her faded blue eye. "Well do I remember it; he tried to kiss me when I had my arms full of clean sheets and couldn't box his ears for him. I squeaked and ran off and I went full tilt into Harry Branch, coming upstairs with two great heavy cans of bath-water; the footmen always did that for us, it was much too hard work for girls, filling and emptying all those hip-baths and saucer-baths. Harry and I were courting then; so the pair of them had a bit of a fight in the stable yard after supper and the other man got a black eye to take back with him to London. Oh! my dear Harry was such a fine fellow in those days, six-foot tall with great broad shoulders and a handsome smiling face; the only thing you could say against him was that he had red hair and that didn't do for a footman. They were all supposed to be dark in those days. Harry could have got a London place any time, if it hadn't been for his red hair, but it didn't matter so much in the country and when there was a big party of course all the men still put themselves into powder."

"Harry and I used to sit opposite to each other at the long table in the Hall. The men were all down one side according to their places, in their fustian jackets or their liveries, while the girls sat opposite in their prints and caps and aprons. I couldn't keep my eyes off Harry and he couldn't keep his off me, whenever I looked up I used to find him watching me. Then he took to hanging about at the stairhead when he brought up the boots and the water-jugs and I'd slip out and get a kiss from him when nobody was looking. When Master Edward was born and I was picked for nursery-maid I thought I'd die, for the nurseries here are all at the back of the house, in the old part, to get the sun and be away from company; but it wasn't long before Harry got himself made nursery footman and then I saw him regularly, six or seven times a day, whenever he brought up the trays and fetched them down again. All the other girls in the house were after him, but I got him. We began walking out regularly on Sunday afternoons and in the end we were married. Her Ladyship was very kind about it, she gave me my wedding dress and a veil and Lord Hornbeam let us have a cottage. Oh! we were as happy as two birds on a tree; but he died quite young, did my Harry and my two children left school and went out to service, so I was glad to come back here when the twins were born and be Nanny again. I've lived all my life in this house or on the estate and when my time comes I hope I'll die and be buried here." Such would have been Nanny's thoughts, if anybody had asked for them, as she showed round the half-crown strangers, or snatched a cigarette behind the door, in the three State bedrooms at Fountain Court.

4

That afternoon had been rather trying. First there had been all the Wilchester Women's Institute loitering and chatting, and then in the late afternoon, a wrinkled shabby lively little man, very inquisitive, wanting to touch and linger and ask questions. He was the last out of each room, he kept holding up the tour while he muttered to himself, pricing everything he saw. "That's a nice little bit of Spode, that screen would fetch money up in London; there's no sale nowadays for the Oriental stuff, there's wood-worm in this chair, it ought to be thrown away. Pity they've let the sun get at these water-colours. They've a few collector's pieces downstairs, but there's nothing up here but bedroom junk. People won't buy these big mahogany wardrobes nowadays, they're only fit to cut up for the sake of the wood." Nanny felt sure that he was a dealer, having a look round against the day when he might hope to attend a big three-day sale of the Hornbeam possessions. She kept a sharp eye on him and her head began to tremble, as it did nowadays when she was vexed.

In the same party were Lady Linden, who greeted her by name, saying, "How are you, Mrs. Branch? We've brought Lucy to see your treasures." Then came Mrs. Holly, elegant and affected as usual, and the daughter, a dear little girl, thought Nanny, but she looked worried, her flannel jacket was done up crooked and her hair wanted brushing. "That's Mrs. Holly all over," thought Nanny, "she thinks of nobody but herself. She'd be no use as a mother." Elsa was being tiresome, going round praising everything in a style which displeased Nanny more than the little man's criticism. "Oh! my dears, these rooms alone are worth the money; too, too period! Fancy waking up among all these roses with a hangover; I couldn't take it, could you? The furniture looks like a herd of elephants, grazing happily in a flowery jungle and all those Oriental curios are pure Rudyard Kipling. That wardrobe's as big as

a cottage, with wooden pegs inside, I suppose, and not a sign of a
mirror; fancy having it bursting full with crinolines!" "Not crinolines, dear, bustles perhaps," said Lady Linden, "when it was new,
I mean, in the early nineties." "And all those delicious nineteen-
hundred Ascot gowns," bubbled Elsa. "Trains and drooping sleeves
and frilly jabots and a kangaroo pouch on the bodice and an Irish
lace coat with a parasol to match. Lord! how it takes me back to
my childhood. Mother never threw anything away, she had cupboards full of garden-party frocks and hats and feather-boas in
dozens. I adored her feather-boas, and she let me dress up in them
sometimes. She had them in every colour, green and pink and
Queen Alexandra mauve and yellow, like fondants; she said you
wore a different one every day at Ascot, and matched it up to a
floppy great hat plastered all over with flowers. Henrietta ought
to lay out one of the old lady's Ascot gowns on the bed, with all
the trimmings; she's been very clever next door with the General's
uniform. I suppose you used to wear all those frightful fussy
clothes."

"They weren't thought frightful at the time," said Lady Linden
with dignity. "We liked to think we looked very pretty in them."
"Oh! girls look pretty in anything, for a few years," said Elsa
crossly, while her daughter listened open-eyed. "I had a blue os-
trich-boa the year I came out, forget-me-not blue," Lady Linden
told them, smiling. "My father bought it for me, on my eighteenth
birthday. I wore it first at Ascot, I remember, on Cup Day. I had
a blue chiffon dress with sweet peas all over it and a blue picture-
hat trimmed to match, I skewered it on with hatpins and they all
hurt my head; then we had the usual downpour just before the
big race. I got soaked to the skin and my hat blew off right in the
middle of the paddock with everybody looking. My dear John
picked it up and brought it back to me; we'd met before at a dance,
but that was the first time he ever really noticed me. I can't think
why, I must have looked a perfect fright. My hair came down,
you know, and the sweet peas on my frock had started to run; I'd

been too vain to carry a coat. John said I looked like a drowned kitten." And the old lady smiled happily, looking back across the dun smoke of two wars to her vanished spring.

"You must have had a fearfully stupid time," vowed Elsa. "It all sounds quite ghastly to me; driving round with mother in the Victoria, leaving cards, going out to endless tea-parties, being fitted for all those tight dresses, wearing stick-up bones in your collars, and black woollen stockings and kid gloves, and never getting the least sign of a drink. Then all that dreary round of being presented, going to Ascot and Lord's and Henley, having programmes and chaperones at dances and never being allowed to dance more than twice with the same man. I don't see how you ever got married at all."

She stared quite rudely at the old lady, with her straight back, her dowdy gown, her honeyed air, but Lady Linden only smiled very sweetly. "It wasn't like that at all, dear," said she. "You've got it quite wrong. We had lovely times. I'm so sorry for all you young ones, not knowing what you've missed. You've no idea how to enjoy yourselves nowadays. When I was a girl I was as happy as the day is long. John was so sweet to me, so proud of me; he thought everything I did was wonderful. Now that he's dead and my two boys are gone and all my real life is over, I'm still happy with my memories. That's why I love to come here," said she, looking round her with her sweet dazed air. "It brings back my youth."

X

THEN ELSA turned her attention to the huge double washstand and began making fun of the earlier generation's arrangements, crying, "Hip-baths and saucer-baths; how completely barbaric!" while Lady Linden murmured, "Oh! it wasn't so bad, dear, with plenty of hot water, in front of a blazing fire; only of course you couldn't wallow for hours, as you do now and it made a lot of work." Lucy was feeling in her pockets in vain hopes of another bit of chocolate, Elsa was laughing and Nanny had glanced at her watch, wondering if she could hurry them, when behind her she heard the tiresome little dealer say, "Commodes . . ."

She whisked round and everybody stared at him, some amused, some affronted as he continued, spreading out his hands, "That's what I'm interested in; commodes. Not the square boxes so much as the other sort that go up like a pair of steps, with a little bit of Axminster on top and maybe a bit of a brass railing round it. The old folks employed 'em as steps to climb up into bed with, as well as for their proper purpose; uncommonly sensible notion to my mind. Nowadays I've got a better use for 'em. I'm always on the lookout for commodes," said the little man earnestly, "and an old house like this, without any proper bathrooms very likely, is just the place to find 'em."

Elsa burst out laughing and Nanny exclaimed indignantly, "Certainly not. You won't find any here, my man; we've done away with all such nasty things years ago." "Ah! but maybe you've got one or two put away upstairs," the dealer persisted. "Astonishing what'll turn up in the attics of an old house. If I had the chance to go up and look round, I bet you ten bob I could lay hands on one or two that would suit me." Two of the women giggled and Nanny exclaimed indignantly, "Now that's quite enough. I don't want any more of your impudence. Just because you've paid half-a-crown to come in and look round, that doesn't mean you can behave as if the house belonged to you."

At this moment Henrietta came in, pale and unsmiling, looking dead-tired, exclaiming, "Oh! Lady Linden, I was afraid I'd missed you. We've had such a crowd, because it's the last day, I suppose. Tea will be in the library at five, we shut the house then and push the last of them out into the garden. I do hope you'll stay, with Elsa and Lucy, and Granny would be so pleased if you'd look in on your way down. About a quarter of an hour would be long enough; this isn't one of her very good days, but she would be so sorry to miss you."

They talked together for a minute, while the remaining half-crown visitors filed obediently past Nanny into the corridor and were directed down the Waterloo Staircase; but the little man hung back, shifting from one foot to the other and turning his inquisitive eyes on Henrietta. All at once he burst out, "Can I have a word with you, madam?"

The tall girl turned on her heel; Nanny, returning, said "Now don't let him bother you." Lucy thought, "He must be mad," and Elsa giggled, "He collects commodes, people will collect anything." The little man turned on her instantly. "I don't collect 'em, madam, I buy 'em for resale, as many as I can get my hands on. People will take 'em off me as fast as I can convert 'em. Take out the front," said he, with a gesture of his broad short-fingered hand. "Pop in a little shelf, rip off the old carpet on top and nail on a bit of leather, polish the whole thing up and call it a fireside bookshelf. They sell like hot cakes, especially to the Americans, I can't get enough of 'em to supply the demand. You can put a dozen or so books into 'em, as many as anybody wants nowadays at a time in a modern flat and stand your ashtray and your drink and your evening paper on top. It's my own invention," said he, beaming round his company.

Lucy stared, fascinated, Lady Linden said, bewildered, "I never heard of such a thing." Elsa burst out laughing, "My dears, he's the White Knight in person!" and Nanny exclaimed indignantly, "Don't your customers know what they're buying?" "Oh! they like 'em all the better for that," the little man boasted. "It's a great joke to tell their friends. I can sell the pots, too, if they're in good condition; Spode Willow pattern, you know, or English Castles, so long as they're not too badly cracked or chipped. It's quite extraordinary," the little man reflected aloud, "what the ladies will use for flower-vases nowadays. Soup-tureens and slop-pails and copper stew-pans and old bedroom jugs. That foot-bath, there," said he, pointing with his finger to the one under King Edward's washstand, "I could get you two or maybe three pounds for that if it's perfect, only that it would be a pity to break the set." Henrietta burst out laughing, she could not help it; and he turned to her at once, as to a kindred spirit, "Now if you'd just let me run up and have a poke round in your lumber rooms, madam, I feel sure I could find something to interest me."

"Don't you let him, dear," Nanny burst out. "Ten to one, he's only here to spy out the land for one of his thieving friends. The next thing you know, we shall have a burglary, like they did at Lambsoot Old Rectory;" and she ended with a toss of her grey head, "Commodes, indeed! I don't believe a word of it."

The little man produced a card with a flourish like a conjuring trick and handed it over to Henrietta. "She's got me wrong," he pleaded. "Indeed she's got me wrong. Henry Ivy, that's me; dealer in second-hand furniture. You may have seen my shop, madam, in Goose Lane, Wilchester, round behind St. Blaizey's. I've been in business there since the end of the war, madam. Cottage antiques, that's what I specialise in; brass, copper, pewter, Staffordshire figures, Masonic mugs, trick teapots, Tunbridge ware, Victorian jewellery; everything marked in plain figures. The chief of my trade is in cottage furniture, any nice little pieces in fruit-wood or yew-wood or mahogany. People won't buy the big stuff any more, madam; they haven't the room in their flats and their maisonettes for all these noble cabinets and bookcases and con-soles, such as you've got downstairs, they're only fit for museums. It's the same all over the country I assure you; everybody wants the small stuff and it's getting scarce. I've a job to keep up my stock," said he, growing confidential. "I've a London dealer coming down next week, four times a year he tours this neighbourhood and I've precious little ready for him; there haven't been as many auction-sales as usual this summer. People pretty well cleared out their surplus furniture after the war, when even old rotten junk would fetch top prices. So if you've any odd pieces you want to dispose of . . ." His loud coaxing voice faltered as he saw Hen-rietta's eyes wander and he mumbled unhappily, "I see you don't like my sales-talk."

She put her hand to her head and said, "It's just . . . I'm rather busy this afternoon." "I'll come back another day," Mr. Ivy offered instantly. "I only looked in on the way back from that sale at Littlecote Home Farm. I've never got round to seeing this house before. Lovely stuff you've got," he added hopefully, "but some of it's shockingly neglected, especially up here in the bedrooms. You're short-handed, no doubt; haven't enough staff to keep things dusted and polished."

Lady Linden interposed, "Don't worry about us, Henrietta, we know our way about. We'll go downstairs and on our way we'll look in on your grandmother; then we'll meet you in the library at five. I daresay we shall find Charles there if you're not quite ready for us. You take this man up to the attics, dear, and let him have a look round for twenty minutes. Nanny will call you if anybody else wants to be shown round, but I expect by this time the house is almost empty." Elsa said in her brittle voice, "It would be a pity to miss a chance to sell a commode or two," and turned to go; but Lucy with her eyes glowing burst out, "Oh! can't I come up with you? I do adore attics. You never know what you won't find. Lady Hornbeam wouldn't want to see me, would she?" She glanced hopefully from one to another of the grown-ups, this was much the most exciting thing that Fountain Court had had to offer. Henrietta murmured, "There isn't anything up there except cobwebs," but Lady Linden told her, "Of course, dear, if Henrietta can be bothered with you," and her mother went out, saying to nobody in particular, "Lucy can help to carry down the commodes."

2

Henrietta had not been up to the attics for a very long time. When she was a child she and her twin brother used to play at pirates and soldiers up there, as other Hornbeam children had done before them, in the part of the roof called the Barrack Room, where the Cavalier troops had slept in the Civil Wars. It was like being between decks in an old man-of-war, great crooked timbers went arching up like giants' knees and pencils of dusty light slanted sideways; in the furthest attic of all was the wild bees' nest. Bats hung like fruit up there among the rafters and swallows slipped in and out under loose tiles; sparrows nested and quarrelled furiously in the gutters, mice lived in the old furniture. There were two or three rooms full of nothing but discarded living-stuff, Henrietta hardly knew what was there. She hesitated at the top of the dark stairhead. "Mind how you go," she told Lucy and Mr. Ivy. "There used to be a lead-gutter running along the middle of the floor somewhere, to take off water in a storm, if it came through the roof. You could break your leg in it if you didn't see it." She had not thought of that for years.

The dealer instantly produced a torch from his pocket and switched on a powerful beam. The corner of a brass bedstead leapt glittering into view, with a surrealist arrangement of a wicker invalid-chair, six croquet-mallets, two archery targets, three fenders and a bundle of fire-irons propped up together in a hip-bath. Lucy gasped with rapture. "It's like a furniture shop," Henrietta heard her say. "You could get lost up here, nobody would ever find you." Then a head popped up from among a heap of old curtains and Victor, scared as a rabbit, blinked at the invaders in the glare of the torch. The little dealer turned it aside instantly and as Henrietta snapped at the boy, "What on earth are you doing up here?" she heard him say, "I do beg your pardon, sir."

Victor scrambled off the bed. "Somebody left a candle here," said he. "I found it." Moving with assurance, they heard him strike a match; he set the round bedroom candlestick on the corner of an old hair-trunk. Candlelight flared and steadied upon a mountain of old luggage, hat-boxes, suitcases, dress-baskets, tin and leather trunks, left over from years of Hornbeam travel and all crowded together under the crooked beams. The two children stared intently at one another while Henrietta, startled and cross, said, "So long as you don't set the house on fire . . . What did you come up for, anyhow?"

"I came to see Jenny's kittens," said Victor uncertainly. "I did stop in the glass-house till Jean and I had planted all the bulbs, but then she went home to her tea, the gardens were full of people and I didn't know where I was supposed to go. So Cook said, 'Go up into the attic and look for Jenny's new kittens'. She's got them round here at the back in an old red velvet chair. Do you want to see them?" He disappeared behind a Sheraton wardrobe and Lucy dived after him; they emerged with the squirming creatures in their arms, two tabbies, a ginger and a tortoiseshell. "They're frightfully wild," said Victor apologetically, as his aunt put out her hand to touch the hard little heads. "But I'm sure I could tame them." At close quarters she saw that he had been crying. "Homesick," she thought; "he came up here to get away from us all, we're strangers." "Put them back again where you found them," she told Victor gently. "They ought to have been drowned, really, but another cat or two about the place won't make much odds. We mustn't upset Jenny." As he turned away obediently she had a recollection which pierced her to the heart of how his father, her dead brother, used to come up here at much his age, on the same errand. "Jezebel," she said to herself confusedly: "a black cat, I hadn't thought of that for years . . . You can choose one for yourself, Victor, and bring it downstairs when it's old enough to leave its mother." She was rewarded by a joyful squeal from behind the wardrobe and an envious wail from Lucy. "Oh! you are lucky, it isn't fair; I'm not allowed to have a kitten in the flat." "It's just the place for a boy to come exploring," the little dealer said in a fatherly way. "My two used to spend half their time in the store on wet Saturdays when they were younger, playing Indians and such. I daresay he knows his way about up here better than you do, Madam. It's amazing what children know and never talk about to grown-ups."

"He's only just come to live here," said Henrietta vaguely. "He doesn't know his way about anywhere properly yet. I don't fancy there's anything up here but junk." Her mind was still on Victor, she only half-heard the little man as he persisted, "It's always worth going through a place like this properly, Madam. There might easily be something valuable hidden away at the back, all covered up with dust and cobwebs. You wouldn't believe me if I told you the stuff I've found in box-rooms and attics. People are too lazy to find out the value of what they've got. You, for instance, I bet you've only insured this lot up here for a lump sum, nothing like what it's worth. You really should have a turn-out one of these days. You'd be astonished how much money there is in what you call junk. All that ugly late-Victorian stuff is coming in again, bead footstools, Venetian blinds, overmantels with little shelves and curly pillars, fire-screens with felt leaves and dead grass in 'em, chairs with buttoned backs like you used to get in old lodging-houses. Fashions've got to change or how would I get my living, Madam? I'll buy almost anything; old picture-frames for the glass, leaves out of big dinner-tables for the wood, broken lustres to mend chandeliers with; why, I'd buy an old grand-piano without any strings for the sake of the legs and the lid. But what I'm interested in to-day," said he, enlivened by Henrietta's laugh, "is really commodes." He was irrepressible.

3

"Come out of there, both of you," said she, raising her voice. "Leave the kittens for now and help Mr. Ivy find these commodes." Victor emerged, with the tortoiseshell kitten still in his arms. "Can I have this one?" he enquired with bated breath. Reassured on this point, he ranged with Lucy among the furniture, till little Mr. Ivy found a row of the admired objects under the window. He skipped from one to the other falling on his knees, lifting lid after lid, tapping and peering inside, saying, "Yes, this is what I'm looking for."

There were five mahogany commodes. Two were square with brass handles, green with verdigris, sunk in their sides; three were stepped and there were four china pots inside, two with broken lids, one common white one, two willow pattern and one adorned with bulrushes and dragonflies. "Pity that's cracked," sighed Mr. Ivy. "It's the best of the lot. I'll take it though, maybe I can convert it into a base for an electric lamp." He got to his feet, dusting his hands and knees and gave a hearty kick to the last in the line. "That one's full of wood-worm," said he. "You should take it downstairs and put it on the garden bonfire, or it'll infect everything up here." Henrietta sighed, "Oh! dear," and at once he turned on her, demanding, "Now, madam, perhaps you'll put a price on these for me, or maybe this young gentleman will."

"They can't be worth anything much, can they?" Victor murmured. "Horrid old things, nobody wants them nowadays." He was answered immediately, "You must never say that, sir; you must make a show of valuing things, in my trade. You can see I want 'em bad, you must try and screw me up as far as I'll go." Victor giggled at this, rubbing his chin on the kitten's black and yellow head. "Six or seven bob you could get 'em for at an auction, when I first went into business," the dealer instructed him, "but people bid 'em up a bit more nowadays, for the sake of the wood. A bit of good mahogany always comes in handy to a home-carpenter. Fifteen, sixteen, eighteen shillings, maybe; I'll give you four pounds for the lot on account of the pots being good, all but one." He rounded on Henrietta, who blinked and said mechanically, "Four-pound-ten." "Where's my profit in that?" he grumbled. "I found 'em, I've got to do the work on 'em, I take 'em away and save you transport and trouble. All right, then; I'll go easy with you, as it's the first time we've done business together. Four-pound-ten I'll make it. That's me all over, can't resist the ladies," said he with a wink. "Now I've got my little van round in your yard empty, I failed to get a piece I wanted at the Lambscot sale. Have you got an odd man in the garden who'll come and give me a hand with 'em to save time?"

Henrietta said doubtfully, "It's Saturday; still, Micky generally comes round about five to fire the furnace for the tomato-houses, we might be able to lay our hands on him. Otherwise you'll have to come back for them. I'll show you the way down the backstairs anyhow; you can pay me for the things and I'll give you a receipt in the office." Lucy already had the bulrush pot in her arms, asking eagerly, "Can I carry this one?" "We'll take one each to save time," Henrietta told her; and after the kitten had been returned to the red velvet armchair they made a solemn procession down the uncarpeted servants' staircase, each carrying a pot.

Half-way down the little man was heard to say earnestly, "You know, madam, you aren't making enough of this place. You should advertise it better, half the Wilchester visitors don't know about it; you ought to have a stall at the entrance to sell fruit and garden-stuff and you really did ought to do teas. There's money in teas, if you set about it right. When people have come a long way and been on their feet for hours they'll sell their souls for a cup of tea and a bun. You could feed 'em by the dozen in that ballroom there, I reckon, with a counter and trays. Ice-cream, too," he said, "all these kids that come, they'd ask their mums for a go of ice-cream the minute they saw the barrow." "And chuck those tubs and papers all over the place, till the gardens look like the Zoo," said Henrietta crossly, butting the baize door open with her shoulder at the bottom of the stairs. "But you needn't give it in tubs," the little man persisted earnestly. "Sell it in slices between a couple of wafers, then they eat the lot; or if they throw half of it down the birds and mice will clean it up for you." Victor said seriously to nobody in particular, "Ice-cream is lovely" and Lucy exclaimed, "I wish I had some now."

They carried their pots along the passage and set them down beside Mr. Ivy's van. The children darted off to retrieve the Irishman from the stable yard and Henrietta and her dealer waited for them in the kitchen. The place was in its late afternoon quiet, with the sun sliding in at the window, the fire damped down, Boffin the cat asleep in the chair, Gladys gone home to the village long ago and Mrs. Peppercorn upstairs, no doubt, listening to the wireless with her feet up in her bedroom. Little Mr. Ivy looked all round and told Henrietta briskly, "Now here, madam, is a chance you've missed. Ever been down to the Pavilion at Brighton? They've got a kitchen there that's hardly bigger than this one, but they've turned every trick with it, got the whole place lined with copper saucepans and kitchen stuff, the whole *batterie de cuisine*, even a couple of plastic chickens put down to roast. It's a real draw, I can tell you, the housewives simply love it. Now if this was my place, I'd doll this kitchen up like a folk museum the way they've done at Sulgrave Manor. I'd hang up all the brass and copper I could lay my hands on, pots and pans, fish-kettles, skillets, jugs, candlesticks, dish-covers; all shined up so that you could see your face in 'em. I'd furnish that great dresser with a dinner-service or two; mason ironstone or something of that, bright and pretty, with great tureens and dishes big enough for a Christmas turkey. You must have stacks of that kind of stuff put away in your cupboards," he told Henrietta. "I'd have all the bygones I could lay my hand on. You know the sort of thing; sugar-nippers, rushlight-stands, little cider-barrels, love-spoons, glass rolling-pins with peppermint stripes inside. I'd have spits and cauldrons and a Dutch oven; I'd use the scullery for the really big stuff, milk-yokes and pails, wash-tubs and kneading-troughs, maybe one of those big box-mangles. People will pay money to see 'em. They like to come round from their council-houses and their new little villas to have a laugh at the way their grandmothers had to work in the old days, before fridges and washing-machines and electricity were invented. It seems funny to them. Hang up the footman's livery on the back of the door, dress a dummy in the maid's print gown with cap and apron. You've made a start on that upstairs with the old General's uniforms, but you've done nothing down here. This could be one of the best things in the house. You're neglecting your opportunities, madam." Stifling an exhausted yawn, Henrietta objected, "Where do we cook our meals, then?" and he came back smartly enough, "Why, scrap this end of the place altogether and put an electric cooker and a sink in one of the pantries; there's sure to be a little room wasted somewhere near the dining-room, in a house of this size. I can't think why that didn't occur to you years ago."

4

At this point Micky appeared and was sent upstairs to lug down the commodes. The children were sent off to the library for tea and Henrietta and the dealer turned into the estate-office. It looked into the stable yard, where all the cheerful racket of hooves and clinking buckets, footsteps and laughter had died down years ago. Henrietta did the accounts there as her father had done before her. That lonely man's life was all about her as she sat at his desk, with his guns behind her in a glass case, his black tin boxes and dusty files ranged round the walls, his broken-down leather armchair on the moth-eaten rug by the fireplace. His face appeared in one faded photograph after another on the walls, in the house-parties, the cricket-week, the polo-team, the school and regimental groups of all ages, with dead men's names underneath; his daughter never looked at any of them nowadays. She rummaged busily in his desk for a receipt book, and while the little dealer lugged out his note-case she admitted, "That's not a bad idea of yours about the kitchen, but you know we haven't any ready cash for alterations."

"No business to be short," said he firmly. "You've enough stuff in the house there to set you all on your feet, surely, if you sold to the right people. Where's the sense in haggling with me about five commodes for four-pound-ten when you've got pictures in the dining-room and the drawing-room worth thousands?" He counted out his dirty notes and took the receipt from her. "Yes, but those are all tied up, settled heirlooms," Henrietta pointed out, locking her cash-box. "My nephew's the heir, the little boy you saw, but he's only nine and all the good stuff is entailed. My grandmother has a life-interest in everything. We can't dispose of anything important without her consent, and she's very difficult to manage nowadays; she's eighty-three and bedridden. She lives in the past, we can't make her understand our difficulties." She blushed brightly, finding herself talking to the little man as if he were an old friend. "We really are in rather a cleft stick for the time being. That's why we show the house, of course."

"You're not making much out of that," he retorted. "It's not to be expected. You don't do teas, you don't hardly advertise, you're right off the map. Oh! I know you'll tell me every little helps. You run it among yourselves, you don't pay any guides' wages, you set it all off against your income tax; but you're not big enough. You're not Blenheim, or Longleat, or Wilton, or Chatsworth; you're just a small house with a few pretty things in it and no particular history attached. People will come once, but they won't come twice; you haven't enough to show. There are hundreds of houses like this up and down the country, trying to catch the tourist trade, but only the big ones are getting anything out of it. I daresay twenty visitors is a good day for you and fifty would be a regular red-letter day? In the end you'll be crowded out of the fight. There's no future in it. What you want is a good side-line."

"If you can show me one I'll take it," said Henrietta. "I'd try anything to keep this place going." He smiled at her and shook his head. "Not you," said he. "You're still a bit too grand, too sorry for yourself. You've got a head on your shoulders, I don't doubt, from all I hear you and that naval gentleman have done wonders; but you've not gone far enough yet. I told you before, you're not in this with your whole heart. You don't realise the times we live in." She uttered a half-choked scornful laugh, but he persisted, "Not yet you don't; you're still on the edge of the water, if you'll excuse my saying so. You can't swim till you've gone in head over heels."

He glanced about him, pulled up a chair, plumped himself down in it unbidden and said, "Now just you listen to me for half an hour, if you can spare the time. I've got a little proposition to make to you. I don't want you to say Yes or No, right away, I want you to let it run round in your head for a bit, talk to anybody you like, take advice on it; I can wait." He bent forward, looked her full in the eye and asked, "What would you say to letting me set up a branch of my business in this house?"

5

She did not stir or speak; a little abashed he continued, "I've got to clear out of where I am pretty soon; the Council are going to pull down my side of Goose Lane to make a car-park. I'm always keeping my eyes open for somewhere to go. I never meant to stop in Goose Lane all my days," he told her confidingly, "The position ain't good enough for me. Wilchester wasn't a bad place to make a start. There's plenty of tourists comes there for a night or two, maybe, at the Woolpack or the Fleece, on their way down West; several of the coach-tours stop the night with us, and we get the Americans driving round England and the men at the base. Wilchester's an interesting old place, there's some good wool merchants' houses and the Roman villa and St. Blaizey's is a fine church. People on holiday like poking round back-alleys and flattening their noses on windows; but my premises are too small. I'm next a fried-fish shop, round behind the brewery, the people who come to me can spend five pound, or ten maybe, if they see something they fancy; but you can't make big money that way. Besides, Aspen's the drapers have a second-hand furniture department that catches the best of the local trade; if a lady wants a table or a sofa she goes to Aspen's first. I've only the one window and you've got to go down three steps from the pavement into my premises; it's quaint enough, I grant you, but I'm always afraid some old woman will tumble down and break an arm or a leg. Besides, I haven't room for my stock. I've built up a nice little business, but I want to launch out now and do a better class of trade." He paused and looked at Henrietta with an eye as bright as a robin's.

She sighed and lay back in her chair. "I don't see how you're going to do it out here," she murmured.

"Well, frankly, I'd rather have stayed in Wilchester," said he, disarmingly. "You're a bit out of the way here, that's one reason why you don't get more visitors, if I may make so bold as to say so. You'd suit me better if you were on a main road; motorists don't care about nosing down side lanes unless they've an object. What would have suited me down to the ground would have been one of those big wool merchants' houses down Cornmarket Street or Staple Lane, you know the kind of thing? Fine stone-work, big windows, vaulted cellars and an archway into the yard. I could have used the downstairs rooms as showrooms and made a flat in the attics for ourselves; but I can't seem to hear of one going. They're all pretty well taken up nowadays for offices. So, as I say, I'm on the hunt; and when I was going through that great empty ballroom of yours this afternoon suddenly it came to me, What a showroom this would make!"

She leaned her cheek on her hand, listened to him. "I know you're out of the way," he admitted. "This isn't the ideal location, still, there's ways and means of getting round that. Two or three big signs we'd have to put up on the main road; One Mile to Fountain Court, half a mile, three hundred yards; Antiques in red letters. Hang up a big copper pot, maybe, or a giant teapot, or a bit of wrought-iron work, just to catch the eye; put up a sign with a picture of the house on it at the end of Pond Lane, anything to tempt 'em in. When they get here they can go over the State apartments in the usual way; then at the end of the round they'd find themselves coming out through the Ballroom, all furnished with stuff for sale. There'd be no end to the trade we could do; people would walk through out of curiosity and before they knew where they were they'd have made a purchase. We'd have good stuff, of course, no rubbish, at first anyhow, everything marked in plain figures. People will give twice the money for a set of chairs if they see 'em set out against the panelling you've got here, instead of having to climb about in the back of a dark shop. You could sell some of your surplus stuff easily enough, customers think more of a purchase if they can spin a yarn about how it came out of a noble mansion. Why, they'd buy your chipped dinner plates for souvenirs! I'd keep you stocked up, of course, with whatever I could pick up at the local sales. We'd advertise ourselves well till we got known, then the London dealers would begin to take us on their rounds."

Henrietta could see that he was getting quite worked up about his idea. "We'd do our best trade with them, of course," said he. "They've got to keep up their stock with what we can find for them; all the good antiques nowadays are found in the provinces and sent up to London for export. I'd lease your old stables from you, put 'em in repair, use 'em for stores and workshop. I'd take over that old kitchen, if you like and pop you in some modern fixings elsewhere, electric cooker, stainless steel sink, anything you fancy. You needn't appear in any of this if you don't want to; my place can be quite separate from the main part of the house if you'd rather have it that way. You can stop in your own rooms and never show your face."

"What, and miss all the fun?" slipped out of Henrietta's mouth. He laughed at that and in a moment she laughed too. "There you are, you see, you're beginning to come round to it," he told her. "Now just you listen to me, madam, while I've got you in the mind for this. I want you to come in with me, I'll take you for a partner. We'll turn it into a company. *Fountain Court Antiques, Limited;* I'll pay you a proper salary and your share of the takings. You'll learn the patter in next to no time, I'll teach you all I can. I've come up the hard way, I've learnt by my mistakes, I'll find the stuff for you if you'll lend your name to it and take your turn at the selling. You and me could work together, we'd make a big thing of it between us." He hardly checked when she said, defensively, "I daresay you'd do better out of it than I should." "Now there you show how little notion you've got of business," he proclaimed, profoundly shocked. "Where would I be if I didn't treat my partner fair and square? I'm upset, really I am; I don't know how you can say such a thing to me?" She had to smile, to say, "You know, this is all very sudden, as Victorian ladies used to put it. I didn't expect an offer of partnership this afternoon; but you know I couldn't do it." "Don't say that," he urged her. "Leave it for now, think it over. I daresay I'm making a fool of myself, but I don't like to see a young woman breaking her back over a load that's too heavy for her to carry. I've an idea we might make this plan work. Now not another word to-day, I've taken up enough of your time as it is; you'll be late for this tea-party of yours. I must be going." He jumped up, shook her cold hand violently and rushed out into the yard; she heard his old car start up and he drove away.

XI

LUCY AND VICTOR went back along the kitchen passage, looking sideways at each other. Without a kitten to unite them they both felt shy again. They found nobody in the library yet, though there was a tea-table set beside the fire. It was a room not much used by the family, except on show days, entirely lined with bookshelves, above which were displayed some of the bronzes brought back by 'Sensibility' Hornbeam from Italy. There was an oriel window filled with coats of arms in bright crude Victorian glass, now illuminated by the setting sun and a bust of the first baron, looking sulky and cold in nothing but a toga. There were also a great many armchairs and sofas, painstakingly covered with Berlin woolwork in the thirties by Colonel "Waterloo" Hornbeam's second wife, an industrious needlewoman; these and the calf-bound histories and sermons all smelt somewhat musty. What had pleased Victor best in the library on former visits were the two great globes, each as tall as a man. The terrestrial globe displayed brown mountains and green lowlands, you could hunt places on it and its oceans were traversed by the voyages of Captain Cook. The celestial globe, of which he did not altogether understand the use, was coloured like an aquamarine and adorned by mysterious classical figures, Orion with his belt and lion-skin, Andromeda stretching out her long white arms, Cassiopeia reclining in the Grecian chair whose shape the little boy could recollect once seeing high overhead on a cold winter's night. He liked to spin the globes about with his finger-tips, as Hornbeam children had done for a hundred years; but Lucy seemed bored with them.

Her eyes travelled round the room. "What a lot of books," she sighed. "Fancy having to read them!" and when he said hastily, "They all look very dull," demanded "Can I go up the ladder?" Quite taken aback, he murmured, "I expect so; what do you want? To get something down from the top shelves?" But she only replied, "I like going up ladders; don't you?"

The thought had never occurred to Victor, he stared dumbly while Lucy seized the mahogany library-ladder from its corner, planted it against the shelves and ran up nimbly. She stood at the top, holding by the edge of the cornice, peering about, nose to nose with a bust of Hadrian. She rocked this to and fro, then snatched at something and waved it. "A penny, somebody's left a black penny up here, underneath this statue-thing." She came down again, dusted her hands and said with a feminine air which sat oddly upon her, "It's filthy up there. I shouldn't think anybody had dusted the top for years and years." In the palm of her hand was a grimy coin. "That's not a penny," said Victor, inspecting it doubtfully; "Not a proper penny." "It's got a king's head on it, anyway," Lucy maintained, "with a wreath on his head and some writing. Look, there's G.E.O. and further along three capital Is." They gazed at each other bewildered, "George the Third," Lucy decided. "Fancy it being up there all that time! Somebody must have hidden it and forgotten to go back for it."

"Perhaps he died," suggested Victor hopefully, putting out his hand for a closer look. Lucy closed her fist immediately. "It's mine," said she, "I found it. At least, I mean, I know it's yours really, but I do think you might give it me." He said quickly, "All right," because she seemed so eager, but he did wish he could have had another look at the mysterious black penny. He would have liked to hold it in his hand and warm it again, after so many years, with a human contact; but Lucy had put the thing in her pocket and turned away. "What else can we look at?" she demanded, putting out her hand to the python skin which dangled beside the bookcase where the sporting books were kept. "What's this snake?"

The dead scales rasped against her enquiring fingers as Victor murmured, "Old General Hornbeam shot it, in Ceylon, he was my great-great-uncle, I think. There's another one on the staircase, but not so big. It was lying in the middle of the path, in a jungle somewhere. It had swallowed a whole goat and gone to sleep; you could see the bulge in the middle where the goat had stuck. My great-great-uncle shot it before it could wake up." Their eyes met and they both giggled. "The elephant's foot was his, too," Victor offered more cheerfully and Lucy fell on her knees by the huge mahogany writing-desk to finger and admire the waste-paper basket, with its wrinkled skin and polished toe-nails. Then, still kneeling, she touched the inkstand, a horse's hoof mounted in a silver racing-plate. Turning it about, she read the inscription aloud. "The Sparrowhawk, winner of the St. Leger" and a date. "That came from Wilchester Castle," Victor was proud to remember. "It belonged to my great-grandfather, the old Duke." She gazed all round her and said, "You have got a lot of funny things in this house. Does it really and truly all belong to you?"

"It will when I grow up," the little boy said doubtfully. "I don't know if it does yet. Aunt Henrietta seems to manage it, sort of and then there's my grandmother upstairs." He was in truth rather bewildered by his legal position and did not know what to answer when Lucy tossed off briskly, "Oh! Lady Hornbeam, Mummy was talking about her this morning. She's fearfully old and quite mad and you're all frightened of her. I suppose the house won't belong to you till she's dead."

"It was my father's house, I think," said Victor. "Mother told me he used to live here when he was a little boy. That's him in the photograph." It stood on the table at his elbow, a debonair likeness in a heavy silver frame of a young man in uniform, with crisp blond hair, a brow clear as morning, a little fair moustache. There was a vase of flowers and berries beside him and his medals and ribbons in a glass case. Lucy gave it one of her piercing glances and said in her off-hand way, "Oh! yes, the one who was killed at Arnhem, I know about him. You *are* an unlucky family, aren't you; all these eldest sons being killed in battle. I suppose you'll have to go into the Army when you grow up and get killed in the next war." He could only mumble, "I suppose so." "Of course you might get killed in an air-raid if you stopped at home," offered Lucy, shaking her curls. "Mother nearly was in the last war, the house next door was hit, but luckily she was down in the cellar." She looked from the photograph to Victor and said with a judicial air, quite as if she were grown-up, "You're not a bit like him, are you? I suppose you take after your mother. Does she live here too?"

He shook his head, conscious of his own insecurity. "We lived at Putney, really, that's my proper home; but now Mum's got married again she's gone away to Stafford and I've been sent here." He hated saying it out loud to this strange girl, it seemed to make the ruin of his child-world more permanent. He looked down and tears brimmed in his eyes. Lucy eyed him sharply. "Don't you like your stepfather?" she demanded. He had not meant to say so, but it all burst out of his mouth, in spite of himself. "I hate him. He's a great red fat man who roars at me. I shan't see Mum any more, except just sometimes in the holidays . . . I've got to live here . . . I don't know any of them. I'm frightened." He stamped his foot, then was ashamed of himself and stopped talking, fighting back his tears.

Lucy said immediately, "I know just how you feel. I don't like Sir James one bit either. He's the man that's going to marry Mummy; at least I think so. I know he pays the rent of our flat. Mummy calls it Knightsbridge, but it's Earl's Court really. It's a horrid dirty shabby place; I hate living there. My own father's in Kenya, I wish I could go back to him, but I can't because of the Mau Mau. I do think it's a shame children can't choose which parent to live with." Victor sniffed, bewildered, stuffed his handkerchief down in his pocket and blinked at her. "But I do think you're frightfully lucky," she burst out, "to be let live in the country. You can have a dog, you can have a pony in the holidays, you can be outdoors all day long. If I were you I'd keep a golden Labrador and take him with me on my rides. You hardly ever see a big dog in London; we can't have one at all in our flat and Mummy's friends only have pekes or poodles. I don't count them." None of this meant much to Victor, who only said dolefully, "I'd much rather have stopped in Putney with Mum."

2

"Oh well, there's no accounting for tastes," said Lucy, tiring of the topic, as children will. "Show me some more things till tea-time." She walked away from him to the fireplace and stood there warming her hands, staring up at the portrait which dominated the room. "Who's that?" she demanded and Victor was able to tell her, "That's Captain Augustus Hornbeam who rode in the charge of the Light Brigade." It was a full length by George Richmond painted after the subject's death. The young officer was dismounted, leaning on his charger's shoulder, surveying the distant battle with a negligent smile. He was a gay coxcomb in all his military glory; the painter had chosen to depict him bareheaded, holding his sabre and plumed busby in his left hand. His spurred feet were crossed in a dancing position, one toe pointed, his right hand toyed with the gathered reins. He had a strikingly handsome stupid face, as red as a raw steak, his brilliant blue eyes bulged as if his gold-laced collar would choke him, his luxuriant auburn curls and whiskers shone with oil. His furred pelisse was so stiff with bullion that it stood away from his side like plate-armour, the tunic beneath it was hung about and concealed by cords, tags, epaulettes and tassels. His waist was as small as a dancing-master's, his shoulders broad as a butcher's under their weight of fur and gold, his pale blue trousers were stretched tightly over his magnificent thighs.

The horse was as fine as its master, a black charger with a wild eye and a flaring scarlet nostril; its ears were pricked to the sound of guns, its forelock and mane tossed by the wind from the battle-field. There was a white sheep-skin under the saddle. Behind this pair of splendid animals the painter had thrown in for good meas-ure all that the newspapers had told him of a Crimean landscape, a glittering brown plain with cavalry squadrons wheeling upon it, a thin red line of infantry advancing towards an escarpment, lines of tents, batteries wreathed in smoke, a loop of river shining in the sun, a distant city twinkling upon a hill. The young man and his mount waited idly under a thin tree; but at any moment, you felt, the man might vault into the saddle, the horse rear, wheel and gallop away with some fatal order towards the fight in the valley below. A sword and sash hung under the picture, the curved cavalry sabre with its gold knot, the crimson silk of the sash, soft enough to bind up a wound, strong enough to pull a horse out of a well.

Lucy gazed at this admired painting and her eyes grew rounder and rounder, she swallowed and turned pale. "He was another of my great-great-uncles," Victor offered politely. "He was very brave, we're all very proud of him." "He was killed in battle, too, I suppose," said Lucy, quite crossly, looking not at the man but at the horse. "I don't think so," stammered Victor, not yet altogether at home with the family history. "Not at Balaclava, anyhow; I think he died of cholera in hospital at Scutari. I know there's a letter from Miss Florence Nightingale about him somewhere. He had a wonderful escape, he rode all through the charge and cut down three Russians and never got a scratch; only his horse was killed under him coming back."

"That horse," breathed Lucy, gazing up at the beautiful wild head and terrified eyes. "Oh! I do hope it wasn't that horse!" "I expect it was," said Victor, quite at sea. "I expect they told the man to paint the right horse. It saved his life, they said." Lucy twisted her hands together and he heard her mutter, "It's a shame."

"They had to have horses," he objected feebly. "They had to get about, they had to ride into battle, you can't have cavalry without horses." He did not know how to appease her and she persisted, turning on him, "It was cruel. They told us about it at school, there was a programme on the wireless and Mummy had a book, I saw the pictures. We all had to learn that horrid poem. *Half a league, half a league, half a league onward*," she chanted, rocking herself to and fro and staring at Victor. "I do so hate it. There were five hundred horses killed in that charge, just think what it would be like for them. They would be so dreadfully frightened," she said. "They would trot down the valley and then gallop and gallop; there would be all that banging and shouting. They wouldn't know what was happening, but they would have to go on, they would get nearer and nearer to the guns. And then . . . and then . . ." Appalled, the little boy saw tears running down her face. "And all for nothing," she said. "For a stupid mistake . . . a wrong order . . . a muddle . . . It ought never to have happened." She stamped her foot at Victor and told him, "I think your great-great-uncle's got a stupid horrid face. I don't like him."

3

Fortunately for Victor the door now opened and Leaf appeared with a silver tray of tea-things, held out at arm's-length. He proceeded to lay the table and mend the fire with great propriety, as if he had never sold an admission-ticket nor conducted a tour in his life. Lucy and Victor approached the table, eyeing strawberry jam, hot scones in a silver dish and Mrs. Peppercorn's renowned gingerbread. "I'm fearfully hungry," Lucy breathed. "I do wish they'd hurry." Victor was hungry too, after planting all those bulb-bowls; he was delighted when his aunt appeared, with

Lady Linden and her niece in tow. Elsa greeted Charles, the next arrival, as if she had been waiting on the top of a glass mountain for him for twenty years. "Darling, darling Charles; I began to think I should never see you. Each room we went into, I said to myself with a beating heart, *Charles* will appear and conduct us round this one; but you never did. I really began to think I'd wasted my half-crown; but here you are at last, and what a pirate you do look in that ducky little shade. Exactly right for your type. One arm and one eye, like poor Nelson on his column." Lucy eyed her mother with disdain and Henrietta coming in later looked sulky. She settled the children side by side at the table, sat herself down with Lady Linden at her right on a massive Regency settee and left Charles and Elsa to find their own level. Charles was making himself extremely charming, fetching tea and tomato sandwiches for Elsa, sitting down beside her on a love-seat just wide enough for two, crossing his legs her way and talking to her about the past. Pouring tea for Lady Linden, watching that the children got enough to eat, answering questions about the hens, the half-crown visitors and the Women's Institute, Henrietta only got their conversation in snatches.

Elsa was flirting furiously, crying out, "You haven't changed a bit, darling, except for that patch and I love it, I adore it; it makes you look exactly like those divine advertisements in the *New Yorker,* the man who sells check shirts, I mean." "Well, I sell lettuces," Charles told her agreeably. "Any time you want a lettuce, Elsa, you've only to come to me." "I'll come over to-morrow afternoon," she promised. "You can take me all round the gardens and give me an armful of veg. to take back to London." "I never give anything to anybody," Charles teased her. "You'll have to pay market price like all the others." "Oh! darling, how unkind you are!" Elsa reproached him. Henrietta was sure that she had expected to get her lettuces for the price of a smile or a pout. "Just two or three dear little baby lettuces for my Sunday supper," she coaxed him. Henrietta saw Charles shake his head at her and

Victor redden right up to his hair. "The boat . . . the island . . ." he stammered with tears in his eyes. "Cousin Charles promised." Henrietta did not know what he was talking about.

"Your dear grandmother wasn't looking quite so well as usual," pronounced Lady Linden and Henrietta had to attend to her for a little. "Of course," said Lady Linden, "one has to remember she's eighty-three." When she was free to listen again Charles was asking Elsa when she was going back to Kenya and she was proclaiming, "Never, never, never. I was simply terrified. There we were out on the farm, miles from everybody, with the natives all round in the woods; we never knew when they mightn't come and rush us. Half the boys might have been Mau Mau for all we knew, it was horrible. I had to carry a revolver round all the time and sleep with it under my pillow." She made eyes at Charles. "Even when Bill sent me down to Nairobi with Lucy he went right back there the very next day, said he couldn't leave the place. So after a bit I simply packed up and came home." She glanced round her with a self-satisfied air and met her daughter's eyes, staring at her reproachfully. "I'm sure nobody could expect me to go back," said Elsa crossly, pleating her skirt on her knee.

4

Charles got up, stretched himself and stood with his back to the fire. "I'm thinking of leaving England myself," said he, prepared to entertain the assembled company. "Had a job offered me overseas, only yesterday. I'm thinking it over, not at all sure I shan't accept it." "So long as it's not in *Africa*," screamed Elsa. "Don't go to any of the black places, darling Charles; or you'll run into trouble. They're all over and done with as far as white people are concerned." Henrietta stiffened markedly and put down the teapot. "No, not Africa," said Charles. "As it happens, it's the South Seas." He observed that Lady Linden was regarding him with horror and smiled agreeably at her. "Coconuts and hula-hula girls," shrieked Elsa, "just too divine, with the winter coming on and coal the price it is. Let's fly together, darling; will you take me under your wing?" "My dear girl . . ." protested her aunt. Henrietta opened her mouth as if to speak, but said nothing; the children were entranced. "You never told me about this plan, dear," faltered Lady Linden, turning to Henrietta, who said severely, "Just some of Charles's nonsense."

Secure of his audience, Charles looked round the circle and smiled gently. "Norfolk Island," said Charles and paused for comment, but obviously none of them had ever heard of the place. "Lucy," said Charles, with his teasing air, "or even Victor, could tell you immediately where it is." He paused again; then placed his finger-tips in a neat equilateral triangle on the table-cloth among the empty cups. "Australia . . . New Zealand . . . Fiji . . ." said Charles, "and here in the middle of them, all by itself is this dear little island, five miles long. Captain Cook discovered it and they moved the descendants of the Bounty mutineers there from Pitcairn Island in the fifties. Not palms and coral, though, you'll be disappointed to hear; just a nice mild climate, rather like the Azores, I fancy, where you can grow every kind of fruit. People fly there for their holidays," said Charles gently, "from Auckland and Sydney. It's quite accessible. Matter of fact, I was there once myself, before the war, just for the day. We landed and played a cricket-match, I remember. Lucy will show it you on the terrestrial globe, when she's finished that doughnut." He gazed at Lucy, who choked on a mouthful. When she could speak she startled her elders by announcing, "I've got a Norfolk Island stamp. There's an Australian girl at school who collects stamps. She got a letter from her father from Norfolk Island and I swapped it with her for a Kenya stamp off one of Father's." She blushed deeply.

"There, you see," said Charles kindly. "Lucy supports me. There *is* such a place as Norfolk Island and real people do go there."

He had an air of gentle mockery. Lady Linden, quite bewildered, appealed to Henrietta, "But is Charles really going out to this place?" Henrietta only shrugged her shoulders, admitting, "It's the first I've heard of it." "What on earth are you going to do there?" shrieked Elsa. "Grow lettuces?"

"I might," said Charles, "or pineapples, or peaches, maybe; I haven't really had time to go into all that. Or I might buy a motor-boat and take people out fishing for tarpon and such, or I might just build myself a hut and sit in the sun." He smiled agreeably at his bewildered audience. "Living's very cheap there, my friend tells me. He married a New Zealand girl, they've got two children. He's going to start a hotel of sorts, I might lend him a hand with that in the busy season, or grow his vegetables. Lots of pleasant people there, he says; nobody's got any money, but they run in and out of each other's houses and play tennis and go for bathing picnics, just as we did in the days of our youth. It's a thousand miles from everywhere, a nice quiet place to end your days," said Charles and had an air of becoming detached from his surroundings as he meditated on his remote island. "No bombs, no nothing; I really must think it over."

Elsa gazed at him bewildered, "Well, I don't blame you," she murmured. "Of course Europe's finished, but how will this place get on without you?" She caused a horrid cold silence, nobody knew what to say. Lady Linden then displayed tact, rising and saying, "Well, dear; I must take my party away. Thank you so much for that delicious tea; nobody else makes gingerbread like Mrs. Peppercorn. Do ask her to let me have a couple of pounds for the Christmas party at the Institute." She swept up Elsa and Lucy and Charles went with them.

Victor stole a look at his aunt, but she seemed unconscious of his presence; she was standing with her elbows on the mantelpiece and her head in her hands, staring down into the fire. He wandered off to the big globe and spun it diffidently, it was so delicately hung that even a child could move it with one finger.

Underneath the polished sphere, going down towards the South Pole, were the Antipodes; New Zealand and Australia, quite empty in the middle when the globe was made and to the east of them an expanse of deep blue sea, powdered with islands, traversed by cobweb-voyages. Victor read the queer and lovely names to himself; the Loyalty Islands, the Friendly Islands, Kermadec, New Hebrides, Vanua Levu, Vanua Vatu; he followed with his finger a thread curving across the deepest ocean in the world. "Captain Cook," said the tiny letters, "1774", and there it was, Norfolk Island, a fly-speck in the blue, he would never have found it except for the name. Victor had a mental image of a single rock, with a seagull perched upon it; but that was silly, Cousin Charles had said there were people upon it, quite a lot of real people, who had picnics and went out in boats. A lump swelled in his throat as Aunt Henrietta came up behind him and said, "Show me." She knelt down beside him and he put his finger on the fly-speck. "It's a very little island," he murmured and so it was. She looked at it and a long, long sigh came from her; he was heartened to say, "I do wish Cousin Charles wouldn't go so far off." At this his aunt put her arms about him and kissed him. "It'll soon be time to take you up to Nanny," said she. "She'll give you your bath and put you to bed."

XII

WHEN CHARLES had shut the door of an old car on Lady Linden
and her party and watched their grey-haired chauffeur drive
away, he took a turn round the gardens to see that the last of the
visitors went away when their time was up. The house shut at
five, in theory, but the gardens were accessible until six and there
were still a few people strolling about in the rose-garden and on
the south terrace, where they could snapshot each other or sit
talking in a pattern of ragged box edging, misshapen topiary,
gravel paths and cracked urns, a display of frosted roses and crimson snap-dragons going fast to seed. The house looked down coldly
upon these last summer visitors. The gilded weather-vane swung
to the north-east and Charles judged that it would freeze that
night. He passed his two American ladies, lingering by the Chinese pavilion in the last of the sun and stopped to speak to them
again. "I certainly do admire this house," the elder one told him
kindly. "It's what I call a nice family house. I can't do with all
the great rambling show-places like museums, we've seen too
many of them on this trip. I'd like to live here, I could make a
real cosy home out of this."

"A mite run down, dear, isn't it?" the young one told her, ignoring Charles. "Reckon you'd find it pretty cold in winter. I wouldn't
call it exactly *cosy*, I saw no heating anywhere." She shuddered
and drew her yellow coat more closely round her, hugging her
thin elbows. "I wish I'd brought my fur cape, or my li'l nylon
raincoat," she murmured. "I left them both in the car and now it's
turning chilly." Charles said that he hoped they had enjoyed the
gardens, but it appeared that they had not ventured further than

the lower terrace. "We didn't feel like walking right down that hill and all round by those temples," the elder one confessed. "We didn't want to get too tired. To-morrow we'll have to make an early start and Corinne doesn't feel so good this afternoon." As Charles said goodbye and left them he heard the younger one saying to herself, "It isn't as though I hadn't seen plenty better gardens in Florida and Italy."

The members of the Wilchester Women's Institute were still getting their money's worth, parading up and down the neglected borders, spreading across the pale lawns, their coach did not leave until five-thirty. They visited the great hump-backed Victorian conservatory, where ferns grew up through the pavement, hiding the cold rusty pipes and a palm tree had poked its tufted head right through the glass roof. They leaned on the parapet of the terrace, pointing out to each other the prospect over the little valley where the Abbot's Brook, escaping downhill from the fish-pond, had been trapped to form a succession of rushy meres. "Those are the Monks' Fishing Lakes," they told each other, "that's the old Decoy, across there's where Hen-and-Chicken Wood used to be when I was a girl. The third Lord Hornbeam shot himself," they still maintained, "in that very wood, and her Ladyship had it cut down afterwards. That must be the Folly, it looks quite different from here." The woods formed an amphitheatre on the opposite slope and above them rose five broken spans of arches, where 'Sensibility' Hornbeam had imitated a Roman aqueduct in brick and stucco on the crest of the hill. There was nothing behind it, the evening sky looked at you ominously through the arches. "You'd think somebody might mend that, or pull it down," the women said.

"There's no water in this fountain," others complained, peering into the grotto beneath the upper terrace, where beneath a roof sparkling with quartz and spar, rough with shells and artificial stalactites, a nymph wept out her centuries of captivity above a broken urn. "I'm sure it was still running last year, or the year before," one of the elder women said. "But nothing here's kept up properly nowadays, they haven't the money. Makes you think, don't it? All those great empty rooms and not a soul living in 'em. Once the tourist-season's over they shuts it all up, I'm told they camps in a couple of rooms at the back and the old lady takes to her bed for the winter. Why don't they sell out and go to the Colonies?"

"Such waste of space," another envious woman said. "My boy and his girl, they can't get married, got nowhere to live, we can't squeeze 'em in anywhere, can't hear of a place to go to. You've got to put yourself down on the list when you marry and have a couple of kids before you stand a chance of a council-house in these parts. A great place like this ought to be divided up," Charles heard them say, "and put to some public use."

Others walked round by the old stables, stumbling on cobbles, peeping in at doorways, eyeing empty stalls and racks, disused coach-houses and harness-rooms, admiring the family coach with its moth-eaten upholstery, the barouche, the dog-cart, the governess-cart, the wreck of an old bath-chair; all standing together, inhabited by spiders, by families of kittens and stray hens. "These are what they used to ride about in," the children were told. "This is where the hunters used to be stabled, this is where they kept the carriage horses; look, Janey," one little girl was told by her grandmother, "this must have been the place where they kept the hounds, before they were moved to Wilchester Castle. They would have slept in straw on those benches and gone out by that door into the yard and there would have been a kennelman in a white coat who called them all by their names."

Most of them rattled the handle of the kitchen-garden door, but Charles always kept it locked on visiting days; he did not want strangers roaming about, leaving the doors of his glass-houses open, or stray children breaking his cloches. So the half-crown visitors had to go on to the Abbot's Chapel, a doubtful eighteenth-century reconstruction upon a few courses of ancient masonry,

where shallow walls and box-edging delineated the ground-plan
and a traceried window framed clouds and sky; there were one or
two broken pillars and some fragments of what might have been
a cloister.

Visitors were usually more interested in the Dogs' Cemetery
beyond. They would read the Victorian pet-names aloud to each
other with real pleasure; Flop, Fido, Ponto, Finette, Neptune the
St. Bernard, Black Nero the Labrador. "That's sweet," they would
tell each other and the children. "Look, Julie, this is where all the
dear doggies were buried. Isn't that a pretty idea? Here's one to
'Rollo, a faithful servant' and another to 'Dear Selina'. Oh! I do
like this! I wonder if there are any pussies." Most of them enjoyed the Dogs' Cemetery as well as anything in the gardens.

2

Beyond the Chapel was the monks' stew-pond, never very popular at this time of year. It was a mournful neglected place, said
to be bottomless and certainly very deep, with three cold springs
in it. There were two islands in it and very old yew trees grew
upon them, trailing their branches in the black water; they made
a sanctuary for the waterfowl who nested there, now that the punt
was rotten you could not get over very easily to the islands. Dab-
chicks bobbed, mechanical and busy, in channels between banks
of weed, their young ones followed them like little black mice;
sometimes huge tench were visible, moving slowly above patches
of clear blue sand and vanishing again into the weeds. Roote's
son had once caught a five-pounder there. The water from the
stew-pond ran out by some very ancient sluices and went down
the valley to feed the lakes. It was a cold sunless place, people
did not much like it. They would walk a little way past the sluices,
until the path was lost in a wilderness of tall grass and interlacing
briars, grumble at the puddles and return, saying, "You'd think

they'd have a boat, wouldn't you? Think they'd make a paddling pool and put a heap of sand for the kiddies, to amuse them? There's nothing much to do here, is there? A waste of money really, I wish we hadn't come on this outing. Let's go back to the terrace, Jane, my feet are getting wet with all this long grass. You'd think somebody might find time to cut it."

A doubtful group hesitated at the top of the steps which descended into the Wilderness, the hillside shrubbery which 'Sensibility' Hornbeam had laid out to display his Italian statuary. It had been exquisite there in other years, in the fine summer weather, when the flickering shade dappled the walks and the many lime-trees hummed like beehives; but in this wet season the azaleas had scarcely flowered and the crimson maples had dropped their leaves without colour. Now it was a melancholy grove, with leaves falling, fungus smelling and damp beginning to rise up from the ponds. Nobody cared to-day to go hunting for the statues, the Dying Gladiator leaning upon his hand under a yew tree, the Venus Anadyomene in a weed-choked cascade, the Pomona in a stone hat trimmed with apples, the buskined Diana catching a stag by its horns. Charles had painted neat white signboards and Henrietta had planted them at strategic points, indicating the various Follies, the Chinese Bridge, the Indian Altar, the Aqueduct beyond the wood, the Monks' Fishing Lodge by the top lake, the Temple of Piety, the Wishing Well, the Swiss Cottage, the Hermitage with its moss roof and windows of coloured glass and the Abbot's Pigeon House with its hundred nesting holes and revolving ladder. They were all good enough to sit down in when the weather was fine, but they were mostly decayed and peeling, used for garden tools, inhabited by spiders and mice; the Swiss Cottage had to be kept locked because the roof was no longer safe.

The Haunted Walk was the nearest and most popular, a whispering grove of ilex, with half-a-dozen curved stone seats. Many people never got beyond it; they would sink down there, rest their feet, take their shoes off, young couples would kiss and whisper, mothers would produce surreptitious sweets and buns out of carrying bags and next day Roote would have to make the boy Joey spike up cartons, silver paper and grocers' bags round each seat. On this melancholy evening the Haunted Walk was deserted early; sitting there alone you really could have fancied that you heard the uncertain footsteps of the club-footed heir who used to limp there with his mother a hundred years earlier; little Arthur Hornbeam who went climbing with the village boys and fell down and was drowned in the moat. "It's a long way down there," the older women said to each other. "My feet ache something cruel, don't yours? I've had quite enough walking for one day already, going round that great house. You'd think they'd do teas, or some refreshment, even mineral waters and ice-cream. Let's go back to the terrace and sit down in the shelter, we can wait there till the rest come back from the ponds. We might get hold of the bus-driver and ask how soon he could start back. I've had about enough of this, haven't you?" Sitting in the Chinese Pavilion, looking back at the apricot-coloured mansion, they summed up against it. "Well, now we've been to Fountain Court. It's a nice house, it's a place you must visit once; I'm glad I've been here; but there ain't much to see, I shan't want to come again."

3

Charles let himself into the locked garden and took his usual evening turn through the steamy glass world of the hot-houses, checking the thermometer and the time-switch of the mercury vapour lamps, running his accustomed eye over the cat's-cradle of string and wire, the lines of water-pipes, the frail foliage of his young plants. There was not very much in the houses at the moment, chiefly tomato-plants in pots, summered out in the gardens and brought in a week earlier. They all had four trusses of green fruit; he would be picking and selling from them till Christmas, then he would sow again for potting in February. The second house, the old vinery, was full of baby lettuces pricked out in rows, as demure and tidy as school-children of various ages all dressed in green for a party. In January he would turn on the heat and draw them up for the early market in March at the same time as his forced tulips. Charles lived a double life in the clear winking light of his glass kingdom, always dividing his attention like a schoolmaster between the present state of his infant plants and their future five or six months ahead. He had never yet said to himself that he might not be at hand when his seedlings were grown, but he found himself saying it now, as he turned out into the cold evening air and locked the door behind him. "Perhaps I shan't be here . . . perhaps Penny won't be here . . . perhaps the place will be broken up."

The sun had already gone down behind the woods. For a short time the sky was full of pink feathers and a light glowed in tree and stone, as if it came from within. Then all faded together and new colours appeared in the borders; the Michaelmas daisies turned a queer electric blue, white and yellow flowers showed themselves, red flowers faded as an immediate chill arose from the damp lawns. As Charles walked back to the house he saw that the garden had become a landscape without figures. Small birds had chosen their places in trees and shrubs and over his head a huge flock of starlings came in with a rush of wings from the empty stubbles. They wheeled and dipped in an orderly formation, rose and settled in hundreds upon their favourite sycamore behind the stable. In a moment the leafless branches were crowded with them, as if with a crop of heavy black fruit. Preening their shining feathers, they fluted, whistled, chattered, croaked and quarrelled like a crowd of schoolgirls, like a coven of witches, exchanging the news of the day before they settled down for the night.

Charles walked past the starlings' roost and through the gap in the yew hedge. The visitors had all gone and there was only one car still standing in the Muses' Grove, but it had not been there when Charles went out and he stiffened at the sight of it. He went up the steps and found old Leaf tidying up the hall, putting away his postcards and bundles of admission-tickets, counting out the entrance money into neat piles of half-crowns and small silver. "Quite a good day for the last one, sir," said he. "It's just gone six, we can shut up now till next year." Charles, ignoring him, jerking his head towards the doorway, said, "Mr. Cornell's back, I see," and Leaf dropped a packet of postcards. "Yes, sir," said he, after a moment's hesitation. "He came back about ten minutes ago. He asked to see Miss Henrietta and I told him she'd gone down the terrace, to put the deck-chairs back into the Chinese Pavilion. So he went after her." They exchanged a look of anxiety and vexation. "I wish he'd left her alone this evening," said Charles crossly. "She's had a pretty frightful day."

4

The Chinese Pavilion was a little gazebo at the end of the south terrace. It had been copied from an unused design by Repton for a summerhouse in the garden of the Prince Regent's Royal Pavilion at Brighton; it had wrought-iron columns imitating clumps of bamboo and a tiled roof curling up at the corners. A couple of kylins in blue pottery guarded the entrance; within, the walls were adorned by a mildewed Chinese paper where pheasants perched among tree-pæonies and little men in funny hats fished from circular bridges over a meandering stream. This paper was peeling from the damp walls in many places and in one corner, where a gutter had been blocked by an old birds' nest, the rain had poured in and made a great brown stain on the ceiling, blackening all its gilt stars. The windows looked down upon the valley and the chain of ponds. This little airy pavilion had ob-

viously been intended for the Hornbeam ladies to drink tea there
out of Oriental porcelain on fine summer afternoons, but now it
only housed two dozen deck-chairs and a heap of rotten fruit-nets.
It smelt forlornly of dry-rot and mice, its uncleaned window-sills
held cobwebs, dead wasps and bluebottles; it was utterly forlorn
and neglected.

Here John Cornell had found his Henrietta. She had collected
the deck-chairs from the corners of the terrace and stacked them
up in the corner, they would not be wanted again till next year;
and now she was standing in the middle of the floor, with her
hands in the pockets of her old tweed coat, doing nothing at all.
If she had seen him striding along the terrace she made no move
to welcome him, she looked at him when he entered unsmiling, as
if he had been a stranger. He did not know what to say to her,
could only look about him in distaste at the neglected place he
found her in and say as he had said before, "I do dislike to see
this old building in such a state. You really ought to have done
something about it, dear. This paper could have been saved, I'd
say, if it had been caught before it got this bad. Of course it's
ruined now."

"Yes, I know," said Henrietta, quite crossly. "You've told me all
that. It could have been stuck to muslin and pulled down and
shipped across the Atlantic, to cover the bathroom walls in a pent-
house in New York. A pity it's gone too far, owing to our laziness."
He scraped delicately at the wall with one finger. "I believe some
of it would travel yet," he said to himself.

"You're welcome to it," she retorted, "if it's any consolation to
you. It's been out here in the damp for about a hundred and fifty
years. I don't fancy it'll look like much when you get it across the
Atlantic." As she turned her back on him and walked to the window she muttered, "I should leave it alone. I should leave the
Hornbeams alone for the future, if I were you, after to-day."

The tall man looked after her mildly. "Now, dear;" he said to
her, "I wouldn't want to hurt your feelings. You mustn't think I

don't appreciate this home of yours. It's just that I can't bear to see it all going to rack and ruin for want of a little care and trouble. I keep feeling I want to lend a hand, prop things up, do some cleaning and repairing; damn it all, I want to help you." He struggled on confusedly, addressing her turned back. "And if things are past mending," said she, looking out of the window, "you may as well pick up a bit of something for yourself out of the ruins."

"You've no call to say that," he said stiffly. "I've done my best, I made you a fair offer, I couldn't tell what that dealer was going to say. I only collected him because your trustees wanted a valuation. I wish to God I'd never brought him down. Now you'll always be vexed with me about it." She relented a little at that, turning back to him and admitting, "It wasn't your fault, John. It was bound to come out some time. I'm sorry you didn't get your picture."

He sighed. "I can't tell you how badly I feel about it all. I'd set my heart on Lavinia. I suppose . . . I suppose you wouldn't let me buy her anyhow, just as a souvenir, you know; just to furnish my study in the new house and remind me of this place." She shrugged her shoulders. "Lav wouldn't be much good to you, would she, even as a souvenir of a European visit? A modern copy of a bad picture by an artist who's going out of fashion? Better keep your money for something you can be proud to show your friends." She added under her breath, "I shouldn't have thought you'd have wanted to be reminded of Fountain Court."

"I certainly won't need any reminding," he told her, staring at her; then burst out, "Henrietta, let's get this thing straight right now. Weren't you going to let me into the secret? Were you going to let me buy that picture, if Birnbaum hadn't spotted it for a fake? Because if you were setting out to cheat me and get my money, just because I'm a fool-Yank who's fallen in love with you, that's something I could never forgive. I wouldn't want to have any more to do with you."

She said then, not looking at him, "I know that's how it must seem to you. It's late in the day now to put the whole muddle right. Charles asked me the very same question, I could see he was dreadfully worried about my leaving you in the dark; but you see, John, Granny had only just told me. I'd really hardly had time to take it all in before you were on the doorstep and the old girl's in such a state nowadays that we don't believe half she says. All through lunch I sat there, wondering what on earth to do." She gave him an imploring look.

"I wondered what was the matter with you," said he. "I was watching you all the time and you did look pretty queer. I never thought of this."

"I truly didn't mean to cheat you," the girl insisted. "I should have told you all about it myself, but Mr. Birnbaum got in first."

"Forget it," said he curtly. "It was just a bit of bad luck for both of us. You know I really wanted the picture because it came out of this house and the woman in it looked like you." "Then hang something else in your new library," Henrietta told him sternly, "and put me out of your mind. I've told you already, I'm no use to you. Better stop thinking about me." "But I can't," he burst out at her, with an endearing simplicity. "God knows I've tried! I'm crazy about you, I can't think of anything else. I love you dearly. All I want is for you to marry me and come back home with me, forget about this dead-alive place and start again new." His gesture included the neglected pavilion, the forlorn and weedy gardens, the mouldering house. "I've told you all that time and again, but you won't listen to me."

He touched her arm, but she only shook her head. "It's no use, John. I've said that to you before, over and over, you won't make me change my mind. You want to pull me up by the roots and plant me in another country, but it wouldn't work. Even with quite a young tree," she said in her low bewildered tone, "there comes a day when you can't move it any longer. You break the tap-root and it dies on you, however much you fuss over it. If you took me to America, John, I should wither."

5

"You could be wrong about that," he pleaded. "It would be
strange to you at first, maybe, but you'd soon settle down, back
home. You'd have no need to be lonely, we'd all make you welcome. I'd do everything I could to make you happy. You just don't
know how badly I feel about all this. Maybe you might change
your mind if you kept on thinking about it, Henrietta. I've sometimes thought you liked me, you know."

"I do like you," said she gently. "I'm very fond of you, but I'm
not at all in love with you; not what I call love," and glancing
round the dark cold pavilion she shivered a little, wrapping her
coat about her, hugging herself with her arms. "I'm afraid there's
nothing I can do about it," she said as if to herself.

He gazed at her seriously. "Tell me one thing, dear. If I'd been
a countryman of yours, would you have thought of me?" but she
only said, with an impatient shudder, "How do I know? It's all
too much mixed up, everything about you is strange to me, we
don't really talk the same language at all. I don't understand you.
I've given this a lot of thought, John, I've tried to be fair to you,
I've told myself what a fool I am. I can't hope for a better chance
in life, I know that; but it's all no use. I can't bring myself to leave
Fountain Court. It astonishes me, but there it is."

"It doesn't make sense to me," said he, honestly bewildered.
"You mean, you're going to stick right here, for the rest of your
days, running the house, managing the estate, scraping a penny
here and a penny there, waiting for the roof to fall down on you;
because that's about what it amounts to, I guess. This place is dead
and done with."

She corrected him gently, "I shall try and keep things going till
my nephew comes of age. After that it's up to him." When he asked
her, "And what becomes of you then?" she only shrugged her thin
shoulders. "I shall be in my forties," she computed. "I shall retire

into the village and do up a cottage with my mother's money. I shall make a garden, I shall help to run the W.I., I shall run fêtes and jumble sales. I daresay I shall get on to the Rural District Council. I shall make friends with Victor's wife, if he has one. I shall have his children down to tea and teach them the history of the family. If he wants to sell the whole place up, which is more than likely, I shan't be able to stop him; but all that's a long time ahead. Meanwhile I look like having my hands full. You see, I'm the only one left who can look after things."

"And you don't intend to marry?" her American demanded angrily. "Well, not to marry you," she told him, kindly but firmly, looking him full in the face. "Don't you see, it would be running away from my job?" He met her gaze for a moment, looked down and moved his foot on the floor. "Not even if I came to live over here," he mumbled, but she only smiled at him. "You know you couldn't," she told him; "and it wouldn't be any good to either of us if you did."

He raised his head, looked mournfully round the little pavilion, at the Chinese fishermen, the pæony-trees, the broken deck-chairs and garden tables, as if he were going to remember them all his life. "So I don't get either the picture or the girl," he said to himself. "Well, this is the damnedest thing. I didn't expect it." She could only repeat, "I'm so sorry, so very sorry. I do like you so very much, I can't think why I'm such a fool as to turn you down. It's just one of those things."

"You don't have to give me a reason," said he doggedly. "You just don't happen to feel the same way about me as I do about you. Let's not fool ourselves; I've given you about all I had to give and it wasn't enough. I did all I could to make you change your mind about me, but somewhere along the line I've made a mistake. Well, if that's the way you want it, it's all right by me. I can take what's coming to me. These things just happen and nobody can do very much about 'em. We'd better say goodbye and call it a day."

He kissed her cold lips, it was like kissing a statue; then he went away. From the pavilion window she watched him walking through the formal garden, one hand in his pocket, staring at the ground, then he went through the archway in the yew hedge, and was lost to her view. She knew that she would never see him again and was ashamed that she cared so little. "Well, I suppose I've been a fool," she told herself. "I've thrown away my last chance, but I can't help it. Henrietta Hornbeam, died unmarried," she said to herself, as she sometimes did when she was melancholy, thinking of her own place in the family tree. "Granny's perfectly right, that's what'll be the end of me."

6

So Leaf was the last person to see John Cornell at Fountain Court. The old man was pottering about on the steps, taking down the signs with *"This Way," "Gardens"* and *"Entrance,"* shutting up and bolting the big double doors. He came pottering down the steps to hold open the door of the big Buick for the departing guest. "Thanks," said John Cornell to him, "thanks again and here's a little something for you, Leaf; I don't suppose I'll be seeing you any more. I've finished my business in this part of the world, I'm on my way, I expect I'll be flying home next week." He stared all round the Muses' Grove in a lost fashion, as if he could not remember why he had ever strayed into it.

Leaf felt quite sorry for him, the old man saw immediately what had happened to him in the last half hour. "I hope, sir," he said gently, "that you will pay us another visit here when next you come to England. Everyone in this house would be glad to welcome you, sir, I feel sure." "No," said the American explosively and again "No," starting up the car, racing the engine furiously. Then he controlled himself and shook his head at Leaf. "You put that very nicely," said he, smiling for the first time. "I do appreciate it; but I don't fancy I shall be over here again for quite a while. I don't think I shall ever come back to Fountain Court." And he circled Apollo's plot and drove away. The old manservant looked round the green circle of yews, seeming to count the battered statues, each in their place, as if to assure himself that none had been stolen. Then he shook his head slowly and went in at the door, saying to himself, "She's better here, Miss Henrietta's better off here. She wouldn't have cared to go away and live in America."

XIII

UPSTAIRS, OLD LADY HORNBEAM had not had too good a day. She had been much more restless than usual, fretting about this and that; wanting her best dressing-jacket of feather-pink wool and her chestnut wig with a lace cap over it, insisting on having her nails polished and her pearl necklace out of the safe for an airing. "Two people are coming to lunch," she told Maria, "and I daresay one or other of them may want to come up and see me." She tired herself with fidgeting about all morning, and was quite in a fever by one o'clock, when Miss Henrietta came down in her best lilac frock, ready for the party. They shut the door and talked together for about ten minutes. Maria could not hear what it was all about, though she listened in vain at the keyhole; she only caught one or two words, "picture" and "American", and twice the word "fool". The old lady was very cross after her granddaughter had gone away, muttering to herself about something or other, beating her thin pretty hand on the pink eiderdown, telling Maria that all the young people nowadays were obstinate idiots. "Henrietta tells me nothing, there's something going on downstairs." Then she must have it that the clock was slow and her lunch late; to pacify her Maria went down early for the tray and had one of her all-too-frequent rows with Mrs. Peppercorn. "Always fussing about," said Cook, "wanting this, wanting that, her Ladyship's turn'll come all in good time, when I've dished up for the company. I've got a lunch-party, I'd have you know, I can't be bothered with omelettes and such. Thinks she owns the house, I suppose. There's chicken cream in the little dish for her Ladyship and some of the bottled peaches with cream and her own special Melba toast that she likes; what more does the old thing want except the rest of the grapes that were saved for her and her special half-bottle of champagne, all chilled nicely in the fridge? You make me tired. Fancies an omelette, indeed, does she? Just when I'm that busy I don't know where to turn. I don't believe there's a thing wrong with her except old age and wickedness."

Maria gave old Doctor Bayes a ring while she was downstairs and could use the telephone without being overheard, but he said much the same. "Wants a visit, does she? Wants a gossip, you mean. Come now, my girl, is there anything really wrong with her? Anything more than usual, I mean? I've got a busy day, I haven't time to come four miles out to Lady Hornbeam just for nonsense." Maria said in her precise foreign accents, "She has been very restless all morning, sir. People have been upsetting her, she dislikes changes. She talks of getting up and going downstairs, she says something is being kept from her. I find her very difficult to manage to-day." She heard the old man groan at the other end of the wire. "All right . . . all right . . . See that she has her usual sedative, maybe she'll get some sleep this afternoon. I'll come when I can, but it won't be till after six. I'll run over then and see how she is."

Lady Hornbeam was certainly better for her lunch and the champagne; she drank it all up and enjoyed it. Then she accepted two of her white pills and slept through the afternoon, while Maria sat and sewed by the window of the room next door, which had once been Lord Hornbeam's dressing-room. He had never used it again after the great quarrel between himself and his wife; he had taken himself away then to a room which had formerly been a spare-room, at the far end of the long passage. There he dwelt till his death, attended by a faithful valet who had been his soldier-servant in his youth, among rows of polished boots and photographs, large mahogany cupboards and a smell of blacking and bay-rum. He never again entered his wife's fine French bedroom after she went away and left him.

2

Maria had inherited his room, after her mistress came home again as a widow. She slept among his massive furniture, in a little bed behind a flowered screen, used his big washstand, hung her rosary on his dressing-table mirror, had her own sewing-chair by the window, where she got the afternoon sun. She still had a dressmaking corner, where an old-fashioned treadle sewing-ma-chine, an ironing board, and a headless dress-stand covered in crimson linen, with a wire skirt, kept each other company on a white sheet, pinned to the carpet to catch threads. This had been her workshop in the past, but she seldom used it nowadays.

All along the north wall were cupboards full of clothes. Lady Hornbeam had been a spendthrift in her youth, but in her latter years had hoarded like a magpie and would never throw anything away. There were dozens of outmoded dresses hanging in there, silk and velvet, beaded chiffon, frills and flounces, with long skirts and trailing sleeves which would have delighted Elsa Holly; sometimes she would take a fad to have them all pulled out and spread about the room. "There's the yellow dress I wore at the last Hunt Ball before the War," she would say, "there's the hobble-gown I had for the Black Ascot, after poor King Edward's death, there's the green dress I wore at Edward's wedding. I shouldn't have chosen that colour, Nanny said it would be unlucky. That geranium satin was one of my Court gowns." Now and again she would ask for her Coronation robes, worn in the Abbey when Edward the Seventh was crowned. It had been a purple ceremony, not a red one; she had worn violet velvet, trimmed with miniver and a robe of silver tissue under it tarnished now with age. She would run her fingers over the silken pile and feel her way back into the past. The Coronation robes were kept by themselves, wrapped up in black tissue paper, layer upon layer; it was always a tiresome business for Maria to take them out and pack them away again, but she enjoyed it as much as their owner.

Underneath the dresses were dozens of pairs of shoes on rails, in brocade or coloured satin, in black, white or bronze leather, beaded and buckled, all with pointed toes and very high heels, all made to measure for a little foot. In the drawers were pile upon pile of underclothes, of stockings, of long white kid gloves in pairs, enough to dress a dozen girls for a fancy ball. There were hats in boxes, haystacks of flowers and feathers for Ascot, for Henley, for Lord's; there were old split parasols in all colours that would never be re-covered. The furs lived in a special cupboard of their own, smelling of mothballs, lined with cedar; twice a year Maria had to shake and beat the heavy bulky coats, the mink, the sable, the seal, the ermine cloak, the cape of seven silver foxes, never to be worn again.

Behind a picture was the safe, built into the wall, with the jewellery inside it; this was opened quite often. Lady Hornbeam liked to have the cases spread about on the counterpane, prop a mirror against her knees and try on one thing after another. She would amuse herself for a whole morning with her jewels, Maria thought that by this time she had almost forgotten how most of them were only paste copies. The big diamond and sapphire tiara, the ruby and diamond dog-collar, given for the birth of the heir, the French pearl and emerald parure of necklace, earrings and bracelets, the old Duke's wedding gift to his favourite daughter, had all been her own property and were sold quietly during her widowhood, when she was short of money. What sparkled on the counterpane nowadays was mostly sham and nonsense, but the senile woman liked the glitter. "I wore the tiara at King Edward's Coronation" she would tell the maid for the hundredth time. "Lord Hornbeam chose the rubies specially when my poor Edward was born, he was so delighted to have an heir to the title. I could wear a dog-collar as well as most women; I had a very long slender neck. My dear father used to say a red-headed woman always ought to wear emeralds at night if she had a white skin." And she would hold the green and white paste under her chin and smile contentedly at her reflection in the glass.

In the corner of the room stood Maria's trunk, black, shining, dome-topped, with a formidable lock and big leather straps; so heavy that it would have taken two men to carry it downstairs. It had not been moved for years, nobody but herself had ever seen it unlocked; she kept the loot of years in it, hidden away among old clothes. She had been helping herself for a long time now to anything small and valuable that came her way. Inside skirts and dresses, wrapped up and poked into the toes of shoes, were rings, buckles, brooches, hair-ornaments; the silver crook of an old umbrella, an ivory cardcase, a sable muff in a box, a couple of good watches, half a string of red amber, a broken earring picked up after a ball, a jewelled snuff-box, a heavy gold bracelet with a broken clasp; a careless footman had been sent away after its loss. None of the other stuff had ever been missed. Maria had been clever about that, prowling about the great house like a cat, taking things that would never be asked for. There was money too in a black tin cashbox at the bottom of her trunk; her savings, her tips, the price of the old gowns which Lady Hornbeam used to throw at her as perquisites when they had been worn for a London season. She used to sell them all at a shop in Camden Town, she used to keep back part of the price when Lady Hornbeam sent her to the jewellers to dispose of some trinket. Maria did not believe in banks or investments, she liked to finger old sovereigns and half-sovereigns and count bundles of dirty notes when she was alone at night, with the passage door locked and her Ladyship sound asleep. When her mistress died there would be a legacy for her, so much for each year of service. Two men from the garden should carry her box down the back stairs and she would walk out of the house, go back to her married niece in Zurich and live in comfort for the rest of her days.

3

Maria had been in service at Fountain Court longer than anybody else. She had come from Wilchester Castle with Lady Hornbeam on her marriage, had been the daughter, they said, of the confectioner-chef there and his wife, both Swiss from the Engadine. She had been a dark girl in those days, plain, fierce and silent, with bright black eyes and a sallow skin, as ugly as a toad. The other servants had never liked her. She talked as good English as they did, though with a foreign accent caught from her parents and she had been born and bred in Wilchester, but she remained outlandish in their eyes. She always kept herself to herself, bit your head off if you spoke to her pleasantly, gave herself airs and looked down on the rest of them; the lady's maid in those days was one of the upper servants and young as she was had taken her meals in the housekeeper's room. She was a man-hater, that was plain, never looked at a young fellow, however handsome; they said there had been some trouble about a footman at the Castle, who had jilted her for a pretty housemaid and the other servants had all known about it and laughed at her. Lady Hornbeam with careless kindness had brought her away from all that; in return she had attached herself to the young bride with a jealous, single-hearted devotion.

Nobody knew just how old Maria was, but she could not have been more than a year or two younger than her mistress. She never seemed to change particularly. She had grown thin and tough as whipcord, yellow as a duck's foot, sour as a lemon; her bony arms were as strong as a man's, she could lift and turn Lady Hornbeam in bed as if she were a child. In the old days she had been deft and clever, could curl and dress hair in the high Edwardian style, trim up hats and clothes, make and mend underclothing, make up the beauty's face in the restrained style of those days and dress and undress her like a child. Nowadays there was little call for these traditional arts of the lady's maid. Lady Hornbeam lay in bed most of the day; if she got up she only sat in her armchair by the fire or the window for a few hours, and never put on anything more than a dressing-gown and cap. She needed endless rubbing, bathing and powdering, enjoyed gossip, scolding and little visits from old friends, but soon tired of them; liked best of all to talk with Maria about the old days.

The maid remembered everything, she knew all the secrets. Sitting in her low chair, mending a dressing-jacket, trimming a cap, running ribbon into a cambric nightgown in the old-fashioned style, she would talk of Wilchester Castle as if it still stood above ground. The great white elephant of a house, which used to stand by the lake outside the town, had been pulled down after the Second World War. The pillars and panelling of the Cedar Room, the coloured marble fireplaces, the drawing-room ceiling with its frescoed Muses by Angelica Kaufmann, had all been taken down, chipped away, packed up and sold across the Atlantic; the lake had been turned into the town reservoir. There was nothing reflected in its waters nowadays except the tennis courts and club house, built upon the old foundations, in the middle of the public park; beyond ran the Wilchester by-pass and the two new housing estates of Castle Meadows and Castle Hill. The last Duke of Wilchester, Lady Hornbeam's great-nephew, had been killed in the Western Desert; his widow had re-married and taken the two little girls to America. Lady Hornbeam would never see them again; but when she and Maria talked of their youth they rebuilt the Palladian house as it used to be, walked through the great rooms, up and down the staircases, in and out of the terraced gardens, just as they used to do when they were a couple of slender girls with all their troubles before them.

Maria knew all the stories and secrets. She knew why her young lady had married that dull Lord Hornbeam, forty if he was a day and cared for nothing but horses. She was twenty-five and afraid of missing her market, she had five sisters, the old Duke her father could not settle anything on her and the man she really wanted had sheered off and married an heiress. She thought Lord Hornbeam was rich and stupid and could be twisted round her little finger. It was not at all a bad match in the circumstances, it might have worked out quite well, Maria would say to herself, mending lace by the window, looking back into the past, Lord Hornbeam had been dull but devoted, his young wife should have been able to manage him. He had adored her at the beginning, let her turn his old house upside down, given her all the new clothes, furs and jewels she wanted. She had given him an heir, named Edward after the Prince of Wales, in defiance of family tradition; two years afterwards there had been a little girl, a Henrietta, called Harriet by her parents, so far so good.

After that had come the gay fashionable years. They had gone up to London regularly for the summer season, to a furnished house in Park Street; there had been all the summer bustle of those days, the Courts and balls, Ascot and Henley, Sundays at Ranelagh, money thrown about as if it were dirt. There had been card-parties and dinners, the Prince and Princess of Wales had taken up young Lady Hornbeam; she was gay and witty and she made them laugh. When the season was over there were the country-house visits, the grouse, partridge- and pheasant-shooting-parties, the hunting all winter. Those were the years when the Hornbeam fortunes were wasted in extravagance, luxury and show; presently the scandals began. Lady Hornbeam had grown into a charmer; she was gay and wild, the men came round her like flies round a honey-pot. The other women could not hold a candle to her, they were all jealous. Everybody watched her and chattered about her. In London at the turn of the century society was no more private than it is in a village; the same people met continually and talked about each other, they all knew when Lady Hornbeam chose her lover. Lord Hornbeam was the last to hear of it, even the servants knew more than he did. Maria understood everything; she had carried notes and messages, watched doors, known about assignations. The young man in question made it worth her while not to give him away, but she would never have betrayed her mistress; in her eyes Lady Hornbeam could do whatever she chose.

They were all at Homburg when the discovery was made in August 1903, meeting their London friends over again in a new setting of green trees, little fountains, shaded walks and German cake-shops. Lord Hornbeam was busy all day long with his cure, drinking glasses of warm water, taking little strolls, being bathed, steamed, rubbed, lapped up in hot towels to sweat the gout out of him; it made him more irritable than usual. There was plenty of time for the lovers to meet and perhaps they were less careful than they should have been; some woman made it her business to open the husband's eyes.

Maria could remember the very day and hour when it happened. She was dressing her Ladyship's hair in the middle of the morning, with the sun streaming through a half-closed shutter and a grey cloth walking-dress laid out for a lunch-party on the red eiderdown of the high-piled German bed, when his Lordship came in with a purple face and ordered her out. He locked the door on her and though she listened through the keyhole she could only hear part of what went on. He was raging and stamping and Lady Hornbeam was answering him back, giving him as good as she got, but not crying, she never cried. When Maria got back into the room again an hour later, there was her mistress sitting still before the mirror in her dressing-gown, with her long red hair over her shoulders and her face pale as death. "Yes, he knows," said she to the confidante in her mirror. "We are to go home tomorrow, you had better start packing;" but Maria had replied, "No need to do that, milady. I will get a message taken to Monsieur, I will pack the small cases and the jewels and we will travel by the night train for Paris."

4

She had managed it all, something outside herself had possessed her. Lady Hornbeam had pretended to be in bed with a headache, Lord Hornbeam had gone down to his dinner and the pair of them, mistress and maid, had walked down the service stairs and out of the hotel to the station, in veils and travelling coats with bags in their hands. The young man had followed them. Maria had been with the lovers, first in Paris and afterwards at a villa in the hills behind Avignon; in the spring they had gone down to Sicily. It had been a wonderful time while it lasted. It did not, could not, go on for long; the young man had his future to consider, Lady Hornbeam was ten years older than he was, he had no money and no wish to marry a divorced woman. After a year he left her.

There was no divorce after all, Lord Hornbeam did not proclaim his injuries; perhaps at the bottom of his heart he still hoped that his wife would come back to him. There was less gossip than might have been expected, and it was given out that Lady Hornbeam had a delicate chest and was spending a second winter in Italy. Her husband was living very quietly in a corner of Fountain Court; the big rooms were all shut up, half the servants dismissed, the children were up in the nursery, nobody was invited inside the place. His neighbours said to each other that the poor man must be trying to pay off his wife's debts. He came out hunting much as usual, but hardly spoke to anybody; he looked old and changed and his temper was worse than ever. In February he broke his neck, putting the grey mare Moonlight at a fence too big for her.

He was buried in the family vault, the undertakers said at the time that there was only one more place left vacant. Lady Hornbeam did not come back from Naples for the funeral. There was some talk about her husband having cut her out of his will, but it was not so. He had been too idle or too loving to make any changes, right up to the last he had pretended that nothing had gone wrong. His widow had a life-interest in the estate and the guardianship of the two children.

They were in the marbled hall to welcome her when she came home at midsummer on her brother's arm; young Edward, now the third Lord Hornbeam, a peaky boy of six and his sister Harriet, in a black dress and a white pinafore, clinging to her nurse's hand. The upper servants were ranged behind; Maria coming in with jewel-cases in her hands, saw a row of familiar attentive disapproving faces. Harriet was too little then to understand this solemn home-coming and shrank from her mother, but Edward hugged her fiercely; he was pale and on the point of tears. She kissed him, put him aside, greeted the servants coolly by name; then she went upstairs and Maria followed her, ignoring them. She was in a glow of pride and satisfaction. They were home again, Lord Hornbeam was defeated, dead and buried; her own dear lady was mistress of Fountain Court and could do as she chose.

Lady Hornbeam did not marry again, though she was still in her middle thirties and beautiful as ever; it seemed that she had had enough of men. She remained at Fountain Court, a commanding dowager, ruling the house with a firm hand, allowing no interference, mismanaging the estate. People gave her the cold shoulder for a time, but she behaved with extreme discretion and made no advances; when her mourning was over she used to appear at dinners at the Castle. Her brother and his wife supported her and gradually she regained her old place in the county; people continued to say that she had been wild in her youth, but they usually added that she had quite settled down.

She made a great fuss of young Edward, his father's heir, and kept him as it were in a glass case. He turned out a delicate bookish boy, a throw-back to her side of the family; the Hornbeams had mostly been simple, hard-riding country squires, but the Wilchester blood, running thin after many noble generations, made Edward nervous and queer. He adored his beautiful mother and she kept him always at her side; Maria could remember how he would come up and sit on a stool in the bedroom, watching her dress his mother's hair, stretching out a thin hand to touch the skirt of a satin gown. Edward had been more like a girl than a boy. He had been shaken to the depths of his being by the anxieties of those two years when his mother went away, he did not understand why, for a long time he could not be sure that she had come back for good. He was like a jealous lover, could not bear to let her out of his sight; they both ignored his fierce stubborn little sister Harriet. It was not a happy situation, though it improved later when Edward went off to his father's old school.

Then came the First World War and Lady Hornbeam, pulling every string she could lay her hands on, got Fountain Court adopted as an officers' convalescent home, attached to the big hospital at Wilchester Castle. She had to spend a great deal of money, had to turn out all the pictures and furniture from the Waterloo wing, and store them for four years; but it was well worth the trouble. She established herself finally among the people of importance in the county, after the war was over, everybody had forgotten her story. There had been the brief interruption of Edward's return from the wars, his coming-of-age, his marriage; but the loss of his wife and his own death had left Lady Hornbeam firmly in the saddle again, ruling over Fountain Court.

She had remained there for thirty years, obstinate, extravagant, never admitting a mistake, letting the house fall into disrepair, every so often selling a farm, cutting down a wood, getting rid of one or two more servants, quietly disposing of a picture, a cabinet, a piece of china or jewellery; in the end she had been the ruin of Fountain Court and now she was past caring. She had let the reins slip out of her old hands; she lay among her pillows, indolent, fretful, shrunk from a tall beauty into a little ugly doll and hardly knew what year it was or who came in and out to visit her.

5

When she woke this day from her afternoon sleep she was quite in a muddle, saying to the maid, in her piping small voice, "You should have come when I rang before, Maria. His Majesty was here. He came and sat beside me for an hour, so friendly, talking about his horses; he particularly told me I must get well in time for Ascot. He was just back from Homburg; he has lost quite a lot of weight, he looks all the better for it, very handsome and jolly. He advised me to be painted by Sargent for next year's Royal Academy. He told me I looked very well and as handsome as ever, he said; we always have our little jokes together when he comes." It was uncanny to hear her talking so placidly about this ghostly visitor. She lifted her thin ringed hand and turned it about, admiring it with a birdlike turn of the head, saying complacently, "He paid me one of his German compliments about my hand." She smiled vaguely; then a tear stood in her eye as she woke a little further and remembered that old King Edward the Seventh had been dead and buried for over forty years. "All gone," she fretted, "all dead and gone; nobody remembers the time when I was young." "I remember, my lady," the Swiss woman said in her smooth false voice. "I remember His Majesty coming down to stay here, how pleasant he was; such a Royal manner and how well he enjoyed his visit. Lift up your head now, my lady; here's a fresh nightcap for you. We must make you look your best, because here's Lady Linden and her niece waiting to come in and see you and after tea we shall have Doctor Bayes." She never listened very carefully when her mistress talked about the old King, all that was too long ago. "Here's your tray, my lady," said she, "with some of the gingerbread you like."

So Lady Linden came in and was just the right kind of visitor, cheerful, composed, ready to talk about the past; though that Mrs. Holly was not much use, standing by the window, watching the half-crown visitors strolling on the terrace, saying disdainfully, "Fools! I can't think why they come, if I were Henrietta I wouldn't bother with them." It was a pity that she ever mentioned Henrietta, for the old lady became fussy and excited saying, "Henrietta does the silliest things. She's trying to sell that picture in the Yellow Drawing-room, the West Indian heiress, you know. I told her this morning she won't get anything for it; why, it's only a copy." Maria could see Elsa Holly pricking up her ears at that, coming back to the bed, saying eagerly, "What, that thing of Lavinia Hornbeam. I thought it was a Lawrence and Lawrence is all the go now;" but Lady Linden shut her up, rising and saying firmly, "We must go down now, Elsa; we promised Henrietta we'd have tea with her and it's struck five. She'll be waiting."

It was a pity really, thought Maria, that she had let them in; she had meant to occupy her mistress's mind with something new, but they had only upset her. She worked herself up, fretting and fuming, during the next hour; by the time that Henrietta looked in to pay her regular evening visit she was in one of her tempers. "You leave me alone all afternoon," was her cry, "with not a soul to speak to, while you enjoy yourself going round lecturing to a pack of strangers, boring them with your stories about the family. Why haven't you been up before? It must be nearly seven." Henrietta sighed wearily. "Oh! Granny, I've been much too busy. We had a perfect crowd today, I suppose because it was such a fine afternoon and people thought it was their last chance before the winter. I'm quite hoarse with talking to them." She dropped down in the armchair which had been pushed up for old Lady Linden and stuck out her legs in front of her like a young man, stretching her arms over her head. "I'm just about dead beat," she confessed and indeed in her lilac gown she looked dreadfully pale. "We got fifteen pounds," she said, "counting the garden-money. I think that's our record."

"Fifteen pounds," said the old woman disdainfully. "What's the use of that? I used to pay twice that for a good dress, even in the old days, before everything got so dreadfully expensive. Where's the sense in turning the whole house upside down and wearing yourself out till you look like a scarecrow, all for the sake of fifteen pounds?"

"Every little helps," said Henrietta, pushing her auburn hair off her forehead and yawning uncontrollably. Lady Hornbeam eyed her balefully. "Sprawling there," said she, "arranging everything to suit yourself, neglecting me all day long, never telling me anything that happens. Charles is just as bad," she added for good measure, putting her handkerchief to her eyes. "Oh! do let poor Charles alone," said Henrietta, getting cross. "He's done nothing to upset you, surely."

"You both do all you can to provoke me," the old lady persisted. "Neither of you remember me except when it suits you. I've been lying up here all day, waiting to hear what happened about Lavinia's picture but nobody's troubled to come and tell me. Did that American buy it? I suppose not, or you'd have been boasting about it already."

"No, he didn't," said Henrietta, biting her lip. "You didn't expect him to, did you? You told me yourself it was a copy and wouldn't deceive a baby. Well, it didn't give Mr. Birnbaum any trouble at all. He just took one look at the front and another at the back; then he scratched in the corner with his finger-nail, which I thought was going pretty far and said it was a fake. I didn't know where to look. John was dreadfully disappointed and poor Charles was perfectly furious with me. He thought I'd let him down." An unwilling smile crossed her face.

The old lady cackled with amusement. "Ah! well, I got a good price for the original, I remember. I sold it at the top of the market. I needed the money badly, I owed every penny of it and more. I was lucky to find a rich buyer." She lay smiling at the ceiling.

"Yes, *you* were all right," Henrietta thought rebelliously. "You enjoyed yourself as long as you had the chance, you spent all the money there was, you thought of nobody but yourself. You sold things right and left, more than I shall ever find out about; the land, the pictures, the jewels, they're all gone now and you never told any of us till it was too late. Now we're driven into a corner, I don't see how we can go on much longer. I've done everything I can, I shall have to give in and it's all your fault." But she did not say it aloud, for she knew the old woman would never listen to her.

"So young Mr. Cornell had to go away without his picture, did he?" Lady Hornbeam said, with an air of satisfaction. "And I don't suppose he asked you to marry him either."

"He's asked me five times," Henrietta said, white to the lips. "I've turned him down every time, because I won't leave Fountain Court. He's gone off now for good. He's flying home on Monday and I don't suppose I shall ever see him again; so please don't let's keep on about him any more." Her voice was not quite steady.

She was surprised to find how much this distressed her grandmother. "Oh! dear, oh! dear," the old woman lamented, "what a dreadful mistake! Why did you do it, dear? You should have taken him, you should have got away from this place. You'll live to regret it, I'm afraid." Tears ran out of her eyes and down her withered cheeks, she beat her hand on the pink blanket. "You're such an odd girl," she fretted, "you come from such an odd family. None of the Hornbeams can look after themselves, I've had such trouble with them all along," and again she cried out urgently, "You should have married him." "But Granny, I wasn't in love with him," the girl protested. Her grandmother rolled her head on the pillow. "Girls think of nothing but love," said she in her faint cracked voice. "What's the use of that? I wasn't in love with your grandfather when I married him, all that came afterwards." "It wasn't much of a success," Henrietta muttered, but too low for Lady Hornbeam to hear her. "I know what I'm talking about," the old woman said. "I've had everything in my time, but it's all over and done with. Finished . . . finished . . . finished . . ." She uttered a long sigh, as if she were utterly exhausted and slipped down a

little in the bed; Henrietta heard her whisper faintly, "What's to
become of you?" Then she turned her head to one side and her
face seemed to crease up and grow smaller. She breathed very
quietly. Henrietta thought that she was dropping off into one of
her sleepy fits and sat quiet for a minute or two, so as not to disturb
her. Then she realised that her grandmother did not seem to be
breathing at all. She turned her head, stared at the hand outside
the bedclothes and saw it twitch once or twice; then it stopped
moving. She jumped up, ran to the bed and called out. The dressing-room door burst open and Maria ran in, exclaiming, "Milady,
oh! milady." She caught up the limp body, sought in vain for the
failing pulse, poured and spilt useless medicine, did all she could
in vain. The old woman had slipped away, in a minute without
warning, as the doctors had said she might; she lay crumpled and
small, like a butterfly on an autumn window-sill, like a dead bird
under a bush.

XIV

OLD DOCTOR BAYES from Wilchester was almost past his work, but still entirely trusted by the group of devoted patients who had been treated by him all their lives. He was a little old man with a big square head, who lived in a tottering house at the back of St. Blaizey's Church with a wife almost as old as himself. Very skilled, severe and silent, he drove himself slowly about the lanes in a shaky car, with a white West Highland terrier bitch in the back seat; she would bite any man or woman who opened the door of the car while her master was away from it. Everybody knew this turnout for ten miles round Wilchester; one villager would say to another "Saw the Old Doctor's car turn in at the Rectory, twice in one day, Parson's bronchitis must be bad again;" or "The Old Man didn't call at the pub today, Joe's missus must be better." The younger people were rather afraid of him, poked fun at him behind his back and told each other he ought to retire. He would not take National Health patients or go out at night delivering babies any longer; but nobody could touch him for skill and kindness and his old patients all hoped and prayed that he would last their time.

Dr. Bayes arrived at Fountain Court in the clear light of the afterglow. He drew up his car, mounted the steps with his stiff gait and rang the bell; but before Leaf opened the double doors he knew what had happened, for the crimson blinds had all been drawn down. "Oh! sir, she's gone, her Ladyship's gone at last," said Leaf with his face puckered up as if he were going to cry. "We tried to get you earlier, sir; Commander Hornbeam rang up Frog Farm, but when we got them you'd just left. It would have been too late in any case; she went very quick and sudden, sir." His face was so pale that the doctor fixed him at once with a sharp grey eye. "This has been a shock to you, my man," he pronounced. "You go back to your pantry, sit down for ten minutes and drink a glass of whatever you fancy, or I shall be having you on my hands next." Leaf smiled feebly, bowed and drew back as Henrietta came quickly into the hall, exclaiming, "Oh! Doctor, I'm so thankful to see you."

He had brought her and her brother into the world; he held her cold hand in both of his and told her, "I'm sorry I couldn't be with you sooner." She pulled him into the library, where Charles was telephoning, but rang off when they appeared. Between them the cousins told the old man all that he needed to know. "I was so dreadfully angry with her this morning," Henrietta confessed with tears in her eyes. "She'd told me something that made me furious. We had a real row about it, I wish I hadn't been so unkind; now I feel as if I'd killed her." She was very pale and could not stop shaking. "I was talking to her when she . . . went," she told him. Charles laid his hand on her knee, Doctor Bayes said briskly, "Nonsense, my dear; don't upset yourself. I've been expecting her to go for some time. It'll be a millstone off your neck." He always spoke his mind as freely as the villagers did, finally he made Henrietta dry her eyes. "She'd outlived her time," said he firmly. "We all do in the end, I've done it myself. It's a long time since I saw her first."

He talked a little, absently, about the days when Lady Hornbeam came to Fountain Court as a bride. "I was only a boy then, it wasn't till I'd finished my hospital training that I came here. My father attended her then, I was only allowed to try my hands on the servants, they taught me my trade. There were no end of people employed here then, upstairs and downstairs. I used to come in by the side door and see them with the housekeeper. I kept my eyes open for young Lady Hornbeam, coming and going about the place but it was a couple of years before I even spoke to her. Afterwards of course I got to know her very well." And his old face softened and changed as he said, "Such a pretty young woman she was then, as pretty a one as ever I saw in my life."

"I always heard she was a great beauty," said Charles doubtfully, and the doctor retorted, "You're going to remember her as a bag of bones with a scolding voice, but you never saw her in her great days. She was tall and slender and very soft-looking; she used to muffle herself up in furs and velvet, with long wrinkled gloves and little suede shoes and ridiculous hats with birds nesting in them; all the women wore them then. She had a small foot and a small hand, all her gloves and shoes were specially made for her; she used to go to Paris twice a year to buy her gowns. She liked to wear great big bunches of violets pinned into her coats and spotted veils tied down tight over her nose; when you went behind her to lift off her coat you smelt flowers and orris root. She had a way of looking up at you," the old man mused, "her eyelashes were so long that they used to catch in her veil; it was extremely seductive. I've never forgotten it. The women all knew how to do it then, surround themselves, I mean, with a cloud of charm and mystery. Nowadays it's all nakedness and paint," he concluded harshly. Charles laughed, Henrietta rubbed her hands over her face as if she were tired out. "Sometimes you remind me of her," Doctor Bayes told Henrietta. "She had red hair like yours and a temper to match. She was very little use in the world, she caused a lot of trouble, but I shall never forget her. Well, we'd better be going upstairs, I suppose. It's getting late."

As they climbed the Waterloo staircase to the first floor, suiting their steps to his, Henrietta told the old man, "Maria's been a bit difficult about it all. I knew we couldn't get the district nurse, because she's got three baby cases, but Charles would have fetched Mrs. Birk; she'd have been glad to help. However, Maria wouldn't hear of it. 'Nobody shall lay a finger on my lady except me', she told me; then she turned me out of the room and locked the door."

She was too dejected to laugh, but the doctor did soundlessly, heaving his shoulders and creasing up his face. "Best leave the woman to it," he agreed. "She's always done everything for her mistress."

Lady Hornbeam's door was still locked when they came to it. Charles knocked and twisted the handle, but there was no sound except running water. Henrietta tapped sharply and called out the maid's name; they heard Maria cry out in response, "Go away, go away; I am not ready." Doctor Bayes then stepped up and hit the door once with his heavy fist. "Come out of that, my girl," he growled. "Open up, I can't stand here all night."

There was dead silence. Henrietta glanced at Charles, who made a comical face, Doctor Bayes's eyebrows drew together into a bristling grey hedge. Then there was a movement within and suddenly the door was flung wide open.

Maria had done everything. She had washed the small body of her mistress and composed it decently; put two silver coins on the wrinkled eyelids, tied up the sagging chin, settled the chestnut wig on the bald head. After that she had dressed the body in the violet and silver Coronation robes of a peeress and spread the train round like a mantle over the feet. She had got out all Lady Hornbeam's jewels and put them in place; the tiara, the dog-collar, the chains, earrings and bracelets; there were rings on each finger of the folded hands and inside the tiara the little gilt and velvet coronet which the dead woman had worn in Westminster Abbey. She lay in full state, with her sharp nose pointing to the ceiling; in the shifting light of half a hundred candles she almost looked as if she were alive.

Henrietta exclaimed, "My God!" and Charles said, "Well, I'm damned." "What's all this?" Doctor Bayes demanded of Maria. The foreign woman only tossed up her head proudly. "I have made my lady beautiful for the last time," she told him, "just as she used to be. I promised her I would do it. I had everything prepared." And she walked to the foot of the bed, knelt down and began to tell her beads.

2

Victor, the heir, was not told that night that his grandmother had died suddenly. Nanny had heard the news when she went down for his supper, but had thought that it could keep till morning. She laid his meal for him beside the fire according to her own traditions, with doorsteps of bread and yellow farm butter, jam with whole strawberries swimming in syrup, sugar-topped biscuits with animals on them and a drink of cold milk with a head of cream on it, in a mug printed with flags and generals of the South African war. He munched it all up and played with the dregs of the country milk, swilling it about in his mug, staring round the walls at photographs of known and unknown Hornbeam children. Aunt Henrietta was there in a velvet dress, gathered over her flat chest; in a school uniform with a sailor hat, a stiff collar and tie; in a Japanese fancy-dress, with a paper parasol open behind her head, looking uncommonly sulky. The mantelpiece was full of her and of his father. They had got Captain Hornbeam downstairs in all his military glory, an enlarged photograph on a table in a silver frame, with his medals in a box underneath, for tourists to peep at and whisper about; but up here in the nursery Nanny had preserved his lost youth. She had all the faded snapshots of a thin boy with fair hair, holding a boat in a sailor suit; screwing up his eyes against the sun as he faced the groom's bowling in the shrubbery; later in a school blazer with a football in his arm, or grinning with a First Eleven cap on his head. There were others of himself and his twin sister, on the sands, in a boat, at a picnic; there was one of him at ten years old with a rabbit in his arms which somehow turned him into a real person. There was even a photograph of Nanny herself, thirty

years back, but looking exactly the same in her plain grey gown
and starched apron, with a lap full of babies; the twins dressed
alike in long embroidered robes and woollen shawls. "That was
just after the christening," Nanny told Victor. "As like as two peas
they were. We used to tie a pink bow on your aunt and a blue
one on your father, to save strangers trouble, but of course I always knew them apart. Miss Henrietta was the quiet one, Master
Harry was noisy; they did everything together, but he was always
the leader."

She folded up her work and stabbed the needles through the
ball of wool, her thin wedding ring sparkled in the light. "Finish
up that milk now, Master Victor," she adjured him. "Don't play
about with it, for goodness' sake! Drink it down, there's a good
boy! it'll make your hair curl, and then you shall have your nice
hot bath and go to Bedfordshire. You're half-asleep as you sit
there, such a day it's been. You'll drop off as soon as your head
touches the pillow." She bustled him into the bath, in its mahogany frame with its big brass taps and the Christmas calendar on
the wall behind it; whisked him out again, dried him on her lap
and put him into the narrow hard bed in the turret-room which
had been his father's. "I'll leave the door on the jar," she promised, "and I'll be here in the day-nursery, eating my supper;
you've only to call out if you want anything."

Victor lay there half-asleep, half-awake, with his toes on the
flabby old rubber hot-water bottle she had given him for a treat.
He watched the line of yellow light on the wall and heard the
curtain flap and suck against the window; the floorboards creaked,
the trees rustled outside in the night-wind. All the sounds and
smells of the old house were strange to him. He wanted to go to
sleep dreadfully, but his head was too full of pictures. He thought
about his mother kneeling on the marble floor of the portico,
about his grandmother lying in her bed, his Cousin Charles up a
tree, and his aunt telling stories to tourists; he thought of the
tabby cat on the kitchen window-sill and the boat on the pond,

the horse in the picture that had been killed at Balaclava and the globe that spun about to show the fly-speck islands in the South Seas. He had almost drifted away across that blue ocean when he was startled broad awake by a queer flapping noise and two or three loud bumps. A shadow crossed the light on the wall and there was a scrabble of claws near him; he sat up and called out wildly.

Nanny came in and clicked on the light; in its cold glare he saw a big soft brown bird, dishevelled and sooty, perched on the rail at the foot of his bed. He cried out again and it rose in the air, dashed itself this way and that in terror and bumped itself against the open door. Then it clung to the window curtain, and turned its head round completely and glowered at him backwards with its flaming yellow eyes. He clung to Nanny, still half-asleep, babbling, "What is it? what is it?" and she petted him as if she had been his mother. "Why, it's nothing to be frightened of, deary, it won't hurt you; it's just one of the owls. The old birds nest in the Abbot's Tower every year, they keep down the rats and mice, they're very useful to the farmers. This is a young bird, it doesn't know its way about yet; at this time of year, they often get indoors. It can't find its way out, I must open the window for it a bit wider. You won't mind if I turn the light off for just a minute, the poor bird's blinded." She darkened the room, drew a curtain, pushed a casement wider. Staring in the soft darkness, Victor saw the strange bird of night appear at the window. It perched there a moment, considering its flight; he saw it outlined, hunchbacked, against a sky quite white with autumn stars. Then suddenly it was gone without a trace.

Nanny drew the curtain. "Well, that was a funny thing to happen on your first night," said she composedly, "For one of your own owls to come down the chimney and have a look at you. It must have been roosting up there lately, I suppose, but I never knew it. This room isn't often lit up at night, I expect that disturbed it. Nobody's slept in here for years, I had quite a job getting it properly aired for you. This was the room your father always slept in. I'll get you a night-light; it's strange here for you, I daresay."

She went away and came back with a treasure, a white china castle whose windows glowed softly from the night-light inside. "Your Great-granny brought it back from Germany for your grandfather," said she, "when he was a little boy. He told me he always loved it and the twins used to have it lit up for them for a treat when they were good." She put the thing on the corner of the chest-of-drawers and it sat there shining quietly at Victor. He felt her old soft lips on his cheek, her bony hand on his hair, as he sank back into the cool pillow which she had turned for him. "This is your own house," he thought he heard her say; "Everything in it belongs to you." "Even the owls?" he asked her sleepily and she said kindly, "Yes, even the little owls." Then she went away. He lay staring at the porcelain castle and it glowed back at him, a warm agreeable presence; whenever he closed his eyes and opened them again it was still there, watching over him. He heard the old house talking to itself, moving quietly, settling year after year into the ground; he heard an owl hoot, a train whistle, far off an aeroplane droning round the sky. When his aunt came up an hour later he was sound asleep with his nose buried in the pillows and his eyelashes making a dark crescent on his cheek.

"Nice to have something in the night nursery again," she said to Nanny, sitting down by the fire. "It's been empty a long time." She looked about her at the old room, sighed, shivered and rubbed her hands over her eyes. "You're tired and no wonder," said Nanny, bustling about, "after all that's happened today. I'll get you a hot drink." She scraped busily, mixing Horlicks in the bottom of the South African mug, filling it up from the eternal kettle on the hob, saying, "The boy's had nearly all the fresh milk, but this will help you to sleep."

"My God! that's the Lord Roberts-and-Kitchener mug," said

Henrietta. "We always got it to drink out of on birthdays. Hideous thing! it ought to have got broken years ago. If it had been Crown Derby somebody would have been sure to smash it up." "It's been in the cupboard all this time," said Nanny placidly, turning back the hem of her skirt to warm her old feet at the fire. "I got it out again, I thought it would be nice for the boy to drink his milk out of his grandfather's mug." She watched Henrietta turn it about, warm her cold hands on it, screw up her face childishly after each burning sip, stare about the walls much as Victor had done. "He's a dear little boy," said Nanny. "His mother's brought him up nicely, you can always tell. He'll be a credit to the family yet. He's taken after her side so far, but there's real Hornbeam in him underneath. In bed there now, he looked just like his father." And she told Henrietta about the young owl. "He was very good about it, didn't make any more fuss than was reasonable, lay down again afterwards and went off to sleep, as good as gold. I was very pleased with him. It was a frightening thing for a town child, I was sorry it happened, he might have been really upset; however, he's none the worse. He's a brave little chap," and again she said, "Just like his father."

"Harry liked owls," said Henrietta sleepily, lying back in the big armchair. "He kept one for a pet. It was a young one that had fallen out of the nest. He brought it in from the Abbot's Tower one day in the summer holidays. We kept it up here for a bit and after that it lived in a cage in the stables, we used to catch mice for it and give it bits of rat and rabbit. We called it Minerva. When it was big enough to fend for itself Harry let it out and it flew away. That was the day before he went back to school. Do you remember?" "Of course I remember," said Nanny firmly, "everything about you children, as if it were yesterday. You were like my own to me."

3

Charles's quarters were over the stable, in the room where the head groom used to sleep; here he had made himself at home in his own fashion with a desk, a big chair, a kitchen table, some bookshelves and a neat kitchen-corner where he cooked for himself when he felt like it, getting his own breakfast always and the odd supper when he had been late on the road. He had his photographs on the walls, ships mostly, and foreign ports; there were polished brass shell-cases on the mantelpiece and a pair of spiky South Sea shells. His bed was a ship's bunk, built against the wall, neatly made up behind a curtain; it had a drawer underneath and a cupboard at the foot. He had designed all this himself and had knocked out two windows, so that he could look into the walled garden on one side and the yard on the other and know where his men were working. This room was his little kingdom and suited him perfectly; it had something of the air of a ship's cabin and was kept as neatly, Charles was an old maid for tidiness. Sitting by the hearth, hearing the wind halloo down the chimney and roar away through the garden trees, Henrietta thought that he sometimes fancied himself at sea.

She did not often go there, but she went over to-night before going to bed; somehow she always wanted to talk to Charles when she was anxious or worried. She found him sitting by the fire, smoking, doing nothing in particular, which was unusual for him and seeming less cheerful than usual; however, he found her a drink and a chair. To take his mind off the old woman's death she told him all about Mr. Ivy. "I do wish you'd seen him, he'd have amused you. He came round the house with one of the afternoon tours, I think really to see if we'd anything in his line for sale. In the end he got up to the attics with Victor and Lucy and me and bought four mahogany commodes." Charles laughed and said, "What did he want 'em for?" He could hardly believe her story about the fireside bookcases. "People don't read now-adays," said he. "They only run their eyes through digests and look at TV." "Well, anyhow, he gave me four-pound-ten for them," Henrietta persisted. Charles said, "Good work, let's hope he comes again. We could find him plenty of rubbish in the attics if he pokes round hard enough." "Seriously, we ought to sell anything we can up there," she told him dryly, "The difficulty is going to be to keep Mr. Ivy off. He's full of notions; he'd like to lease the ballroom for an antique shop. He talked to me about it for what seemed like hours," said she, rubbing her eyes. "I got quite hypnotised, I think; he went on and on and I didn't seem able to stop him. There never was such a man for talking. I tell you, Charles, I got quite sold on the idea. It might work, you know."

"Well, if you want to lose what money you've got left," said Charles, quite crossly for him, "I daresay that's as good a way as any other. You're a good business woman, Penny, but you don't know the first thing about antiques."

"The lunatic would do the buying," said she quite eagerly. "He'd run round the sales and pick up the stuff; I should do the selling, in the ballroom . . . everything marked in plain figures . . . warranted genuine from a Noble Mansion." At his shocked face she began to laugh uncontrollably. "I know, I know; he told me I was too much of a lady to take good advice. I can't even manage to plant a faked Lawrence on a fool who's in love with me, I'm too grand to sell Toby jugs to tourists, or unload our chipped plates and old spoons on them . . . crest and all, warranted genuine . . . straight from a lord's kitchen. You can mix in a few fakes once you've got your name, I'm sure. I should soon get round to thinking that quite clever. Mr. Ivy said I'd make a good saleswoman with time and practice. He offered to train me, he said he'd make me a partner." "I hope you told him where he got off," said Charles severely, but she only shook her head. "You don't understand," said she. "He was a decent man, an honest little fellow according to his lights, he was really sorry for me. I liked him, he meant well. He kept saying 'No offence', and I didn't take any. I thought, 'Well, maybe he's got something there'. You know, Charles, we're almost at the end of our tether. We really are in a hole, we can't go on much longer. It might be worth trying, don't you think?" He only shook his head. "Oh! well," said she, losing heart, "I daresay it's no use, I wouldn't know. Sometimes I get desperate and feel I'd do anything at all to save the place."

Charles did not answer immediately. She thought that he looked very tired. "You know," he said slowly in the end, "you're getting this thing out of proportion, Penny. You're killing yourself over it. The best thing you could do would be to set fire to this house, and the next best thing would be for you all to get together and make some proper arrangement; get the leave of the court to sell most of the heirlooms and let the empty house, or sell it, or pull it down if everything else fails. That's what you'll have to do now that your grandmother's dead." He paused, but Henrietta sat like a marble statue, not moving a finger. "And as far as you're concerned, Penny," said he savagely, "you'd better marry that decent chap who wanted to buy Lav's picture and go off with him to America."

She gave him a look which he hardly understood, full of reproach and surprise. "Now you're talking just like Granny," said she. "Poor John, I've turned him down. He's gone off full of despair, he thinks he's had the disappointment of a lifetime. He'll forget me in six months."

"I don't know about that!" Charles objected. "You aren't being fair to the man, or yourself for that matter. It would take me more than six months to forget you if I were in his shoes." His cousin gave him a very peculiar look, almost as if she were vexed with him. "But you're one of these truly faithful people, the sort that have died out, really," she told him, and then she startled him by saying, "It's more than ten years since she died, but you haven't forgotten Margery."

He turned his head in spite of himself to the photographs which hung over his writing table, where he could see them whenever he looked up from his work. In one he himself was in full naval uniform, descending the steps of a church under an arch of swords, between groups of cheering people, with a girl in white on his arm. In the other the same dark curly-headed girl was sitting in trousers at the helm of a boat, with an expanse of reeds and water behind her and a dog at her feet; no doubt it had been enlarged from a snapshot. "That's frightfully good of Margery," said Henrietta, staring at his dead wife. "What a pretty creature she was!"

Charles's face twisted, "I don't look at it very often now," said he. "Yes, she was a pretty girl and a good one; we might have had longer together. We had all sorts of plans, you know. We'd worked out what we'd do together when the war was over, we'd even got round to settling what she was to do with herself and the boy if anything happened to me. That was always on the cards, but we never thought of her being killed." He made an impatient gesture with his clenched fist, "I thought I'd got her safely tucked away in that boat on the marshes. There were raiders going over all the time, of course, but she was miles from any place that could be a target. She'd have been all right if she'd only stayed put. She'd got no business to go up to London, once the flying-bombs had started."

"I don't remember her very well," Henrietta confessed. "I think I only saw her about twice. Very gay, with black hair and blue eyes, always laughing. What on earth made her go up to London?"

"She wanted a new hat," said Charles, twisting up his monkey-face in a reluctant grin. "It was all in a letter she sent me. I didn't get it till weeks after she was dead, or I'd have written and forbidden her to go up to town. It was just about the time I was wounded, I'd always ragged her about not wearing a hat, she was lazy about it, couldn't be bothered to turn herself out properly. She wrote to me that if I was really going to get ashore for a bit she must go up to Knightsbridge and buy something very special, poor dear! She needn't have taken the boy," he added under his breath, looking at the ground. "You know, what with one thing and another, I never saw him. I can't even imagine what he would have been like."

Henrietta had begun to say, "Perhaps he was too little to leave," when Charles told her suddenly, "I went to look at the place the other day, where it happened. I'd never been there before. It was down beyond Sloane Street, somewhere at the back of Harrod's. It was in the middle of the morning; she was on her way to leave the boy with that aunt of hers, they told me, while she went off to do her shopping. You can't give your mind properly to getting the right hat, I suppose, with a child on your hands. Poor dear Margery, she hadn't even got to the shops." He concluded with a grimace, "There was nothing to see, you know, after all these years, just a hole in the ground, with a lot of willow-herb in seed, and some foundations and an old empty static-water tank. I thought I'd go and see what the place looked like, before they start building on the site. They're going to put up a block of flats, I believe. I'd always kept away till now and I don't know that I did myself much good by going. It didn't look like a place where people had been killed, but there were half a dozen buried in the ruins. She can't have had any time to think, you know. She might have heard the thing coming, but then it would just cut out and dive and before she knew what was up the house would have come down all over the pavement. It fell on her . . . on both of them." He stared hard at his cousin. "It really wasn't worth going," said he. "There was nothing left there of her. I couldn't face it before, then lately I felt that I wanted to go there and say goodbye to her." He added with a bleak stare, "I suppose it means I've got over it."

The coals fell together in the fire and he bent down and mended it, glad perhaps to turn his back. Behind him Henrietta said, "I remember I was frightfully upset when I heard you were going to be married."

If she had wanted to change the current of his thoughts, she succeeded. He stood up, turned his back to the fire, stood looking down at her, screwing up his marred face, amused and puzzled. "I had rather a feeling for you at the age of fifteen," said she in a dry detached tone, lying back in his deep chair and looking up at the ceiling. "One must make a hero out of somebody at that age. You were our handsome naval cousin who used to turn up in the holidays, play cricket with us, improve our tennis, dance with me at Christmas parties, take us out into the garden at night and teach us to name the stars. Andromache, Cassiopeia, Capella," said Henrietta, "I know them all still. Harry and I both admired you enormously. I used to tell the other girls all about your noble deeds at St. Olave's. Most of us had photographs of Noel Coward and Ivor Novello hidden away, but I had one of you in uniform looking very handsome, with your cap on one side. It was much admired."

"Ah! I had all my face then," said Charles pleasantly. "I don't wonder the girls thought well of me." He looked sideways at her out of his good eye, interested but perplexed. For the moment she had all his attention, he had forgotten the bomb-site in Chelsea. "Two or three of them were deeply in love with you," Henrietta assured him with her most sardonic inflection. "There was a very pretty one called Penelope who was quite desperate about you; but I told her I'd made up my mind to marry you when I grew up, so she quite understood it was hands-off. It was a dreadful come-down for me when Granny wrote and said you'd got yourself engaged to Margery. I was sick all night. Matron couldn't think what was the matter with me; I had to pretend I'd been stuffing coconut ice and they stopped my pocket-money for a fortnight. It was all your fault for being so handsome, Charles."

He laughed, but still looked worried. "You never told me any of this before," he grumbled.

"I'd have died sooner than speak of it," Henrietta retorted. "I was frightfully ashamed of myself, but I couldn't help it. I was always sick in those days when life was too much for me. Shock, I suppose. I couldn't help it any more than one can help falling in love. I'd got it all planned so carefully, you see, I always thought you'd wait for me, but that of course was too much to hope for. You were thirty and I was fifteen and Margery got you." She added, "You've no idea what fools schoolgirls can be. It's a very long time ago, but it meant quite a lot to me at the time." She glanced at the wedding photograph.

"1938; Munich year," said Charles. "We all knew war was coming, so we got married while we could. You were there, I suppose." He had honestly quite forgotten. When Henrietta murmured, "Don't you remember? I got measles," his mind was still full of uniforms, white lilies and champagne. He murmured absently, "Oh! bad luck" and quite jumped when she told him, "Bad luck, nothing! I got it on purpose." That made him turn back from the photographs and look at her. "I wasn't coming to see you married, Charles," said she. "I couldn't take it. Granny had got it all taped, of course, I was to be one of the bridesmaids. I was going to be paired off with a very pretty cousin of Margery's, just my age; we were to wear the most frightful frocks, pink taffeta, very enlarging with rows and rows of frills right down to the ground, and carry Malmaison carnations. You can imagine what it would have done to me, with my red hair, but I had to match the others. When the dress came home and was laid out on the bed I couldn't stand the thought. It was just in the summer holidays. I knew Roote's little girls all had measles, so I went down to the cottage. Mary Roote was in bed, her mother had gone round to the village shop, so I sat on her bed and played two games of snap with her and then I put my arms round her and kissed her two or three times. I never told anybody. I got measles all right, just in time. I came out in spots ten days later, the very night before we were going up to London. Granny was wild!"

Charles put back his head and laughed out loud. "You were a little devil in those days, Penny; always got your own way, didn't you?" "Not always," she retorted, "and not by a long chalk, where Granny was concerned, but I did beat her that time. She never could think where I'd picked the germ up. She went to London all right, she wasn't going to be done out of her fun by any nonsense about quarantine. Grace Thorn went too and had a heavenly day, she was always sentimental about weddings. She told me the whole story with tears in her eyes; Holy Trinity, Brompton and that hotel in Hans Place and an arch of swords and so forth. She said Margery's little cousin had walked by herself and looked lovely. She brought me back a piece of wedding cake and a flower out of the bridal bouquet. Nanny put them on the table beside me and I threw them into the fire when she was out of the room. Thorny cut out all the *Tatler* photographs and stuck them in that frightful album of hers, she used to sit beside my bed and show them to me. I had quite a bad attack, I remember; fifteen's a bit late to get measles. Harry got them over at his prep-school, but I'd always had such a sheltered life. I got my chest bad and missed nearly all the holidays. I had to take the pink frock back to school for dancing class, but I spilt a bottle of ink down the front as soon as I got the chance, so that was all right. Yes, Charles, that was how I dodged your wedding," and she laughed, got up and went off to bed, leaving Charles with something new to think over.

XV

ABOUT MIDNIGHT a strong north-west wind got up and swept the sky clean; there seemed to be about three times as many stars as usual, thought Charles, taking a look out of his window before he went to bed. He was dead-tired and slept like a log, in spite of the aircraft which kept droning round in circles over Wilchester. He woke about three in the morning from a dream of disaster at sea, but he could not remember what it had all been about and he lay awake for a few minutes, still thinking himself afloat on the Atlantic, climbing one wave after another, listening to murmurs in the sky. Then he was startled broad awake by a new noise, like drums rattling in the distance. It approached rapidly, there was something unusual and terrifying in its violence; he had jumped from his bed before he realised his thought, "Something wrong with that one."

He rushed to the window and leaned out, but saw nothing, only the noise went over him like an express train, like the Day of Judgment. He did not see the American aeroplane go screaming over the yard, though he got out on the head of his wooden staircase faster than he had ever moved in his life; but he heard it hit the house. Empty, out of control, with its crew floating in air five miles behind it, flying all by itself, the thing came down upon Fountain Court, trailing fire like a blow-lamp. It landed on the south-west corner of the house, ploughed its way among the chimney-stacks, broke off a wing and dropped it on the south terrace; then, still burning, skated forward over the parapet. It broke in half and the tail stuck flaring on the roof, while the whole fore-part of the aircraft stood on its head in the rose-garden, outside the Red Dining-room. There it remained, a crumpled brazier, with flames streaming up through it as high as the roof.

Charles clung to the rail of the outside stair, he heard but did not see the crash, which was hidden from him by the bulk of the house. At that time he thought there were men in the thing and wrote them off as dead. At first he was deafened by the explosion, then he began to hear all round him bricks, tiles and metal falling to the ground. He scrambled back into his room, stamped into trousers and gum-boots, snatched his duffel coat and his big lantern-torch and ran to the house. The back door was locked but he broke the kitchen window with the boot-scraper off the back step, luckily there were no shutters. He tumbled over the low sill, bruised himself on a couple of taps and fell over the sink on to the floor inside, but did not break his torch. He struck his hand down on the electric switches as he ran through the door, but in vain, evidently the lights were all fused. The kitchens were connected with the main part of the house by quite a long passage, about which tray-carrying footmen used to grumble in the old days. Charles dumped his lantern on the floor by the telephone, pulled the receiver off and let it dangle, dialled feverishly with his one hand. As he picked up the receiver and began shouting into it he was aware of Nanny coming down the back stairs, with Victor in her arms, wrapped in a blanket. The child was sobbing with fright and only half-awake, but Nanny was perfectly calm, though Charles scarcely recognised her in her grey dressing-gown, with her white hair in two short pigtails and her stockings down over her ankles. "We'll go into the kitchen, Master Charles," said she in quite an ordinary voice. "I'll poke up the range and get kettles going. I've told Mrs. Peppercorn and that Maria to come down quick. It's the other end that's burning so far." And she disappeared down the stone-flagged kitchen passage.

Charles heard a distant resentful squeak, shouted "Fire" again and smelt smoke very strongly. "Fountain Court," said he. "We've got a Yank plane burning on the roof." "Then you want the base," said the tiny voice in his ear, squeaking like a cross doll. "I'll put you through." There was a rattle and silence, while he shouted "Don't cut me off", and "Fire Brigade".

He heard Victor wailing in the kitchen and Nanny soothing him; then with an enormous gush of relief he saw Henrietta at his elbow, in a green fisherman's jersey and slacks, with her hair standing out round her head like flames. "Take this damned thing, Penny," said he, thrusting the telephone at her. "I can't wait while they play the fool. Then get everybody into the kitchen and tell them to wait till I come."

He did not wait for her reply, but left her and ran along the passage to the entrance hall. Smoke met him there in a visible wave, curling down the Waterloo staircase, mixed with sparks; he heard the fire roaring in the distance like a pride of lions. He saw the door of the Red Dining-room standing open and dashed through it; but when he struggled to open the big shutters with his one arm he had to bang them to again as fast as possible. The wood was hot to his hand and so was the shutter-bar; all the window panes on that side of the house were broken and he was stamping bits of glass under his feet. Outside the fire was hot and bright, like the mouth of hell: it glittered through the joints of the shutters. When he turned round there was old Leaf at the sideboard, in a plaid dressing-gown, without his false teeth, lighting candles with his trembling old hand as if for a dinner party. He was pulling spoons and forks out of the drawers in handfuls and rolling them up in a baize cloth, mumbling, "My silver . . . my silver . . ."

"Don't stay too long at that," Charles advised him. "The shutters will go pretty soon, you've only a few minutes. Damn the silver; it's insured. You'd better get along to the kitchen, man; that's where the rest of them are. We shall have the firemen along presently, it'll have to burn itself out." Yet a freakish impulse made him reach down, one-handed, as he went past it, the little Stubbs by the doorway, of the three race-horses at morning exercise with their yellow-jacketed grooms. "Take that away," said he to Henrietta, meeting her in the marble-flagged hall and dumping the picture into her bewildered arms. "Mr. Birnbaum says he can get us a thousand pounds for it any time." And he grinned in her bewildered face and said, "No time to get any big stuff out. It's a good thing we don't need to bother about saving Lav's portrait."

She clutched the picture as if it had been a child. Her face was dead-white, her eyes staring. "Maria," she said. "Nobody's seen her. I'm going up to look for her." A sudden thought made him almost jump out of his skin. "The jewels . . . the old woman's diamonds." Henrietta had dropped the picture and started for the staircase, he seized her arm and pulled her back. "You stay here till I come down," he told her in a voice of fury. "Understand, Penny, I won't have you up there. The roof may go at any minute." He went upstairs two steps at a time, leaving Henrietta like a statue at the foot. He heard her cry out something, but could not tell what it was, for the roar of the fire.

2

The smoke was pretty thick already in the first floor passage. As he went past the General's bedroom he saw through the open door flames pouring in through the broken windows; the curtains were already alight and floating up to the ceiling. He banged the door to as he went by for what that was worth, ran down the passage and round the corner into the south front and burst into Lady Hornbeam's bedroom. The dead woman lay there in all her bejewelled splendour, with the candles burning about her; in the moving light she almost looked as if she were alive, but Maria was no longer telling her beads at the bed's foot. Charles found her in the dressing-room, clawing and burrowing like a wild animal in her big black trunk, flinging out on the carpet old shoes, old gowns, old knots of gloves and stockings, cramming a pillow case with her treasure. A diamond buckle dropped from her fingers and rolled on the carpet at Charles's feet. When he shouted in her ear, "The jewels . . . get her jewels . . ." she spat back at him the one word "Paste". It came to him then that this was what Henrietta had been trying to tell him, if he had listened to her. "Get out of here," he told the Swiss woman. "Do you want the roof to fall on you?"

She stumbled to her feet, clasped the bundle in her arms and ran from him through the far doorway. He heard a crash as the blazing wreckage on the roof burst through the tiles and fell into the empty bedroom above. All the candles in the bedroom flared in the draught as he darted back there and thrust his hand into the gaping wall-safe, but there was nothing in it but a heap of old empty cases. He saw the plaster darken above him as he turned away, then the ceiling opened in the middle and a shower of burning fragments fell through upon the corpse. Charles took to his heels and bolted after the Swiss woman down the servants' staircase; as he clattered past a broken window he heard bells ringing and saw the first fire-engine turn into the gate.

He found the front door open and Henrietta on the steps, looking very pale in the glare of the head-lamps. There were three scarlet engines in the drive by this time, as Charles came out he saw one of them smash through the end of the yew hedge and sway round the corner of the house into the rose-garden. Another followed full tilt through the gap that the first had made. "They'll break down all the rose-bushes," exclaimed Henrietta faintly; then she laughed out loud and said, "Well, who cares? the whole place is going, I suppose." He put his arm through hers and squeezed her elbow tightly. "Did you get Maria?" she asked and when he nodded said, "The jewels are mostly paste; Granny told me this morning she'd sold them years ago, at the same time as the Lawrence. Pretty well everything we've counted on was a fake. Oh! let it burn; let it burn." She shuddered from head to foot. Charles said firmly, "You'll catch your death out here; come along to the kitchen while I see if there's any chance of carrying some stuff out."

He put his arm round her waist and pulled her indoors. Back in the kitchen Nanny and Cook had got a kind of crazy tea-party going already; they were sitting round the table with Leaf, all in their dressing-gowns. Leaf had a black iron cash-box on his knees, which he fingered anxiously; Mrs. Peppercorn had a man's cap on her head and Boffin the cat purring on her knees, she was stirring her cup as cheerfully as if it were mid-morning and eating biscuits from a tin. Maria was in an armchair by the range, fully dressed in her black uniform, she even had an apron on; there was a sable coat draped round her shoulders and an astrakhan cape across her knees. Her arms were round the pillow-case, stuffed, Charles knew, with loot; she kept her back turned to the other servants. Victor was in the second armchair, smothered in blankets, he cried out and turned over, Charles thought that he said, "Want to go home." "Well," said Nanny rising like a hostess, "that did sound like the end of the world, but here we all are, none the worse. Sit by the fire, child and drink a cup of tea to warm you. You can't do nothing more for the present." She fussed over Henrietta. Roote the gardener was stamping his old feet on the doormat. "I knocked up Micky," said he, "and sent him down to the farm to get hold of a couple of chaps so's we can carry stuff out; but them Yanks is all over the drive, they won't let me by. You'll 'ave to talk to the officer, Mr. Charles." Mrs. Peppercorn lifted a teapot as big as a football, with a hospitable gesture, she poured a mugful for Charles. "Just like the war, ain't it?" she said cheerfully. "All the boys'll be in presently; I'd best put another kettle on for luck."

Charles gulped the tea, patted Victor on the head and bolted round by the gap in the yew hedge into the Muses' Grove. Here a fantastic ballet was already in progress, illuminated by the glare of headlights. The scene was as clear as day, cars and lorries had followed the engines and the place was alive with men in uniform, struggling with hoses and ladders; round the corner, where the engines stood among the trampled rose-bushes, the lawn was a sea of foam. The fire was getting a steady hold on the east end of the house, sheets of flame were gushing out of the upper storey, clouds of black smoke rushed out of the chimneys and billowed down from the roof. There was a hospitable glow from the open doorway, the columns stood out black against it and all the windows were lighting up, one after another, as if the Hornbeams were giving a farewell party inside. Charles heard the whole place roaring and crackling, the hiss of foam and water, the rattle of falling tiles; the heat scorched his face as he stood by the broken statue of Clio. He understood that this was the death of Fountain Court.

He found an American officer, shouting at some men who were jumping off the tailboard of the last lorry. "Everybody out of the house, buddy?" this young man demanded briskly; and when Charles said, "In the kitchen, seven of 'em, women mostly," said "Then keep 'em there, for Pete's sake and don't bother me. I've got no time to talk to you." Charles said, "Look here, I've got a couple of chaps from the garden and farm-hands coming; can I take 'em round and pitch out some of the furniture while there's time?" "You'll have your work cut out to save anything," the officer told him. "All right, buddy, it's up to you; but don't go getting cut off and having to be rescued." Charles laughed and promised, "I'll see nobody plays the fool. We'll go round by the terrace and break in through the french windows."

He collected reinforcements from the kitchen, Henrietta, Micky, Jean the landgirl and a couple of farm-hands, who had been roused by the crash and come over in a hurry. They broke into the Yellow Drawing-room, which was furthest from the fire, carried out the chairs and tables and dumped them among the flower-beds on the terrace; the women ran in and out with the smaller pictures and the best of the china. Two men got down the portrait of the Crimean captain from the library and propped him against the parapet; then they went back and carried out the ivory-and-ebony cabinet from the Green Boudoir. They could not get anywhere near the Red Dining-room, which was well alight, but among them, in under half an hour, they got out a number of family relics, about enough to furnish a small room.

Charles, stopping once to take breath, found Leaf at his elbow and heard the man cry out, "Oh! sir, the old place is done for," as the flames gushed from a new window; then falter, "The body, sir; has nobody thought of the body?" He had quite forgotten himself about Lady Hornbeam's corpse. "That room's well alight, man," said he, pointing. "Only look at the window, Leaf. I was in it myself half an hour ago when the ceiling began to drop; even then it was too late. We can't do anything more than we have done." The old butler shuddered, passed his hands over his face and stared at the burning building where he had worked all his life. "My clothes are gone," he lamented, "and so's the money I had in my trunk; I was going up again when I'd fetched out the silver, but there wasn't time. Oh! Master Charles, it's enough to break a man's heart to see the place go like this; I loved it as if it were my own, it was such a beautiful house." The young American officer came running along the terrace shouting, "Get back there; do you want the place to come down on you?" and Charles took it up, "All out; all out." He counted heads one by one on the terrace and stood with his arm through Henrietta's elbow; presently they saw the roof fall in and a fiery fountain of sparks go up to the stars.

3

Back in the kitchen there was a whole crowd of people come to see what they could do, all excited, all talking at once. The farmer's wife, Mrs. Wood, was there in a fur coat, crying, "Jim's got the vet. out and a cow calving, but I've got the big car outside and I'm to bring back anybody that wants a bed." There were two or three American officers by this time, arguing with one another and breaking off to tell Henrietta, over and over, "We feel dreadfully about this, it's terrible to see your lovely house burn." Grace Thorn was there, come through the night on her bicycle, wind-blown and wild, lamenting "The Queen's Room, the Queen's Room; there's nothing left of it. Oh! how awful; we can never build it up again." Grace was really a perfect nuisance. She kept wanting Henrietta to go back with her and set off Mrs. Wood to offer the same hospitality, but Henrietta was stubborn with both of them, saying over and over, "I can't leave."

In the middle of all this there was a frightfully pretty young American woman in slacks and a scarlet parka, crying out to Henrietta, "You don't know me, but I know Nanny and this little boy. I'm Helen Hazel from the base and I've got six flasks of coffee and a basket of what you call doughnuts for the boys. As soon as they've eaten them I'm going straight back and what I want is to take your little boy right back with me and put him into bed with my Elmer. They're just of an age. It's warm as Florida in our place, I've got five kerosene stoves burning, because we can't take your British climate. Your Nanny's coming too, it's all arranged." She flung her arms round sleepy Victor and hugged him to her. "He's too little," she told them passionately, "to stay here and watch his own house burn." Henrietta seemed quite stunned by the situation; Charles said firmly, "Very sound. You take him away till morning, Mrs. Hazel, and then we'll settle what to do with him. I expect his mother will come rushing to fetch him away." Victor, quite dazed, turned in the strange woman's arms and settled himself to sleep against her shoulder, as if he had known her all his life. "You come on home with me, honey," she said to him, "and tomorrow you shall wear Elmer's cowboy suit. You're just of a size."

So she took Victor and Nanny. Mrs. Wood carried off Maria and Mrs. Peppercorn, Leaf went over with old Roote to the cottage and poor Grace bicycled home alone. The American airmen bundled into their trucks and rattled away, leaving only a few men to watch the dying fire and Charles took Henrietta up to his own room over the stables. There was still electric light to be had there, the stables had a separate supply from the house; he was able to turn on all three bars of his fire, light up a radiator he had for very bad weather and boil his kettle. He was worried about Henrietta, she looked so pinched and cold. However, he sat her down by the fire and mixed them both a steaming mug of tea with rum in it. She made a face at the smell and a worse one at the taste of it, complaining "What on earth's this?" but he told her firmly, "Nelson's blood, proper thing after a shipwreck. You put it down; first it'll warm you up, then it'll make you sweat, then it'll put you to sleep. It's good stuff." He spoke with much the same tone of authority which Nanny used to use when she said, "Drink up your milk, Miss Henrietta, and then you can go to bed." Henrietta gave him the smile he was working for. "Well, I shan't make a habit of it," said she, "but I'll drink it just this once to please you. I shan't sleep though," she vowed obstinately, with her eyelids drooping already, like a child, he thought. "Nothing else to do till to-morrow," said he. "The fire's got to burn itself out."

"It *is* tomorrow," Henrietta contradicted him. "Sunday already," and she yawned enormously. He took her glass from her and said, "You're asleep now. You can tuck yourself up in my bunk." He pulled her up from the armchair, sat her down on the edge of the tumbled bunk, lifted her feet into it and pulled the grey blankets up to her ears. "Turn your face to the wall," said he, "then the light won't bother you." She snuggled down obediently. He heard her say, "Don't leave me," and promised, "I'll be here if I'm wanted." Then he kissed her forehead as if she had been the child he remembered, turned out the light and sat down by the fire to wait for morning under the photograph of his own wedding.

4

At seven he woke from an uneasy doze, heard church-bells at a distance and was glad to think that he need not go out with his vegetable-lorry. Henrietta was still dead asleep, breathing quietly; she did not wake when he rose up, stretched himself and tiptoed out to look at the damage. In the chill air of morning he walked round by the south terrace, where the heads of scorched brown palm-trees rose out of the smashed conservatory and a few yellow chairs and a japanned table were set out in the morning sun under the blackened walls, as if for a ghostly tea-party. Under the Drawing-room window, in a trampled flower-bed, he found the weather-cock, a battered gilded object as big as a lamb, split down the middle of its metal back and standing on its head in the earth, astonishingly undamaged. He picked it up and leaned it against the tea-table, wondering if it would ever turn in air again.

A sentry stopped him at the entrance to the rose-garden, which was blocked by a tangle of wreckage, but he got round by the path on the edge of the ha-ha. Downstairs the shutters were burst and split, hanging from their hinges, so that he could see into all the rooms. The east wind had swept the fire right through them, plasterwork and panelling alike had been destroyed, the floors were a foot deep in black ash and fallen brickwork. Here and there were bits of burnt furniture, empty picture-frames which had slid down the wall and smashed themselves, rags of black-

ened curtains hanging down like mourners' crape. In the Yellow
Drawing-room the grand piano was a tangle of curled wires in a
ribbed and charred case and Lavinia's portrait had fallen from
the wall. The big sofa which the men had not had time to move
still stood before the hearth, a recognisable heap of springs and
ashes, with the fallen chandelier perched upon it; Henrietta had
sat there yesterday after lunch. The Red Dining-room upset
Charles most of all, because the ceiling had come down upon the
table and the whole floor was strewn with turquoise-and-white
china fragments of the celebrated dinner service; Leaf would not
find one whole plate left. Wisps of smoke rose up from the ruins
and there was a horrid smell of water on burnt wood, the rose-
garden was a disgusting swamp of dirty puddles. On the north
side the portico had come down with a run and the Muses' Grove
was choked with lumps of apricot-coloured stone. Sky shone
through empty windows; the whole house had gone, more or less,
except that at the west end one or two Victorian rooms on the
ground floor were still standing. Nothing else had escaped except
the Abbot's Tower, rosy in the morning sun, and the neat square
of the old stables, closed on the east by the kitchen wing. All else
was now a pile of ash and rubble, with somewhere underneath
an old woman's bones.

Charles was surveying the broken columns, heaped like spilli-
kins one upon another, all down the steps, when he became aware
of Henrietta at his elbow. "This is a nice mess, Penny," said he
ruefully, not looking at her. "Have you been round the other side?"
She sighed, "I've seen it all, Charles, and I don't want to look at
it any longer. Come and have breakfast."

She was a good girl, he thought; she had tidied up the room
over the stables already, made the bed, lit the fire and started the
percolator for coffee. Now they boiled eggs and fried bacon and
had breakfast together, talking of anything but the night's work.
Charles exerted himself to entertain her, stealing glances at her
out of his one eye. He had expected to find her broken-hearted,

but she was perfectly calm; her morning face was pale and dry-eyed, there was even a faint smile on her lips when she put her elbows on the table among the dirty cups and plates and said firmly, "Well, where do we go from here?"

He had been thinking that out as he wandered among the ruins. He was able to tell her, quite steadily, "Well, you know, my dear, things might be worse, from your point of view. The whole place was all fully insured, rather over-insured, in fact, what with the Lawrence and the diamonds and such. We shall have a bit of a fight with the insurance company, of course; but the policy does cover damage from the air. I looked that up, as it happens, a bit ago; I'd wondered about it, with all those chaps flying round us night and day. We shall get some dollars from the Americans, I fancy, too. A pity we didn't sell that dealer of yours the junk he wanted, before the whole lot went up in smoke; still we should get enough to build the place up again, after a fashion. Not that it would ever be the same," he admitted ruefully.

She did not speak immediately. He busied himself with lighting his pipe and did not look at her; in the end, slowly and reluctantly, she did shake her head. He admired her for it. "I don't suppose anybody would want us to do that," said she. "What's the use? it wouldn't be the same Fountain Court. It would only be a sham. No, Charles dear, we shall have to face it, the thing's over and done with. The house has been a burden on all of us, for years and years; times are changed, it had to go. The fire has really been a godsend, if I can only make myself see it."

She leant her head on her hand, he did not dare to speak to her. "Last night," said she, "I thought I'd die, watching it burn, I wished I'd been in it, but I've got past all that. In a way, I'd rather see the place destroyed than have it cut up and turned into something it was never meant for. I don't really want anybody but the Hornbeams to live in Fountain Court. I don't believe now that Victor would ever have been able to keep it going. We shall have to invest the money we get for his use and when he grows up he can have it to start something different."

She put out her hand and Charles squeezed her fingers in a hard grip, it was all he could do for her. "We shall have plenty of time to work it out," said she in a sleep-walking voice, "you and I with the lawyers, about what to do with the ruins. I don't suppose anybody would buy the site, but you never know. The gardens are a going concern, about the only thing that has paid its way for ages. Some rich fool might buy the site for the sake of the gardens and build a new house on the old foundations." She glanced at Charles imploringly, "Do say something," she murmured.

"Well," said he slowly, "you can certainly try it. Meanwhile you can be thinking about something else; I mean, letting me take over the gardens altogether. I could launch out quite a bit, if I had the chance. I could use the borders for market-flowers, grow more wall-fruit, go in for standard roses, put up a couple of modern glass-houses where that frightful palm-house used to be, make the whole thing into a proper nursery-garden. I'd have to borrow money, take in a partner perhaps, anyhow employ more labour. I've been thinking about it a good deal lately, before all this happened. Of course, if you pulled down the main part of the ruins you could make a good little house and some packing-sheds out of the bit that's left, if you feel you can stand going on living here. I don't see why the whole thing shouldn't pay its way, at any rate till the boy's old enough to say what he wants done with it." He was running on, talking aloud, trying to see his way, when Henrietta pulled him up short. "But, Charles, you won't be here. You're going to Norfolk Island."

He stopped, stared at her, smiled gently, shook his head. "Oh! no, I'm not," he assured her. "You said you were, yesterday," she objected quite crossly, but he waved that aside. "I was only teasing that fool Elsa, teasing you too, if it comes to that. Anyhow, you're just as bad. You let us all think you were going off to America." She shook her head indignantly. "You knew perfectly well," said she, "that I shouldn't and so did poor John. When it came to the point, I couldn't tear myself away from Fountain Court." "And you don't think I'm going off to the other side of the world when you're in all this trouble?" Charles reproached her. "Not on your life." He added, "I may not be much use in the world, nowadays, but I think it's my job to look after you, as long as you need it." "I need it dreadfully," said Henrietta under her breath. "When you said you were going away I thought I was done for. I don't see how I'm to get on at all without you." The colour came up in her cheeks; as it had done in the night, she said to him, "Don't leave me."

At that he got up, walked round the table and pulled her to her feet. "I'll never leave you, as long as you want me," he promised. "We'll see this business through. We'll pick up the pieces and set the old place in order, somehow or other we'll come out on the right side. We won't be beaten." He looked over her head at the photograph of his wedding and said farewell to his own youth. He had only one arm, but it was strong enough to hold Henrietta; he kissed her and she returned his kisses. "And one of these days, when we're not too busy," said he firmly, "we'll go across to the church and get married."

THE END

Oct. 1954
June 1955